the
church → ✝

Miss
Blalock's
place

Tupelo Landing

Three Times Lucky

by Sheila Turnage

SCHOLASTIC INC.

ISBN 978-0-545-50844-5

12 11 10 9 8 7 6 5 4 3 2 1   12 13 14 15 16 17/0

Printed in the U.S.A.   23

First Scholastic printing, November 2012

Book design by Jasmin Rubero
Text set in Carre Noir Std

*For my parents—Vivian Taylor Turnage
and A.C. Turnage, Jr.—who taught me to love books.*

Contents

CHAPTER 1: *Trouble in Tupelo Landing* *1*

CHAPTER 2: *The Colonel* *13*

CHAPTER 3: *The Three Day Rule* *28*

CHAPTER 4: *Meeting Up at Lavender's* *40*

CHAPTER 5: *At the Carolina Raceway* *51*

CHAPTER 6: *Keep Your Windows and Doors Locked* *69*

CHAPTER 7: *Desperados* *86*

CHAPTER 8: *Miss Lana* *98*

CHAPTER 9: *The Cousin Information Network* *106*

CHAPTER 10: *At the Tobacco Barn* *115*

CHAPTER 11: *Murder Weapon to Go* *122*

CHAPTER 12: *Stay Away from My Crime Scene* *132*

CHAPTER 13: *Don't Call Me Baby* *144*

CHAPTER 14: *Deputy Marla* *157*

CHAPTER 15: *A Spiritual Curveball* *164*

CHAPTER 16: *Lavender Blues* *177*

CHAPTER 17: *Mr. Jesse's Final Contribution* *184*

CHAPTER 18: *Miss Lana!* *194*

CHAPTER 19: *Listening to the Stars* *209*

CHAPTER 20: *A Suitcase Full of Cash* *215*

CHAPTER 21: *Ransom* *224*

CHAPTER 22: *A Town Full of Nobodies* *236*

CHAPTER 23: *Creative Chaos* *248*

CHAPTER 24: *Right Under Our Noses* *264*

CHAPTER 25: *A Hurricane Party* *271*

CHAPTER 26: *Sorry* *277*

CHAPTER 27: *Storm Break* *285*

CHAPTER 28: *Didn't See It Coming* *296*

CHAPTER 29: *Dear Upstream Mother* *302*

Chapter 1
Trouble in Tupelo Landing

Trouble cruised into Tupelo Landing at exactly seven minutes past noon on Wednesday, the third of June, flashing a gold badge and driving a Chevy Impala the color of dirt. Almost before the dust had settled, Mr. Jesse turned up dead and life in Tupelo Landing turned upside down.

As far as I know, nobody expected it.

As for me—Miss Moses LoBeau, rising sixth grader—trouble was the *last* thing on my mind as I crept across Dale's front porch at six o'clock that morning. "Hey Dale," I whispered, pressing my face against his sagging window screen. "Wake up."

He turned over, tugging at his sheet. "Go 'way," he mumbled. His mongrel dog, Queen Elizabeth II, stirred beneath a hydrangea at the porch's edge.

Dale sleeps with his window up in summer partly because he likes to hear the tree frogs and crickets, but mostly because his daddy's too sorry to bring home any air-conditioning. "Dale!" I bellowed. "Wake up! It's Mo."

Dale sat bolt upright, his blue eyes round and his blond hair spiking in all directions.

"Demons!" he gasped, pointing vaguely in my direction.

I sighed. Dale's family is Baptist. "It ain't demons, it's me," I said. "I stopped by to tell you: The Colonel's come home and he ain't up to cooking."

He blinked like a stunned owl. "You woke me up for that?"

"I'm sorry, Dale, I got to open the café today."

"Oh," Dale said, his disappointment riding the word to the ground. "But we been planning this fishing trip forever, Mo," he said, rubbing his eyes. "How about Miss Lana? Can't she whip up some craps, or—"

"*Crepes*," I said. "It's French. And no, she can't. Miss Lana slammed out just after the Colonel slipped in. She's gone."

He swore, his voice soft as a breeze through the reeds. Dale started swearing last year. I haven't started yet, but the way things are going, I could at any moment.

"I'm sorry, Dale. We'll have to go fishing another time. I can't let the Colonel and Miss Lana down."

The Colonel and Miss Lana are the closest thing to family I've got. Without them, I wouldn't have a home. I probably wouldn't even have a name. I am bereft of kin by fate, as Miss Lana puts it, washed into my current, rather odd life by Forces Unknown.

Just then, Dale's bedroom door creaked open and his mama leaned into the room, her green eyes soft from sleep. "Dale?" she whispered, clutching a faded pink housecoat to her throat. "You all right? You aren't having nightmares again, are you, baby?"

"It's worse than that, Mama," he said gravely. "Mo's here."

Miss Rose used to be a real beauty, back before time and Dale's daddy got hold of her. That's what people say: coal-black hair, a tilt to her chin, and a sway that made men stand taller.

"Morning, Miss Rose," I said, pressing my best smile against the window screen.

"Lord have mercy," she said, staggering back. "What time is it, Mo?"

"A whisker past six," I said, smiling. "I sure hope you slept well."

"I did," she said, "for a shockingly brief period of time." Like Dale, Miss Rose doesn't necessarily wake up good. Her voice took on a silky, dangerous tone. "And you are on my porch before the sun has wiped the sleep from its eyes because . . . ?"

I took a deep breath. "Because the Colonel's back but

Miss Lana's gone, so I got to open the café, which means Dale and me can't go fishing, and I feel like it would be rude not to let him know. I'm just trying to do what's right," I concluded.

A tiny frown creased her forehead.

Fortunately, Miss Rose is a person of manners and, as Miss Lana says, manners will tell. "Well," she finally said, "as long as we're all awake, won't you come in?"

"She can't," Dale said, swinging his legs over the side of his bed. "Me and Mo are opening the café today."

"Mo and I," she murmured as he stood up fully dressed and stepped into a pair of sandals that looked way too big. She blinked. "What happened to your pajamas? And why are you wearing your brother's old shoes?"

"Sleeping in my clothes saves time, and my feet are growing," he replied, shoving his black T-shirt into his shorts and running his fingers through his hair. The men in Dale's family are vain about their hair, and with good reason.

"He's growing feet first," I added. "The rest of him will catch up later." Dale is the second-smallest kid in our class. Only Sally Amanda Jones is smaller. Dale's sensitive. "Gotta go!" I shouted, and grabbed my bike and headed across the yard.

Dale caught up with me just outside town. We coasted past the mayor's new sign—Welcome to Tupelo Land-

ING, NC, POPULATION: 148—and skidded to a halt in the café parking lot, kicking up a rooster tail of oyster shells and sand. "Holy moly," he said, dropping his bike. "Looks like the Colonel's got a new car."

"A '58 Underbird," I said modestly. "Original paint."

"You mean a Thunderbird," he said, strolling around the car.

Dale's family knows cars. In fact, his big brother Lavender, who I will one day marry, races at Carolina Raceway. Dale kicked a tire and squinted at the silvery letters sprawling across the car's fender. "Used to be a Thunderbird," he announced. "Looks like the *T* and *H* fell off."

"Well, it's an Underbird now," I said, waving my key in front of the café's door.

"I don't see why you do that," he said, watching me. "Everybody in town knows that door won't lock."

"I don't do this for everybody in town; I do it in case of strangers. You can't be too careful about strangers. That's what the Colonel says."

Dale grabbed my arm. "Wait. Don't open up today, Mo. Please? Let's go fishing. I was going to surprise you, but . . . I got us a boat."

I froze, the door half-open. "A boat? Where'd you get a boat?"

"Mr. Jesse's," he said, rocking back on his heels.

I tried not to sound impressed. "You stole Mr. Jesse's boat?"

He studied his fingernails. "I wouldn't say *stole*," he said. "But I did borrow it pretty strong."

I sighed. "I can't, Dale. Not today."

"Tomorrow, then." He grinned, grabbing the CLOSED sign and flipping it to OPEN.

Dale's my best friend. By now, you can see why.

We barely had time to rev up the air conditioner and click on the ceiling fans before our first customer stumbled in. I won't say our patrons are an ugly lot, but at 6:30 a.m., they ain't pretty. I stepped up on the Pepsi crate behind the counter as Mr. Jesse came sauntering in, thin-shouldered and round-bellied, wearing a faded plaid shirt, khakis, and last night's whiskers. "Morning, Mr. Jesse," I said. "What'll it be?"

"Hey, Mo," he said, grabbing a menu. "Shouldn't you be in school?"

"School ended last week, Mr. Jesse."

"Oh? What grade will you . . . ?"

"Sixth."

"Sixth grade? Good gracious, girl," he said, looking at me for the first time. "You *are* growing."

I sighed. "I'm standing on a Pepsi crate, Mr. Jesse. I ain't grown that much since yesterday. You want to order? I got other customers to think about."

He looked around the deserted café as the 7UP clock ticked loud and lonely on the far wall. "Other customers? Where?"

"On their way over here."

"Oh. Lessee then," he said. "I don't know what I'm in a mood for. Some jackass stole my boat last night, took my appetite with it." Dale dropped a glass. "Big-footed buzzard, too, from his prints," he added. "I'm guessing he's at least six foot four and a good two hundred twenty pounds." Dale kicked his oversize sandals under the counter. Mr. Jesse licked his thin lips. "Miss Lana take her biscuits out of the oven yet?"

I made my voice gentle, the way Miss Lana does when I have a fever. "We ain't having biscuits today, Mr. Jesse," I said.

"Oh," he said. Then: "Oh!" He sniffed the air like a hound, and a frown flashed across his unshaven face. "Doesn't smell right in here," he announced. "No coffee, no bacon, no biscuits . . ."

"Miss Lana's taking some time off," I said, keeping my voice low. "It's probably for the best. Her biscuits are awfully fattening and you could stand to lose that belly, Mr. Jesse. You know you could."

His eyes darted to the gray double doors leading to the kitchen. "Is the Colonel back there?" he demanded. I couldn't blame him for being nervous.

"Want me to see if he's in?" I offered, stepping off my Pepsi crate. I won't say I'm short, but without the crate, I'm not tall.

"Disturb the Colonel?" he gasped. "No! Heavens no. I just like to know when he's in town." He dropped the menu. "What do you suggest this morning, Mo?"

I stood up straight, the way Miss Lana taught me, and draped a paper napkin over my arm. "This morning we're offering a full line of peanut butter entrées," I said. "We got peanut butter and jelly, peanut butter and raisins, and a delicate peanut butter/peanut butter combination. These come crunchy or smooth, on Wonder Bread, hand-squished flat on the plate or not, as you prefer. The special today is our famous peanut butter and banana sandwich. It comes on Wonder Bread, cut diagonal on the plate, with crust or without. What can I start you with?"

"The special," he said.

"An excellent choice. Hand-squished or fluffy?"

"Fluffy," he said. "No crust. And . . ." He gazed at the coffeemaker, his pale eyes hopeful. "Coffee?"

I shook my head. "Our drink du jour is Mountain Dew," I said. "I got a two-liter breathing in back."

His shoulders slumped.

"Morning!" Mayor Little sang out, the door slapping shut behind him. He smoothed his ice-blue tie over his pudgy belly and flashed an unnaturally white smile.

"Hush!" Mr. Jesse barked. "Miss Lana's gone and the Colonel could be in the kitchen!"

Mayor Little tiptoed to the counter, his polished loafers *tick-tick-ticking* across the tile floor. "Miss Lana gone? The Colonel back? An unfortunate turn of events, but put in an historical context, it's nothing the town can't handle," he murmured. "Morning, Mo. Give me a special and drink du jour. No ice. My gums are giving me fits."

"Coming up," I said, turning away.

We always choose a Little for mayor in case a television crew ever comes to town. Littles like to talk and they're naturally neat; even their babies dress good. As the mayor sipped his Mountain Dew, the breakfast crowd trickled in.

Grandmother Miss Lacy Thornton parked her Buick by the Underbird and strolled to a table by the window. Grandmother Miss Lacy Thornton always wears a navy-blue suit and shoes. Their color offsets her white-blue hair, which she sweeps up in a halo around her heart-shaped face. She stands just a little taller than me, but somehow looms above everyone in the room.

Tinks Williams darted in next to grab a sandwich, leaving his John Deere tractor idling in a patch of shade. Then came slow-talking Sam Quinerly, Lavender's racing partner and mechanic. He already had grease on his hands. Before Dale could make Sam's sandwich, in strolled Reverend Thompson and his boy, Thessalonians.

"Hey, Thes," I said, sliding him a glass of water. "How's summer school?"

He grinned, his carrot-colored hair glistening. "Wouldn't know. I ain't going."

Like me, Thes doesn't over-study. Unlike me, he's F-prone. I keep my borderline straight A's to myself, preferring to spring my brainpower on others when they least expect it. I take after Miss Lana that way. "How'd you wiggle out of that?" I asked.

"Makeup tests, and prayer," Reverend Thompson muttered.

Thes beamed. "Hey Mo, we got three potential hurricanes off Africa this morning. I figure we got a thirty percent chance one will make it all the way to us." Thes is a weather freak. He dreams of being a TV weatherman, and updates for practice. As far as I know, there's no way to stop him.

"A couple of specials, please, Mo," Reverend Thompson said.

"Coming up."

By 7:30 half the town had crowded into the café and rising seventh grader Skeeter McMillan—tall, slender, freckles the color of fresh-sliced baloney—had claimed the counter's last spot.

"Morning, Mo," Skeeter said, propping her law book open. "I'll have the alleged special, please." Skeeter, who hopes to one day be an attorney, loves to say "alleged" and "perp." Rumor has it she's already written to Matchbook University for a paralegal course under an assumed name. She won't say if that's true or false, only that unsubstantiated rumor won't hold up in court.

"Hey Skeeter, the Colonel's back," Dale told her, speeding by.

She swept her law book into her bag. "Make mine to go," she said.

The Colonel hates lawyers. We allow Skeeter to come in, since she's only in training, but she keeps a low profile out of pride.

By 8:30, Dale and I were tearing around like our shirttails were on fire. I am permitted to serve meals since the café is a family business, but not to use the stove, which the Colonel says could be dangerous for someone of my height and temperament. The pre-lunch lull found me opening jars of Miss Lana's Practically Organic Garden Soup—which, fortunately, serves up good cold in the bowl. "Miss Lana better come home soon," I said, twisting the ring off a quart jar. "This is the last of her soup, and I ain't no gardener."

"You can say that again," Dale muttered.

Dale gets his green thumb from Miss Rose. I, personally, am practically herbicidal. I've killed every plant I ever met, starting with my lima bean sprout in kindergarten.

As the lunch crowd drifted in, I plugged in the jukebox. The lunch crowd is the breakfast crowd shaved and combed, plus the Azalea Women, who call themselves the Uptown Garden Club. There's six of them, all told. Add the Azalea Women to our regulars, and the café was bustling when the stranger parked his dirt-colored Impala out front and pushed open the café door.

"Afternoon," he said, and the place went still as well water. I glanced at the clock. It was exactly seven minutes past noon.

Chapter 2
The Colonel

The stranger looked slow around the café, his eyes the color of a thin winter sky. "Give me a burger all the way and a sweet tea," he said, strolling to the counter.

Already I didn't like him.

Didn't like the starch in his shirt, or the crease in his pants. Didn't like the hook of his nose, or the plane of his cheekbones. Didn't like the skinny of his hips, or the shine of his shoes. Mostly, I didn't like the way he didn't smile.

I stepped up on my Pepsi crate. "Sorry, we're out. You want the special instead?"

"What's the special?"

I hooked my thumb toward the blackboard.

Carnivore's Delight:
Miss Lana's Practically Organic Soup served up cold, Baloney and Cucumber Sandwich, Mountain Dew/$2.75
Vegetarian Special:
Miss Lana's Soup, Peanut Butter and Cucumber Sandwich, Mountain Dew/$2.50

He frowned. "That's all you got?"

"It's good enough for us," Tinks Williams growled from the stool beside him.

His eyes narrowed. "Give me the Carnivore's Delight, then."

Tinks handed me three dollars. "Keep the change," he muttered, slapping his green John Deere cap on his head. "We tip good around here," he said, directing his words in the stranger's direction.

It was a bald-faced lie, but I appreciated it. "Thanks, Mr. Tinks," I said.

I hadn't even raked Tinks's crumbs to the floor when Mayor Little took his spot at the counter. "Mayor Clayburn Little," he said. "Welcome to Tupelo Landing."

The room relaxed. The Littles are good with strangers.

"Starr," the stranger said, introducing himself as he flipped open a gold badge. "Detective Joe Starr."

The mayor formed his mouth into a perfect O. "A detective!" he said, shaking Starr's hand. "Isn't that wonderful? We don't see many detectives around here."

"My boat got stole last night," Mr. Jesse said from down the counter. "You come about my boat?"

"It'll show up," Dale shouted, his voice raw and panicked.

Mayor Little forced a smile. "Your boat's a local matter, Jesse. I'll look into it." Then to Starr: "Where are you out of, Detective, if you don't mind me asking?"

"Winston-Salem," Starr said.

"My, my. You're a long way from home. Passing through, I imagine. On your way to . . . a crime scene, of some sort?"

"Something like that," Starr said. He gazed at me. "What's your name?"

I swallowed hard. I'm not good with authority figures. "Mo," I said, a blush walking up my neck. Sometimes I could kill the Colonel for giving me a name like Mo.

"Unusual name," he said.

"It's Biblical," I told him. "Don't take this wrong, but the last person to make fun of it got swallowed by the Red Sea."

An Azalea Woman tittered.

Dale slid Starr's paper plate across the counter. "There you go: a Carnivore's Delight. I gave you a cucumber strip, on the house."

"Thanks, son," he said. Starr's gaze traveled from the dollar bill over the kitchen door, to the Colonel's hand-lettered sign over the coffee urn: No LAWYERS. Starr picked up his sandwich and studied Dale. "What's *your* name?"

Dale blanched. "Me? My name is . . . Phillip. Sir."

The café gasped, and I gave Dale a sharp kick in the shin. "I mean, it's Dale," he said, his eyes filling with tears. Dale's family is like that. Let the Law come within twenty yards of them, and every male over the age of six—uncles, brother, father, cousins—starts lying his fool head off. Dale says it's genetic. Miss Lana says that's poppycock.

"So," Mayor Little said. "To what do we owe the honor, Detective Starr?"

"Just passing through, like you said," Starr said. "Headed for Wilmington. Who's that?" he asked, glancing at a black-and-white photo on the wall.

"Miss Lana," I said, ringing up Tinks's bill and dropping the extra into my tip jar. "She doesn't always look like that," I added. "She's dressed up like Mae West."

Mayor Little propped his elbow on the counter and beamed at Starr. "Hollywood Night here at the café, don't you know," he said, crossing his chubby legs and waggling one loafer. "We're a wonderfully creative community."

"I see that," Starr said, glancing around the room. "Miss Lana own this place?"

"Goodness, no," Mayor Little said. "The Colonel does. He's not in today. A bit under the weather, I suppose."

The crowd's attention swiveled to Starr, who sauntered toward the photograph. As he passed the Azalea

Women they leaned away from him, like rabbits shying away from a bobcat. "She looks familiar," he said, squinting at the photo.

"Well, that was the idea, Detective," Mayor Little said in a pained voice. "We had Hollywood Night here at the café, and we all dressed up. The whole town. Miss Lana came as Mae West, I chose Charlie Chaplin. I went silent for once, you see. Sort of an inside joke. We made an evening of it. Skits. Impressions."

Dale seemed to have regained his composure, even with a detective within arresting distance. Or so I thought until he opened his mouth. "The boobs aren't real," he squawked.

Mayor Little frowned. "Dale!"

"In Miss Lana's photograph, I mean. Those boobs aren't real," he babbled. "Neither is the hair."

"Dale, go check our Mountain Dew supply," I said, giving him a shove. The kitchen door swished shut behind him.

"Well, sir, what are you investigating?" Mayor Little asked as Starr settled back onto his stool. "Anything exciting?"

"A murder," he said, and the Azalea Women shuddered.

"Where?" Mayor Little asked.

"Happened in Winston-Salem, a couple weeks ago,"

Starr said, picking up his soupspoon and leaning over his bowl. "Good soup," he muttered.

"Miss Lana put it up last summer," I told him. "It's practically organic."

Mayor Little smoothed his tie. "Who is the, uh, dearly departed?" he asked.

"Fellow named Dolph Andrews. Ever hear of him?" Starr pulled a photo out of his shirt pocket and slid it down the counter. The mayor and I leaned over the counter, studying it. Even upside down, Dolph Andrews was a good-looking man.

"Looks a little like George Clooney," Mayor Little said. "No, Dolph Andrews has never been here. I'd remember." He slid the photo back. "Who killed him?"

"Don't know." Starr nudged the photo toward me. "Go ahead, pass it around. Let everybody take a look." The photo went from hand to hand, around the café.

"Somebody slit his throat?" I guessed, and an Azalea Woman dropped her spoon.

"Interesting thought, but no—somebody shot him dead," Starr said. "Cut his phone line, came into his house, and pulled the trigger." At the end of the counter, Mr. Jesse studied the photograph for a long moment. His hand shook as he passed it on.

"Who would kill a nice young man like that?" the

mayor sighed as Starr polished off his sandwich and pushed his plate away.

Starr shrugged. "Somebody who thought Dolph needed killing, I guess," he said. "Could have been right too, for all I know. What do I owe you, Biblical Mo?"

"Two seventy-five, plus tax."

"Don't be silly," Mayor Little said, reaching for his wallet. "Lunch is on me."

Joe Starr handed me a five. "Keep the change," he said, a whisper of a smile in his eyes. "And that spooky kid in the kitchen—"

"You mean Phillip?"

"I mean Dale," Starr said, slipping the photo into his shirt pocket and buttoning the flap. "Tell him the next time I come in here, I expect to see shoes on his feet."

He strolled to the door and stopped, looking out over the parking lot. "Nice Thunderbird," he said. "Whose is it?"

I hesitated. The Colonel always says not to lie, but sometimes the truth doesn't feel like a good fit. "Well," I said, my voice trailing off.

Fortunately, at that moment, the kitchen doors behind me swung open, slamming against the wall. The dollar bill over the door tilted. The café jumped. "It's my car, you nosy son of a gun," the Colonel growled from the doorway. "What's it to you?"

"Colonel!" I cried. The Colonel opened his long arms and scooped me in.

Miss Lana says hugging the Colonel's like hugging a turning plow, but I like the scrawny steel of his muscles and the jutting angles of his bones. "I thought you'd still be in bed, resting," I said.

He tightened the belt of the green plaid robe I gave him for Christmas the year I turned six. "Dale told me you had a stranger," he said, eyeing Starr.

I pointed. "That's Joe Starr," I whispered. "He's a lawman." Everyone in the café pivoted to squint at Starr, who stood stock-still, the way you do when a mad dog comes near. "He looks like trouble," I continued, keeping my voice low, "but he's nothing I can't handle." I smiled at Starr. "No offense," I said.

"None taken," Starr said easily.

"Except for that, everything's going great. Well," I added. "There's been a murder and we're out of soup."

At the end of the counter, Mr. Jesse leaned forward and cleared his throat. "Oh, and Mr. Jesse's boat went missing," I said.

The Colonel patted my shoulder. "Good job, Soldier," he said. "You are temporarily relieved of duty."

"Thank you, sir."

An uneasy silence fell over the café.

"My goodness, where are my manners?" Mayor Little

sputtered from the counter. "Detective Starr, this is Colonel LoBeau, proprietor of the Tupelo Café. Colonel? Detective Joe Starr, from Winston-Salem. As I believe Mo mentioned, he's looking into a murder."

"Afternoon," the Colonel said.

Joe Starr's gaze drifted from the Colonel's close-cropped military haircut, to his acorn-brown eyes, to his rough beard. He scanned past the frayed bathrobe to linger on the Colonel's tan bedroom slippers. "Colonel," he said, and from his tone I knew he would have tipped his hat if he'd been wearing one.

The Colonel faked a thin smile.

Everybody knows the Colonel handles authority figures even worse than I do. Some say it's because of a tour of duty in Vietnam. Or Bosnia. Or the Middle East. Miss Lana says it's because he's an arrogant fop who can't tolerate somebody else being in charge. Either way, the lunch crowd fluttered like nervous wrens.

"Colonel LoBeau," Starr repeated, and glanced at me. "So, that makes you . . ."

"Mo LoBeau, with the accent at the end," I said. "It used to be Mo Lobo, with the accent up front. But Miss Lana changed it when I went to first grade. She says it makes us practically French."

"Plus, *Lobo* means 'Wolf,'" Dale chimed in. "Who wants to lug around a name like Mo Wolf when you're headed for something like first grade? That's like heading for Niagara Falls with a cinderblock strapped to your ankle."

Starr ignored him. "Colonel, you look familiar to me," he said. "Have we met?"

"Not likely."

"Ever visit Winston-Salem?"

"Not that I recall."

Mayor Little swiveled on his stool. "The Colonel? In Winston-Salem?" He barked out a little laugh. "Unlikely indeed. The Colonel's avoided cities since when . . . Bosnia?" He looked at Dale, who shrugged.

For some reason, Starr ignored him too. "Know a fellow named Dolph Andrews?" he asked the Colonel, flipping Dolph's photo onto the counter.

"Nope," the Colonel said. "Is he your murderer?"

"He's my victim."

"I'm afraid I can't help you," the Colonel said, turning toward the kitchen. "So if there's nothing else. . . ."

"One more question," Starr said.

The café went tense. The Colonel had already been polite longer than anyone expected, and when he turned back, the smile had slipped from his face. He put his hands on his hips and jutted his chin forward. "Let me ask a couple questions, if you don't mind," he suggested. "Am I under arrest?"

"No sir."

"Do you plan to take me in for questioning?"

"No sir."

"Are you hungry?"

"No sir."

"Then please help me understand what business remains between us."

The café relaxed. That wasn't bad at all, not for the Colonel.

"It's about your Thunderbird," Starr said. "Where did you get it?"

"Robeson County, I believe," the Colonel said, his voice glassy smooth. "Cash transaction. Is there a problem?"

Starr shook his head. "No problem. When was that?"

"A couple years ago, maybe."

Dale's face reflected my shock. The Colonel just got that car! What on earth? The Colonel never lies. My shock went molten in a heartbeat. "You stop picking on the Colonel," I shouted, stepping on the Pepsi crate for extra height.

"I'm just asking a few questions," Starr said. "Dolph Andrews here collected vintage cars and a couple seem to be missing."

Mayor Little's mouth dropped open and he gaped at the lunch crowd, inviting everyone to share his horror. "Surely you're not suggesting the Colonel's—"

"I'm not suggesting anything," Starr said. "There's nothing wrong with driving old cars. I like them myself."

The mayor forgave him with a wobbly smile, and the café relaxed again. "If you like old cars, Detective, eastern North Carolina's perfect for you," he said, smoothing his tie. "We have oodles of vintage vehicles around here, don't we, Colonel? In fact, I like to think of them as one of poverty's little perks."

Starr didn't smile. "Thanks again, Mo," he said. "I'll be seeing you. Soon."

"Another visit?" Mayor Little said, holding out his hand. "I know we'll all look forward to that."

I bet we won't, I thought as they shook hands.

As the door slapped shut behind Starr, the Colonel shuffled toward the kitchen, yawning. "Give a man a badge, and he thinks he owns the world," he muttered to no one in particular. "Only thing worse is a lawyer." Like I said, the Colonel hates lawyers.

Outside, Starr slowly circled the Underbird.

"Can you handle checkout, Soldier?" the Colonel asked, and I nodded. "Very well, I'll take the supper patrol."

Dale stood on his tiptoes, trying to see over the Azalea Women's hair and into the parking lot. "What's Starr doing?" he asked.

"He's squatting to write down the Colonel's license

number," Grandmother Miss Lacy Thornton said from her table by the window. "For a man of his age, he has excellent balance."

The Azalea Women murmured in agreement.

As Starr settled into his Impala and began scribbling on a clipboard, the lunch crowd stampeded the cash register. Only Mr. Jesse hung behind. "Don't see why folks care about a murder a half day from here when they don't give a Fig Newton about my boat," he said, pushing his three dollars across the counter and holding out his hand for change.

"Yes sir, that's a pity," Dale said, straightening the salt and pepper shakers. "Too bad there's no way to get your boat back. Hey!" he said, his blue eyes flying wide. "Maybe we could . . . No," he said, his face falling, "that would never work. I guess I really *am* dumb as dirt, like my daddy says."

"I'll be the judge of that," Mr. Jesse snapped. "What's your idea? Spit it out."

"Well," Dale mumbled. "I was just thinking if you offered a reward . . ."

A reward! My heart leaped like the cheerleader I will never be. Dale shows glimmers of genius at times, no matter what our teacher, Miss Retzyl, says.

Mr. Jesse scowled. "You think I should pay a thief to return my own property?"

"Don't you listen to him, Mr. Jesse," I said, dropping his change into his hand. "The thought of rewarding somebody for bringing your boat back. . . . That's wrong. Shoot. It would be better if they kept it, and that's the dog-honest truth. You don't need a boat. Besides, you can use that dab of reward money for . . . for . . ."

"For canned goods," Dale suggested.

"Right. For tuna," I said. "That way you'll still get plenty of fish in your diet." I buffed a napkin holder to a high sheen with my shirttail. "Too bad, though, losing a nice boat over a little finder's fee."

Mr. Jesse drummed his fingertips against the counter.

"A finder's fee," Dale said mournfully. "See? That's smart."

"Sure," I told him. "A reward is like welfare, which Mr. Jesse here has said a million times will bring about the end of civilization. Isn't that right, Mr. Jesse? But a finder's fee! That's more like a minimum wage job."

Mr. Jesse squinted at me, his eyes glittery hard. He snagged my pen and scrawled a notice on my order pad:

$10 Finder's Fee for the return of my boat. Jesse Tatum.

"Put this on the bulletin board," he said, and slammed the door behind him.

We watched Mr. Jesse cross the parking lot, giving Starr a wide berth as the Impala roared to life. "Think

Starr will really be back?" Dale asked as Starr's taillights disappeared around the curve.

"Yeah," I said, thinking of the Colonel's Underbird. "Me too."

I could feel it in my bones: Trouble had come to Tupelo Landing for good.

Chapter 3
The Three Day Rule

That evening, as the Colonel puttered about our living room, I settled on my bed and printed a title across the bright blue cover of a new spiral notebook. *THE PIGGLY WIGGLY CHRONICLES, VOLUME 6. TOP SECRET. If you ain't me, stop reading.*

As far as I know, I'm the only kid in Tupelo Landing researching her own autobiography. I'm also the only kid who needs to. So far, my life is one big, fat mystery. At its heart lies this question: Who is my Upstream Mother, and why hasn't she come for me?

Fortunately, I'm a natural born detective, hot on my own trail since birth. I mostly decorate my room with clues.

The *Piggly Wiggly Chronicles*, volumes 1 through 5, line the bookshelf over my flea market desk. The sprawling map of North Carolina, which Miss Lana helped me tape on the wall above my bed, pinpoints my search for my Upstream Mother. Using the process of elimination and a set of color-coded pushpins, I've marked all the places I know she's not. By now, the map bristles like a neon porcupine.

My bedside phone—a heavy, black 1950s model with a genuine dial—jangled. I scooped it up on the second ring. "Mo LoBeau's flat, Mo speaking," I said. "A message in a bottle? Yes sir. It's mine. . . . You found it where?"

I hopped onto my bed and studied the map. "Cypress Point? I see it on the map, sir. . . . No, I'm not upset that you're not my mother. Thanks for calling."

I jammed a green pushpin into Cypress Point and settled on my bed.

How did I wind up short a mother? Good question.

I was born eleven years ago, during one of the meanest hurricanes in history. That night as people slept, they say, the rivers rose like a mutiny and pushed ashore, shouldering houses off foundations, lifting the dead from graves, gulping down lives like fresh-shucked oysters.

Some say I was born unlucky that night. Not me. I say I was three times lucky.

Lucky once when my Upstream Mother tied me to a makeshift raft and sent me swirling downstream to safety. Lucky twice when the Colonel crashed his car and stumbled to the creek just in time to snatch me from the flood. Lucky three times when Miss Lana took me in like I was her own, and kept me.

Why all that happened is Mystery on a larger scale. Miss Lana calls it Fate. Dale calls it a miracle. The Colonel just shrugs and says "Here we are."

Behind my back, Anna Celeste Simpson—my Sworn Enemy for Life—says I'm a throw-away kid, with no true place to call home. So far, nobody's had the guts to say it to my face, but I hear whispers the way a knife-thrower's assistant hears knives.

I hate Anna Celeste Simpson.

The Colonel knocked on my open door and peeked in from the living room, his gray stubble glistening in the lamplight. "Busy, Soldier?"

"Sorry, sir," I said, closing my notebook. "I'm contemplating an intro to Volume Six. It's Top Secret."

"I'm sure I haven't got the clearance," he said. "But as a dedicated member of your mess crew, I'm contemplating popcorn. Thoughts?"

"Excellent strategy, sir." I hesitated. "Colonel, has Miss Lana checked in?"

"Not yet," he said. "But she only left this morning. We're nowhere near the Three Day Rule."

Miss Lana and I made the Three Day Rule last year, after the Colonel got turned around in the Appalachians and didn't check in for a week. Miss Lana went frantic, dragging half the town along with her. Now whenever he or Miss Lana leaves, which is often, the Three Day Rule automatically kicks in.

It's a no-brainer for Miss Lana, who naturally checks in almost every day. When she leaves, she visits her cousin Gideon, in Charleston. Usually, they shop. Twice last year, she took me with her. I have the plaid sneakers to prove it.

The Three Day Rule's harder on the Colonel. When he leaves, he leaves to sleep under the stars—usually on a mountainside or at the seashore. Cell service along North Carolina's wild fringes remains as patchy as it is here in Tupelo Landing—where, except for scratchy blips, we ain't got none. For him, calling every third day is a tribulation.

The Colonel glanced at my phone. "Lana loves talking to you, Soldier," he said. "I believe you have Cousin Gideon's number."

"Yes sir, I've seared it into my brain," I said. "But I don't want to over-dial."

He nodded and slipped back into the living room.

I opened Volume 6, skipping the intro in favor of a quick note to Upstream Mother. I've been writing to her ever since I learned to print (Volume 2). I used to think she could somehow read my unsent letters. Now, of course, I know she can't. I still write, partly out of habit and partly to settle my thoughts. Besides, my teacher, Miss Retzyl, says personal letters make rich research material for autobiographies—in my case, an obvious plus. I picked up my pen.

> Dear Upstream Mother,
>
> Miss Retzyl claims my vast experience in discovering where you're not helps me zero in on you. But frankly, my map can't hold many more pushpins. Neither can my heart. Eleven years is a long time to search. Drop me a line or pick up the phone. I'm on the verge of puberty.
>
> Mo

Eleven years is no lie.

Miss Lana mounted the first search when I was a week old. She dialed her way upstream, targeting churches and town halls as far west as Raleigh. No one had lost a baby. When our neighbors went out of town they asked too: "Anybody missing a lucky newborn?" My map's 167 yellow pushpins mark the places people said no.

The green pushpins are Bottle Pins, which I started adding the summer I turned eight. Me and Dale had plundered our way down to the creek, to escape the heat. As we lolled in the water, a leaf drifted by. "Look," I gasped, pointing.

It was so obvious! Why hadn't I thought of it before?

"Dale, what do we know about my Upstream Mother?" I demanded.

"She ain't here," he said, standing and emptying the mud out of his pockets.

"We know she lives by the water," I prompted.

He sat back down, the mud rising in the water like smoke. "So?"

"So, if water took me away from her, water can bring us back together," I said, watching the leaf swirl away. "I'll send her a message by water, so she can find me. This is brilliant. Let's go tell Miss Lana."

Moments later, I stood in the café, creek water puddling around my feet as I explained my plan: I'd put messages in bottles and release them far upstream, letting them float down to my true mother.

Miss Lana studied me like I was a star chart and she had crashed on Mars. "I don't know, sugar," she finally said. She rang up Tinks Williams's bill and handed him his change. "It seems like a long shot to me. A very long shot."

"But Miss Lana," I said, "we have to. The water's all I got."

"I'm going to Goldsboro for a tractor part," Tinks said. "I'll sling a message off the bridge for you, if you want me to."

Grandmother Miss Lacy Thornton dabbed her lips with her napkin. "I think it's a fine idea," she said. "I'm going to Raleigh tomorrow. I'd be glad to release one if you'd like, Lana." She smiled. "You have to admit, some things *do* look better sailing away," she'd said, and Miss Lana had nodded.

So far my bottles have failed. Every once in a blue moon someone finds one and calls, but most just disappear. Like Miss Lana, I now recognize them as long shots. Still, I keep them ready for folks heading west, with my standard note inside: *Dear Upstream Mother. You lost me during a hurricane 11 years ago. I'm ok. Write back or call. 252-555-4663. Mo.*

Sometimes I still dream she floats an answer back to me. But I always wake up before I can make out the words.

The Colonel *rat-a-tat-tatted* against the door. "I've located Lana's cooking oil and a popcorn pan," he reported, looking frazzled. "Popcorn front and center in five."

"Message received, sir," I said.

The Colonel's a wizard in the café kitchen, where he organizes things in neat lines and stacks. Miss Lana organizes our personal kitchen by "intuitive whim"— circus-worthy towers of plates and bowls, canned goods stacked by color, a refrigerator of health foods possibly gone toxic. The Colonel says he can't find a dad-blamed thing in there. He would say more, but Miss Lana doesn't allow cursing.

The phone rang again. "I got it," I shouted, scooping it off the hook. "Hello? Miss Lana? . . . Oh, hey Grandmother Miss Lacy Thornton. How are you?" I asked, trying not to sound disappointed. "Fine. . . . No ma'am, not yet, but she'll call. . . ."

Miss Lana says the good thing about living in a small town is everybody knows your business, and they pitch in. The Colonel says the *bad* thing about living in a small town is everybody knows your business, and they pitch in. It cuts both ways.

"Yes ma'am," I said, "Anna Celeste's party *is* Saturday, but I don't need a ride. . . . No ma'am. It's because Anna Celeste is my Sworn Enemy for Life and I'd rather go face-down in a plate of raw chicken entrails than go to her party. Plus I'm not invited. . . . Yes ma'am, I'll tell the Colonel you called. Good-bye."

Anna Celeste Simpson—blond hair, brown eyes, perfect smile—became my Sworn Enemy for Life our first day of kindergarten.

Miss Lana had walked me to school and fled, crying. As I waited for the bell that would spell my doom, I spied a princess-like girl across the muddy playground. A new friend! I started toward her. Her pinch-faced mother grabbed her arm. "No, honey," she said in a pretend whisper. "It's that *girl* from the café. She's not one of us."

Not one of us?

Until that instant, everybody in my world had been "one of us." Still, I might have regained my Legendary Poise if little Anna Celeste hadn't squinted at me and shown a faint, pink crescent of tongue.

For one sickening moment, I thought I would cry. Then I had a better idea.

I lowered my head and charged like a bull, the blood pounding in my ears as my white sandals pounded across the playground. My head slammed into Anna's tender belly just as the bell rang. I trotted toward my first time-out, leaving Anna Celeste wheezing in the mud.

For me, it was a Gold Star day. I'd identified an enemy, and I'd made a life decision: I might come home tore up from fighting or late from being punished, but I'd never come home crying. So far, I ain't.

The Colonel took my educational debut in stride. Miss Lana was a harder sell. "Hold on, sugar," she said, pulling out her dog-eared copy of *Suddenly Mom*. "Let's see what the experts say." I leaned against her as she ran her finger across a page. "As I suspected, there are better ways to express baby rage," she said, taking my hand. "We're going to the Piggly Wiggly."

At the grocery store, she bought my first spiral

notebook—a bright red one—and the *Piggly Wiggly Chronicles* were born. I filled Volume 1 with scribbled portraits of Anna Celeste in mud.

The phone rang again. "Mo's place. Mo speaking."

"Hi, sugar," Miss Lana said. "How are you?"

I smiled. "Fine," I said, closing Volume 6. "How's Charleston?"

"Beautiful. And hot." Miss Lana's voice is the color of sunlight in maple syrup. "How did things go today?"

"Fine." A long silence crackled through our line.

"What's wrong?" she asked. Miss Lana reads my voice like a Gypsy reads tea leaves.

Should I mention Mr. Jesse's boat? Detective Joe Starr? The murder in Winston-Salem? The Underbird? The Colonel's lie?

"Nothing," I said. "How's Cousin Gideon?"

"Fine. Well, a little nervous. His play opens this evening. And the Colonel?" She doesn't say so, but Miss Lana worries about the Colonel, maybe because of his background. Or the fact that he doesn't have one.

The Colonel came to town the same stormy night I did, crashing headfirst into a pine at the edge of town. Some people say he lost his memory in the wreck. Others say he lost it *before* he got in the car, or he wouldn't have been out in a hurricane. Either way, he climbed out of that car free of every memory he'd ever owned.

Rumors swirl around the Colonel like ink around an octopus: that he's a retired warrior, or a paper-pusher. That he's from Atlanta, or Nashville. That he came to town broke, or carrying a suitcase of cash.

I suspect he started most of the rumors himself.

"The Colonel's just fine, Miss Lana," I said. "He's making popcorn."

"Oh dear," she said, and I could hear her smile.

"Popcorn, front and center," the Colonel barked from the living room.

Miss Lana laughed. "It sounds like he survived," she said. "Run along, sugar. Tell the Colonel hello for me. I'll see you in a couple of days."

"Yes ma'am." I grabbed Volume 6 and made a beeline for my favorite chair as the Colonel folded himself onto Miss Lana's velvet settee. He looks as out of place as a coyote in a tuxedo among Miss Lana's Victorian curlicues.

Our fancy house surprises people used to the café's plain, cinderblock face. The Colonel built the café and our house together, in one building. The café faces the street. Our home faces the creek.

Anna Celeste calls our place the Taj Ma-Gall, because she says you got to have gall to talk about a five-room house the way we do. Miss Lana calls her room a suite, and the Colonel's room his quarters. Last year, the Colonel and Miss Lana gave me my own apartment. Anna Celeste says it's just a closed-in side porch with a bathroom stuck on the side. I say I'm the only kid in Tupelo Landing with her own flat.

"Miss Lana called," I told the Colonel, and he smiled. "She's fine."

"History Channel?" he offered, handing me a bowl of popcorn. The Colonel enjoys reliving battles he may or may not have been in. "Any progress on your intro?"

"Autobiographies are tough when you're clueless," I admitted, settling in. I picked up my pen.

Miss Lana says her life's a tapestry. Mine's more of a crazy quilt stitched together with whatever happened to be at hand. Then there's the Colonel.

"Excuse me, sir," I said. "Do you feel more like a tapestry or a quilt?"

He tossed a handful of popcorn in his mouth. "Wool blanket," he said. "Warm, scratchy, too ugly to steal."

"Thank you, sir," I said, closing Volume 6 and settling in.

I glanced out the window, at Mr. Jesse's lights flickering a couple hundred yards down the creek, like they had every night of my life.

It's funny, the things you think you'll always see again.

Chapter 4
Meeting Up at Lavender's

Mr. Jesse lingered over lunch the next day. "This pudding ain't right," he said, a fleck of meringue clinging to his unshaven chin. "Take it off my bill."

I eyed the half-eaten dessert du jour. "The Colonel's banana pudding is county-renowned, Mr. Jesse," I said. "You're just suffering from sticker shock. It happens every time you order dessert."

Dale rolled his eyes. The Colonel says if you handed Mr. Jesse a two-dollar sandwich wrapped in a twenty-dollar bill, he'd still complain about the price.

"I can't take back half a pudding, Mr. Jesse," I said. "You know I can't."

He slapped four George Washingtons on the counter. "Count whatever you charge for that pudding as your tip," he growled, and stalked off glaring like the afternoon sun.

The Colonel strolled in from the kitchen and tossed his apron on the counter. "You two have performed above and beyond the call of duty," he said, watching

Mr. Jesse disappear down the lane. "You're at liberty for the rest of the afternoon."

We sprinted for the door before he could change his mind.

"Want to go fishing?" I asked Dale as the door banged shut behind us.

He drained a soda and crumpled the can. "Not until Mr. Jesse settles down about that boat. It's not that I'm scared of getting caught," he added, giving me a quick look. "It's just that I'm too pretty to do hard time. Lavender already told me."

Lavender, as I may have mentioned, is Dale's big brother.

"Hey," Dale said, flipping his empty can to me. "Practice me."

Dale dreams of being the first rising sixth grader to be drafted by a high school football team. This is because he sings in church, which his daddy says is sissified. Football ain't. Dale may not know much from the classroom, but his recess skills are legendary. He's small, but he's a wildcat of a receiver and fearless when he goes up for a pass. I sighed. "Buttonhook on three," I said.

He set up to my left.

"Set!" I said, looking right and left. "Down! Hut-hut-hut!"

Dale sprinted across the parking lot. I dropped back

three paces and he did a neat buttonhook. My pass sailed high, but he climbed into the air like a cat scrambling up a tree, and snagged it. Touchdown!

"I'm going home to check on Mama," he called, veering across the parking lot to his bike. Dale's protective of Miss Rose. "You want to meet up at Lavender's?" he asked. "We can watch him work on his car."

Visit Lavender? The day went golden.

"Sure," I said, trying to sound casual. "See you there."

We got two streets in Tupelo Landing: First Street, where the café sits, and Last, where Lavender lives. We like to say if you're looking for somebody in Tupelo Landing, you'll find them, First and Last.

I discovered Lavender working in his front yard, the hood of his faded red Monte Carlo up. While he tinkered, I settled in the cool, dense shade of a water oak and told him about Joe Starr's visit—even though he'd probably heard it from five other people before me. He stayed quiet until I got to the Colonel's lie.

"He *lied* about the Underbird?" He peered across the car's engine, his blue eyes soft and thoughtful. "Why?"

I shrugged, and he pushed his wheat-colored hair back with his wrist. Lavender is tall and hound-dog skinny. He wears his hair combed up in front, like he's speeding through life. "Have you asked him?"

"No," I said. "Mostly the Colonel won't talk 'til he's ready."

Lavender's handsome in the NASCAR way, and if I was old enough I'd snatch him up and marry him before sundown. I've asked him plenty of times already, starting the day I turned six. He always laughs and says I'm too young. Lavender is nineteen, and dangerous close to being a man.

"It's not like the Colonel to lie," he said. "Of course, he's always been a mystery. We don't really know where he's from, or who his folks are." He flushed. "I didn't mean that the way it sounded, Mo," he said quick. "What I mean is . . ."

"I know what you mean." I tossed an acorn at the birdbath. "The Colonel and me ain't true family. Everybody knows that."

"You *are* family," he said. "You're just not blood, is all. And blood don't count for much anyway. Look at Macon and me." Lavender calls his daddy by his first name, but as far as I know, he's never called him that to his face. Lavender slammed out of his daddy's house the day he turned eighteen and hasn't been back. He moved here the same day.

Lavender's house is old, with a patched roof, but his pride shows in the way the porch stays swept and the daylilies never want tending. His hand-lettered business sign stands in the front yard: Auto Doc—We Make House Calls. He keeps the Azalea Women's wheels turning and has Grandmother Miss Lacy Thornton's Buick purring like a kitten. But everybody in town knows Lavender is just scraping by.

"Maybe you're right," I said. "Maybe blood ain't all that much. I guess the main thing is, the Colonel's good to me."

"No," he said, picking up a pack of spark plugs. "The main thing is, the Colonel loves you. Miss Lana does too. Speaking of Miss Lana—"

"She's fine," I said. "She's in Charleston, with Cousin Gideon."

"Don't worry," he said easily, "she can't stay away from you very long."

"I know. I just wish she wouldn't go away."

He dove back under the hood. "How's your autobiography coming?" he asked.

"I'm still in the research stage," I admitted. "Miss Lana gave me a newspaper article before she left, about my coming to town. Your daddy's got some quotes in it."

"Really? I'd be curious to see that."

Lavender? Curious about me?

I smiled. "Truth is, autobiography is harder than I expected. Maybe because I got so many fill-in-the-blanks."

"Yeah," he said. "I'm more of a multiple choice man, myself."

An easy silence fell between us.

"Hey, Lavender," I said after a while. "That new girl-friend of yours—what's her name? Candy? Taffy? You may not know it, but a girl like that will rot your teeth out. How about you marry me?"

He tossed a screwdriver in his battered toolbox. "You? You're a baby." He grinned. "Hand me that ratchet. I got to get this car right for tonight's race. Where's Dale, anyway? You guys are usually like get and got, one right behind the other."

"Gone home to check on your mama," I said as he leaned over the engine.

I haven't mentioned it to Lavender yet, but if we adopt children after we're married, I'll want to name them myself. Naming Good runs scarce in the Johnson family.

Lavender's full name, for example, is Lavender Shade Johnson. No lie. Miss Rose says she named him during her Early Poetry Stage. When Dale come along, Mr. Macon named *him* Dale Earnhardt Johnson, III—after Dale Earnhardt, maybe the most famous racecar driver in history. The "III" in Dale's name stands for Dale Earnhardt's car, the Immortal Number 3.

Dale runs opposite his daddy on most things, but he

too believes in Naming for the Famous. His dog, Queen Elizabeth II, is living proof of that.

"Dale's back," I told Lavender, and he looked up as Dale skidded to a halt, sending up a spray of fine white sand.

"Hey, little brother," Lavender said.

"Hey yourself," Dale replied, ditching his bike and plopping down beside me in the shade. He leaned back in the cool grass and crossed his tanned legs. He'd slipped into a fresh shirt—black, as usual.

"How's Mama?" Lavender asked.

"Fine. She's out in the garden. Daddy came by—for a few minutes, anyway."

Lavender shot him a sharp look. It was awful early for a farmer to be home, even one sorry as Mr. Macon. "Everything okay?"

Dale's shrug said it all: Mr. Macon had come home drinking again. Lavender tossed his ratchet in the tool-box harder than he needed to. "What you hooligans doing this evening?" he asked, slamming the Monte Carlo's hood.

"Tonight's Karate Night at the café," I said. "Mr. Li's coming over from Snow Hill to teach everybody some new moves." I tried to sound modest. "I may not have mentioned it, but I'm a yellow belt."

Dale sighed. He hates Karate Night, but he hates Mr.

Macon's drinking more. "Yeah," he said, his voice dull. "Karate Night. That's probably what I'm doing too."

Lavender wiped his fingerprints off the Monte Carlo's hood. "Sounds good," he said. "In fact, it almost sounds better than fine-tuning this car for the Sycamore 200."

"The Sycamore 200?" Dale said, sitting up straight. "That's big time!"

Lavender smiled. "I wouldn't say big time, but it's a step up—and good money for the checkered flag. All I got to do is check out this engine."

"Since when do you race for money?" I asked.

He closed his toolbox. "There's nothing wrong with money if you know how to spend it," he said. "Anyway, I'm short somebody to time laps tonight, and I'd hoped you two might help me out. You two *can* tell time, can't you?"

"Us?" Dale yelped. "Time laps?"

It was an undreamed-of honor.

"I'll ask the Colonel if I can go," I said, jumping up.

"Sam's taking the car over on the flatbed," Lavender said, looking at his watch. "We'll take my truck. Let's leave at four o'clock. That'll give us an hour to get there."

"Count me in," Dale said, grabbing his bike. He leaned close. "I'm going to see Mr. Jesse. We could use the pocket money," he whispered, and winked. The reward money! "Pick me up at the bridge," he shouted.

Lavender nodded. "Mo, tell the Colonel I promise to have you home by ten."

"I'll wait for you at the café," I said, setting off at a dead run.

"Hey, bring that newspaper clipping," Lavender called after me, and I waved without looking back.

I pounded home, changed shirts, and stuffed my laminated newspaper article in my pocket. I bolted for the kitchen, where I found the Colonel dressed in faded fatigues, a bag of spuds at his feet. He smiled as I skidded across the floor and hurled myself into a chair by the stainless steel work table. "Afternoon, Soldier," he said.

"Afternoon, Colonel," I panted.

"Thought I'd make some garlic potatoes tonight. Steamed turnip greens with fresh green onions, grilled chicken. While I was away I picked up a teriyaki baste I think you'll appreciate. Broth, ginger root, sesame oil, a dash of teriyaki. . . ."

"Sounds great," I said. "Actually, Colonel, I was hoping you might handle the supper crowd on your own tonight. That is, if you wouldn't mind."

He raised his right eyebrow. "You're here to request leave? On Karate Night?"

I nodded.

"Reason?"

"Deployment to the Carolina Raceway," I said. "Me

and Dale been asked to time laps for Lavender. Don't worry, sir, it's not dangerous," I added.

"I see," he said. "Transport?"

"GMC pickup driven by Lavender Shade Johnson."

"Always liked that boy," he mused. "Pity about the name. Time of departure?"

I studied the clock, trying to do the math without moving my lips. Four o'clock is a tough one. "Sixteen hundred hours?" I guessed. "I already changed shirts," I said, smoothing my purple T-shirt. "I know you like me to look good in a crowd."

He nodded. "Return time?"

"Twenty-two hundred hours."

He tossed a potato into the pot. It made a bald, rolling sound. I held my breath. Miss Lana wouldn't let me stay out until ten o'clock if the planet's fate depended on it. "Very well, Soldier," he finally said. "I suppose I can draft someone to help me if we get too busy. Permission granted. But I expect you back on time."

"Yes, sir," I said. I crossed to the Colonel and gave him a quick kiss on top of his head. He smelled like ginger and Old Spice. "Colonel, I don't know what you and Miss Lana got crossed up about, but don't you worry. She'll be back."

He sighed. "I know," he said. "I just wish she'd stay put. She's so . . . flighty."

"A little, maybe," I said. "But she's crazy about you." Just then, Lavender's GMC roared into the parking lot, horn blaring. "There's Lavender!" I cried.

"Run along, then, Soldier."

I stopped at the door and turned. The Colonel looked thin and old and lonesome among the dented pots and pans. "Colonel?"

"Yes, Soldier?"

"I think I know what you mean about Miss Lana."

He looked up at me, his expression suddenly as fragile and vulnerable as a new fawn. "You do?"

"Yes, sir," I said. "I miss her too."

He smiled. "Move along, Soldier," he said. "Never keep a comrade waiting."

Chapter 5
At the Carolina Raceway

Lavender leaned across the seat of his 1955 GMC pickup and pushed the door open. I hopped up on the running board and dove in. "Hey," I said.

"Hey yourself." The truck bumped into gear as he eased off the clutch.

"Truck looks good," I told him.

It was true. Lavender found her in a junkyard last year. He restored her piece by piece, and dressed her broad curves in a coat of deep blue paint. I scooted forward to scan the roadside. "Dale ought to be out here somewhere," I said at the edge of town. "There he is, by the Crash Pine."

Dale jumped in almost before we stopped rolling. "Sorry about the mud," he muttered, scraping his black sneakers together. I glanced at the creek's dark waters. I could just make out Dale's bike on the bank, hidden in a tangle of kudzu.

"How'd you get your feet wet?" Lavender asked.

I changed the subject before Mr. Jesse's boat came

up—which it would if Dale started talking. "Hey, you reckon that's where the Colonel found me?" I asked, peering over the bridge rail. "Because I'll want a good description for my autobiography."

"Your *what?*" Dale yelped, looking like I'd handed him something dead. "You ain't writing during summer vacation, are you?" he demanded. "Because I'm pretty sure that's against the rules. Aren't there rules against that, Lavender?"

Lavender shifted gears. "Calm down, Dale. Mo's doing research, that's all."

"*Again?*" Dale said, his voice accusing. "You try to figure out your life every time you get close to a birthday, Mo, and you ain't done it yet. I wish you'd leave it alone," he said, slumping against the door. "I'm tired of hearing about it. There's nothing wrong with the people you got."

"Well, others are interested in the Mystery of my Upstream Family even if you ain't," I said, pulling the newspaper article from my pocket. I cleared my throat and read:

BABY GIRL FOUND

Macon Johnson, of Tupelo Landing, found a newborn girl at the edge of Contentnea Creek last Tuesday while helping a man who had wrecked in the hurricane.

"The old coot in the colonel's uniform was holding a

baby when I found him," Johnson said. "Said he found the baby floating downstream on some debris. He named her Moses. She's darned lucky to be alive, if you ask me."

Anyone with information about the man, who had the name Lobo on his pocket, or the baby should contact Mayor Little.

"Yep, that sounds like Macon," Lavender said. "I'm surprised there's not more about the Colonel, though."

"He's got his own article," I said, slipping the story back into my pocket and buttoning the flap. "Miss Lana's keeping it for him."

Dale looked back over his shoulder. "Daddy was right, Mo. You were lucky to get out of that creek alive."

"Mo's always been lucky," Lavender said. The truck chugged good-naturedly through her gears and settled into a steady hum.

An hour later we rumbled across grassy, rutted acres of parked pickup trucks, and through the crew gate of the Carolina Raceway. Lavender let the GMC glide to a halt. "Here you go, little brother," he said, pulling a twenty-dollar bill out of his pocket. "You two get us some eats and meet me in the infield." He stretched. "Listen, Sam brought a couple of ladies, so don't skimp on the food, okay? Don't worry about drinks. We brought a cooler. All right? Can you handle it?"

"Sure," Dale said, stepping out onto the running board. I slid out after him. "Lessee," Dale muttered as we headed for the concession line, which wound down the drinking side of the bleachers and halfway across the family seats. "You, me, Lavender, Sam, two ladies. That makes six."

"Don't waste your money buying food for those girls," I told him. "If I know Sam, he's brought a couple of ex-baton-twirlers trying to starve themselves into cheerleader-size jeans." I peered at the line ahead of us. "Hey, I'm going over to Potty Palace. I'll be back before you get to the front of the line." Dale nodded, straining to see the menu board, and I trotted into the crowd.

I got my first shock of the evening just after exiting Potty Palace. I rounded the corner at near Olympic speeds, slamming square into a tall, slender woman who wheezed like an out-of-sorts accordion. I careened off of her, jumped a medium-size azalea, got my feet tangled, and landed in a crumpled heap by the gravel walk. "Jeez Louise, lady," I shouted. "Why don't you look where you're going?"

"I *was* looking, Mo," the woman said, trying to stand up straight. "Were you?"

"What?" I rolled onto my back and squinted into a shockingly familiar face: Miss Retzyl, my fifth-grade teacher from last year. She's also my sixth-grade teacher for next year, having suffered the dreaded Curse of the Combined Grades. "Miss Retzyl? You should be careful! You could have killed us both!"

She smoothed her starched white blouse, then her hair.

I sighed. The truth is, I adore Miss Retzyl, who is tall and willowy, with red hair and brown eyes. She's smart and poised, and always on time. She has an average house and drives a dark blue convertible. When it comes to Predictable, a quality rare in my life, she's the real deal. Plus, she likes me. I cast about in my mind for something brilliant to say. Sadly, I came up empty. "Good Lord," I muttered instead, pointing to her legs. "What are those?"

She stepped back nervously, looking at her sandals. "What do you mean?"

"Knees," I answered. "You got knees."

She frowned. "Of course I have knees, Mo. Everyone has knees."

"Right. But I never saw them before. You always wear those old-lady dresses. And shorts!" I cried. "Miss Retzyl, you're wearing shorts!"

She smiled uncertainly. "Are you all right, Mo? Did you hit your head?"

"I'm fine," I said, swiping the gravel off my shins. "What are you doing here?"

"I'm . . . here for the races."

"Really? Dale's brother is in the next one. Me and Dale are timing laps for him."

"Dale and I," she murmured.

"Right. You remember Dale? Third row, fifth seat from the front? Blond hair, bad at math, wears a lot of black?"

"Of course I remember Dale."

"His brother, Lavender, drives the thirty-two car."

"I'll be sure to watch for him," she said, edging away. "Well, this has been nice, Mo, but my friend is waiting, and—"

"Friend?" I gasped. "You got friends? I figured when the school year ended you'd go home and watch TV, maybe read. I never considered friends."

She smiled. "Of course I have friends, Mo. See you soon," she said, and faded into the crowd. I wound my way back to Dale, who stood just one person away from the concession stand.

"You won't believe who I ran into," I said. "Miss Retzyl."

"That's nothing," he said. "Look over there." I followed his gaze.

The second shock of the evening fell like an ax. "Miss Retzyl and . . ."

"Joe Starr," he said, his voice grim. Detective Joe Starr handed Miss Retzyl a hot dog, and smiled. The hair on the back of my neck stood up.

Miss Retzyl and Joe Starr? Together? Had the world gone mad?

"What'll you have, baby doll?" the lady behind the counter rasped, her cat-eye glasses sliding down her narrow nose as she glanced at Dale.

"Six fried baloney sandwiches, three orders of fries, and as many M&M'S as I can get with whatever's left," he said, pushing the twenty-dollar bill toward her. "You want anything else, Mo? I got our reward money from Mr. Jesse," he said, tugging his pocket open to show off two five-dollar bills.

I snagged a five and shook my head.

We made our way to the infield clutching greasy bags of race chow. I was right about Sam's friends: a couple of big-haired, thin-faced twins named Crissy and Missy. They sat on lawn chairs in the back of the GMC, sipping Diet 7UPs and winking at Lavender and Sam. Dale stepped gallantly forward. "Care for a baloney sandwich?"

Crissy peered into the bag. "No thank you, sugar; we're dieting. But *you're* so sweet, I could eat you with a spoon."

Dale turned red as their nail polish, shoved his bag at me, and bolted for Lavender. I sauntered behind him, queen of the eats. "Watch the inside of the fourth turn," Sam was saying, over by the car. "It's running loose, you're liable to slide."

Lavender grabbed a sandwich. "Mo, Dale, I want you two on the truck."

"With the twins? Buffy and Muffy?" I asked, passing fries to Sam.

"Their names are Crissy and Missy and I'm not marrying either one of them, so play nice," he said. "Dale, I'd like for you to time the laps," he said, handing him a stopwatch. "No rounding off. Mo, I need the times in this ledger, please, ma'am. I want to see how we're running, lap by lap. Okay?"

I nodded. Dale stuck out his hand. "You can count on us."

Lavender hid a flicker of surprise. "I know I can," he said, shaking his hand. "That's why I asked you."

As Dale and I settled on the GMC's tailgate, our backs to the twins, Lavender stepped into his well-patched race suit, wiggling it over his hips and shrugging it across his shoulders. He clamped his helmet on, swung his legs in through the driver-side window of number 32, and fishtailed onto the track.

"Look," I said, elbowing Dale. Across the way Starr plowed through the tide of race fans like a tugboat, Miss Retzyl bobbing along in his wake. "They're gonna miss the race," I said as they exited the gate. I caught a flash of siren-blue light in the parking lot. "I hope Miss Retzyl ain't under arrest," I gasped as a siren wailed.

"For what?" Dale asked. "Bad taste in boyfriends?"

Lavender jostled in the pack, revving his engine. "He's headed to the starting line!" Dale shouted. "Here we go."

The flag fell.

The night roared.

The race was on.

Dale called out the times, lap after lap. On the twenty-eighth lap, Sam waved Lavender in, shouting and pointing at the rear left tire. Lavender slammed his palm against the dash and roared back into the race, tires screaming.

Sam stomped over and grabbed a soda from the cooler. "What's wrong?" Dale asked. "Why's Lavender mad?"

"Oh," Sam fumed. "It's probably nothing. That rear left tire don't look right and your brother's so damn stubborn. . . ." He took a deep breath. "Don't pay any attention to me, Dale. Lavender's right. I worry more than your mama does."

The crash came three laps later. Lavender skidded sideways through the fourth turn, his back tires billowing smoke. The crowd rose like a thousand open-mouthed puppets played by the same string, and I held my breath as Lavender hung sideways on the track—sliding, sliding, sliding—cars swerving miraculously by. Finally the number 45 car clipped his bumper, spinning him headfirst into the concrete barrier by the stands.

The night fell into slow motion as Lavender's car somersaulted down the wall, bounced right side up, and wobbled to the infield. I found myself running toward him before I knew I was standing.

Dale sprinted past and lunged through the driver's window. He and Sam pulled Lavender free, but he lay still in their arms as the EMTs rushed toward them.

A half hour later, Lavender sat in the rescue truck door, Doc Aikin turning his arm in the flat, yellow light. "It's a wonder you walked away from that crash," Doc said. "You could use some stitches in this arm. You got insurance?"

Lavender winced. "Are you kidding? Just tape it up, Doc."

Doc nodded. "I'll give you some antibiotics, then. As for your head . . ." he said, tilting Lavender's head back and shining a pin-light in his eye. Again.

"What's wrong with his head?" Dale asked, his voice wavering. He had barely spoken since Lavender came to sputtering and kicking on Doc's gurney.

Doc's a walrus of a man, tall as Lavender and twice as wide, but he gave Dale a kind smile. "He may have a concussion," he said. "It's too soon to tell." He fished his card out of his wallet and stuck it in Lavender's shirt pocket. "He needs to rest. But if he can't stay awake or starts throwing up, you call me and I'll meet you at the hospital. Pronto. Insurance or not. Understand?"

Dale and I nodded like dashboard dogs.

"Now, Lavender, where are you headed from here?"

Lavender was watching Sam winch what was left of the race car onto the flatbed truck. "I thought I'd take my crew home and go by Sam's . . ."

Doc followed his gaze. "Nope. No alcohol, no women. Especially no twins."

Dale touched Lavender's hand. "You could stay at the house," he said. "Just for tonight. Mama would be glad of it, and Daddy . . . probably wouldn't mind."

"Excellent," Doc said. "Here's my offer, then. Go to your mother's with my appointed deputies here, or go to the hospital."

"Deputies?" I repeated, standing tall. "Are badges involved?"

"It's your choice, Lavender," Doc said. "What's it going to be?"

Lavender frowned. "I guess one night at home won't kill me," he muttered.

"Good. Of course you're not driving with a head injury, so . . ."

I felt it coming: a phone call to the Colonel, begging him to collect us up like a pack of slick-nosed kids. I had to act fast. "Actually, Doc," I said, "those big-haired twins over there are pining to drive us home. Crissy can take us three in the GMC, and Missy's wild to drive the flatbed if Sam's too upset. Those twins are willing, plus they're sober out of their minds from sipping Diet 7UP all night. Don't take my word for it. Give them a blood test. I don't mind."

It worked like a charm.

"You sure you know how to drive this truck?" Lavender asked Crissy a few minutes later as she slid behind the wheel of the GMC. "Because she's a classic, and—"

"Ready!" I shouted, plopping down beside Dale and leaning against the cab. Crissy ground the gears, and we lunged into the night.

Dale and I dozed until an artless downshift woke us at the outskirts of town. "Must be taking the shortcut over Fool's Bridge." Dale yawned, peeking around the cab. Swirling blue lights swept the night. "Looks like a roadblock."

"Maybe they're breathalyzing everybody," I said.

He shook his head. "Nah, too many lights. Cop lights, rescue lights, headlights. An accident, maybe," he said. "Looks like they're turning people back."

Sure enough, a white Cadillac purred up the narrow road toward us and oozed to a stop. The window whirred down. Pinch-faced Mrs. Betsy Simpson—mother of my archenemy Anna Celeste—squinted in the dark. "Hey, Mrs. Simpson," I said. "It's Mo. How are you?"

"Mo," she said, her eyes following the GMC's lines. "In a jalopy. Not my taste, exactly, but how nice for you."

Mean runs in the Simpson family. "It ain't a jalopy, it's a classic," I said.

"Whatever it is, you might as well turn it around," she said, glancing at Crissy. "Fool's Bridge is closed. The police won't let you through."

"Closed?" Dale said. "Why? What happened?" But her window whirred back up, and she was gone.

Crissy did a surprisingly nice three-point turn and we detoured to Miss Rose's house. As we lurched to a stop, Dale vaulted over the side of the truck. "You all wait out here while I see if Daddy's up," he said.

"Sorry to ruin your plans, sugar," Crissy said, hopping out. "But I got to pee. So does Missy, I'm sure," she said as Missy wheeled into the drive. The four of us traipsed onto the front porch, where Dale held the screen door for the twins.

"Mama," he called. "I'm home."

Miss Rose sat in her armchair, scribbling on a legal pad and listening to the radio. "Hey, baby," she said without glancing up. "How'd it go?"

"Evening, Miss Rose," I said, stepping into the lamplight.

"Hello, Mo." She saw the twins for the first time. "My goodness," she said, jumping to her feet. "I didn't realize you'd brought company home, Dale."

"They ain't Dale's, they're Sam's," I said. "Miss Rose, I'd like to introduce you to twins. This one's Crissy and that one's Missy. Or the other way around."

"I'm pleased to meet you," she said. "Won't you sit down?"

"They can't," I said. "They got to pee." I pointed to the hall. "Bathroom's on your right. The light switch is in the hallway, by the door. Miss Rose," I continued, "I think you better sit down yourself."

Dale nodded encouragingly, and Miss Rose drifted to the settee. Miss Rose is the most graceful person I know. "Mama, where's Daddy?" Dale asked.

Miss Rose hesitated. "He's resting."

Dale looked relieved. "In Lavender's old room?" She nodded.

Dale's daddy sleeps in Lavender's room when he's had too much to drink, because Miss Rose can't stand having him around her. I know that because Dale told me. It's not something Miss Rose and me talk about. "He's sleeping pretty sound?" he asked.

"Sleeping pretty sound" is their code for "passed out cold."

She nodded slowly. "What's this about?" she asked.

"Let me tell her, Dale," I said. "The way you tell things, you'll kill her."

"Tell me what?" she asked, her green eyes suspicious.

I took a deep breath. "Miss Rose, I hate to mention it, but your firstborn's crashed headfirst into a cement wall at maybe a hundred miles an hour, which we can all be grateful hard-headedness runs in your family. He's outside right now hoping his daddy will let him in without any nastiness, and *we're* hoping he don't get medically no worse, because Doc Aikin says if he goes concussion, we got to rush him to the hospital. Dale and me are Doctor Appointed in this," I concluded.

Miss Rose was already halfway across the room. "Lavender Shade Johnson, you get yourself in this house this instant," she said, pushing the screen door open.

Lavender stepped in, looking embarrassed. "Hey, Mama," he said.

She gasped. The bruise on his forehead had run dark, hungry fingers to his eye. "You sit down," she said, pushing him onto the settee. "Dale, get me a towel and some ice. And bring a pillow off my bed." She leaned down to tug Lavender's boots off, pausing when she got a look at his socks—one gray and one black. "Thank God you *didn't* have to go to the hospital," she said. "Where's Dale? Where's that ice?"

"Hey, Miss Rose," Sam said, stepping gingerly into the room. "Can I help?"

Miss Rose stood up and slugged him in the arm. Hard. "You've done enough," she said. "Getting my son into racing. What on earth were you thinking?"

Lavender grinned.

"Me get *him* into racing?" Sam said, rubbing his arm and backing toward the door. "Miss Rose, I never—"

"He might have been killed," she snapped.

"That's the truth," I added. "Doc Aikin said so. More or less."

"And who's responsible for those twins?" she demanded as the toilet flushed. "What do you have to say for yourself, Sam Quinerly?"

"I . . . What I mean is, I'll just show the ladies out the back way," he said, edging toward the hall door.

"Well, don't wake up Lavender's daddy," she said. "And don't you drive, either. You smell like a brewery. And tell Dale to get in here with that ice."

"Yes, ma'am," he said. "Mo, you want a ride home?"

"Go on, Mo," Lavender said, winking. "You've saved me enough for one day."

"Wait," I said, grabbing Miss Rose's hand. "Let me call the Colonel and see if I can stay over. Please," I begged. *"I'm Doctor Appointed."*

For the first time since Lavender walked through the

door, Miss Rose actually looked at me. Her face softened, and she reached up to brush the hair from my eyes. "Sometimes I think you love Lavender near as much as I do," she said.

"Gag me," Dale said, handing his mother a towel full of ice.

"Call the Colonel, then," she told me. "Tell him you're invited."

I darted across the room and scooped up the phone. The Colonel answered on the first ring. "This is the Colonel," he said. "Speak to me."

"Hey, Colonel," I said. "It's Mo."

"Soldier," he said. "Where are you?"

"I'm at Dale's. I'm invited to spend the night, and—"

"I want you home," he said.

"Yes, sir. The thing is—"

"I want you home. Now. That's an order."

"I see. Hold on a second, sir." I covered the mouthpiece. "Miss Rose?" I said. "The Colonel would like to speak with you, to work out the details of my visit."

Miss Rose glided toward me, reaching for the phone. "Good evening, Colonel," she said. "I hope you're well. We'd be delighted for Mo to stay with us tonight if—" She nodded as she listened, her smile fading away. "I see," she finally said. "Sam is just leaving. I'll send her with him."

Her face went ashen. "No, I hadn't heard."

Her knees buckled and she sank onto the high-backed chair by the phone. "Certainly," she said. "I'll keep her safe until you arrive." She let the phone clatter into its cradle, and a sharp-edged silence filled the room.

"What's wrong?" Lavender asked, swinging his feet to the floor.

For a moment, she looked at us as if we were strangers. "There's been a murder at Fool's Bridge," she said, her voice distant and off pitch. "Jesse Tatum is dead."

"Mr. *Jesse?*" I yelped. "*Our* Mr. Jesse?"

"Who killed him?" Lavender asked.

"They don't know who killed him, or why. Or where the murderer is, for that matter," she said, glancing toward the door. "They found Jesse's body adrift in his own rowboat. The one somebody stole . . . when was it . . . Monday? Tuesday?"

I looked at Dale.

The blood fell from his face in a single, swift curtain as Lavender stood up, crossed the room, and locked the door.

Chapter 6
Keep Your Windows and Doors Locked

The Colonel's face looked gaunt in the dashboard's glow as the Underbird bounced out of Miss Rose's drive and onto the blacktop heading to town.

"Dead? Are you sure they mean *our* Mr. Jesse?" I asked.

"I'm sure."

I settled into the Underbird's bucket seat and took a deep breath. It felt like a thousand spiders had spun their silk inside my head. "Somebody's made a mistake," I said. "I served Mr. Jesse his lunch not eight hours ago. He stiffed me on the tip, just like always. He's fine. Turn by Miss Blalock's barn up here," I said, pointing. "We can take the back way to Mr. Jesse's, through the woods. He'll straighten this out."

"I'm afraid that's not possible," he said, cruising past the turn.

My anger jumped like a cat and took a few quick, hot

paces around my chest. "Turn around," I heard myself shout. He didn't blink. "Fine," I muttered, scrunching down in the seat. "I'll take my bike. I'll find Mr. Jesse myself. Or the police will find him. You'll see."

The Colonel placed his hand on mine. "The police have already found Jesse Tatum," he said. "That's how we know he's dead."

They're rough hands, the Colonel's, with a touch soft as nightfall.

"Death always shocks, even when you expect it," he said. "This is your first experience, and Jesse's death is anything *but* expected. Take some time to get your bearings."

I slumped, watching the pines flicker by in the headlights' glow. "You may not know this, but Mr. Jesse was like a father to me," I said. The Colonel's right eyebrow drifted up. "Okay, not like a father," I said. "More like an uncle, maybe. A stingy, selfish uncle who was secretly nice inside."

The Colonel sighed. "Jesse Tatum was a miserly, fetid old goat. The truth is you didn't particularly like him and neither did I. Still, we are accustomed to him," he said. "He's part of our world. I will miss him and I expect you will too."

We rode in silence to the edge of town. "Colonel, who would kill Mr. Jesse?"

He shook his head, and his lips went tight. "I don't know. The police are wondering the same thing," he said, "not that they have enough sense to figure it out. Never underestimate the idiocy of our criminal justice system, Soldier."

"No sir, I won't. But—"

"Listen to me," he said, his voice suddenly urgent. "Keep your eyes and ears open, and keep your opinions to yourself. Bring anything you learn about Jesse to me. Or, if I am away, to Lana. To no one else. Stay close to us until further notice. We are safe, but there is a killer among us. We must prepare to defend ourselves if necessary. And the best defense is what, Soldier?"

"A good offense," I said. "You've told me a million times. I just don't see how—"

"Leave the 'how' to me. Here we are," he added, hanging a right at the café. "Maybe my spot by the door is still open."

I surveyed the packed parking lot. "Karate Night," I muttered as the Underbird shuddered to a stop. "I forgot."

He nodded. "And other people have stopped by to see about Jesse. They're scared. Nothing like this has ever happened in Tupelo Landing." He opened his door and gave me a quick smile. "Mr. Li's karate class is nearly over, but maybe you'll feel better if you practice your kicks."

"Maybe," I sighed, heading for the café door. "I can't feel much worse."

Mr. Li started Karate Night at the café two years ago. The Colonel keeps just the counter open after the supper rush, and lets Mr. Li push the tables to the walls and use the floor space. In return, Mr. Li gives Dale and me free lessons for life. Dale hates it. I enjoy kicking others, but would do better in an art that allows spitting.

The Colonel offers Karate Night as a public service, same as Jaycees on Tuesdays and Miss Jennifer's Ballroom on Mondays. Wednesdays we hold open for Emergency Bridal Showers. As we entered the café, the Colonel draped a wiry arm across my shoulders. "Keep your wits about you," he whispered. "There is an enemy among us, and you are new to the ways of war."

Mr. Li, dressed in his trim white gi and faded black belt, spotted the Colonel at once. *"Rei!"* he shouted, and his students turned to the Colonel and bowed. We bowed back.

Some say the Colonel earned his black belt in Okinawa, and killed a man to get it. Others say he bought it used at a Fayetteville flea market and never had a lesson in his life. Either way, Mr. Li always bows—just in case, Miss Lana says.

"Miss Mo, will you please join us?" Mr. Li said. "Miss Anna needs a partner. No spitting." I grabbed a set of pads and sprang in front of Anna Celeste Simpson.

"Hey Mo-ron," she whispered, an evil glint in her eyes.

"Hey yourself, Attila Celeste," I hissed.

Mr. Li clapped. "Ten-way block drill. Begin!" I went at Attila, swinging with all my might. Sadly, she blocked every punch. Mr. Li blew his whistle. "Roundhouse kick! Lean and twist your body when you kick. Throw your weight behind it. Begin!"

"What's that smell?" Attila panted after our third set.

"Sweat," I said. "Didn't your mother tell you?"

"At least I have a mother, Mo-ron," she said. "And I don't mean the sweat."

I sniffed. "Seaweed salads," I said. "Miss Lana stocked them for Karate Night. She says they're thematic. The Colonel's giving them away before they go bad."

Mr. Li clapped. "Mo! Stop talking!" As we practiced, more townsfolk drifted in, hungry for information and the comfort of friends. At quarter past nine, Mayor Little burst through the door, glistening and out of breath. We froze.

"Everyone settle down," he gasped, fanning his red face with both hands. "Don't panic. Detective Starr has things well in hand. The man is a God-send. Stay calm, and have faith in your civil servants. We'll get past this little speed bump in no time."

Attila Celeste raised her hand. "I don't think it's fair to

call Mr. Jesse a speed bump just because he's dead," she said. "It's not like he can defend himself."

For a brief instant, I almost liked her.

The mayor zigzagged by, holding his tie to keep it from brushing our sweaty arms.

"Is it true, then, Mayor?" Grandmother Miss Lacy Thornton warbled from the end of the counter. "Is Jesse Tatum officially dead?"

"Dead is such an unflattering term," he said, sliding onto his stool. "I prefer to think of Jesse as . . . passé."

The Azalea Women gasped.

"What's *passé* mean?" Tinks Williams asked the Colonel, his voice low.

"Dead," the Colonel said, refilling Tinks's iced tea.

Mr. Li clapped his hands, snapping the class back to attention. "Line up for kick drills!" he commanded. "Upper belts first!" Thes, in his green belt, and legal whiz Skeeter McMillan, in her brown, stepped to the line along with three high schoolers. "Fighting movement number one!" Mr. Li said. "Front kick, punch–punch, round kick! Begin!"

They set off in perfect unison, slinking across the floor like a band of lethal ballerinas. "Next group! Begin!" The café door swung open as I kicked at Attila's head. She lunged out of range just in time, lost her balance, and crumpled to the floor.

"Nice round kick, Biblical Mo," Detective Starr said from the doorway. He gazed around the café as if he could freeze-frame the faces staring back at him. "I could use a cup of coffee, Colonel, if you've got one," he said, strolling to the counter.

The Colonel hid a scowl as he reached for a clean mug.

Starr's eyes looked tired, and his gray pants were stained black with mud. "I know you have questions, and I'll answer all I can," he told us, tossing his hat on the counter and sitting down. He opened his notepad. "First," he said, "I have a few." He glanced up. "If you don't mind, Sensei, I'll start with you."

Mr. Li nodded. If he was nervous, it didn't show.

"Your class started when, sir?"

"Eight o'clock. After the supper crowd left."

"Was everyone on time?"

"Everyone except Mo."

I took my place behind the counter, by the Colonel. "I was late from being Doctor Appointed," I said. "I can get a note if needed." I stepped up on my Pepsi crate and peered at Starr's notepad. "Is that all the clues you got? It doesn't look like much."

He moved his notes. "Did any of you pass by Mr. Jesse's tonight?" he asked, scanning the café.

Attila raised her hand. "That's Attila Celeste," I whispered, propping my elbows on the counter. "She lives down the creek from Mr. Jesse. Her parents drive her around like she's a princess. If she didn't take karate, you'd never even guess she had feet."

He didn't look at me. "Colonel, could you do something with her, please?"

"Hey," I snapped, but the Colonel put his hand over mine and shook his head.

Starr picked up his pen. "What time did you pass Mr. Jesse's place, Miss . . . ?"

"Miss Anna Celeste Simpson, and I'm pleased to meet you," she said, tossing her hair. "My mother and I drove by Mr. Jesse's a little before four o'clock. We came into town early because we wanted to go to the Piggly Wiggly, plus I needed a trim. Unlike some people, I won't tolerate split ends," she added, shooting me a nasty look.

"Right," Starr said. "Did you see anyone near Jesse Tatum's house?"

"A boy, maybe," she said. "By the creek. He was pulling something, or . . . I don't know. I only saw him through the trees. Who knows what boys do? It's a mystery to me."

My heart lurched. She'd seen Dale returning Mr. Jesse's boat, sure as my name's Mo LoBeau. I put my hand in my pocket and closed my fingers around my half of Mr. Jesse's finder's fee—money we tricked him out of. Suddenly I felt sick.

"Can you identify the boy?" Starr asked.

I tried to slow my heartbeat. What if Attila realized she'd seen Dale at Mr. Jesse's just before the murder? What if Starr found out Dale had swiped Mr. Jesse's boat? How much trouble would he be in? How much trouble would I be in? I needed time to think. I turned to Starr. "All boys look alike to Anna Celeste," I said. "She's boy crazy."

"*Soldier,*" the Colonel snapped, clamping his fingers into my shoulder. "At ease."

Attila blushed. "I am not boy crazy," she said. "All I saw is light hair and a dark shirt. Black, maybe. I didn't stare. Why would I? I didn't know Mr. Jesse was dead."

"Maybe it was Thes," I suggested. "He's a boy."

"It wasn't me," Thes yelped. "I got red hair. And a dark shirt, well, that could be half the boys in town."

Starr looked around the café. "Did anybody else see him?"

Skeeter looked at Attila, then at me. I could see it in her eyes: She knew it was Dale. Panic swirled through me like a flock of blackbirds banking into a tree. I shook my head. She nodded so faintly, her nod could have been mistaken for a breath. She wouldn't say anything. Not yet, anyway.

"Anna, I'll need to talk to your mother," Starr said.

"Betsy Simpson, she's in the book," the Colonel said,

finally pouring Starr's coffee. "You don't really think a kid killed Jesse, do you?"

"I'll ask the questions," Starr said without looking up, and the vein in the Colonel's forehead jumped to attention. Now I reached over and patted the *Colonel's* hand. "Colonel, did Jesse Tatum come in for supper tonight?"

"Negative," he growled, picking up a dishtowel.

"Well, that's twice a pity," Mayor Little said. "The Colonel's teriyaki chicken is simply out of this world. And if Jesse had come in for dinner, he might not be so passé. Oh my gosh," he added, slapping himself on the forehead. "What am I thinking? Detective, you must be famished. I'm sure the Colonel would be glad to scare you up some supper, even with the kitchen closed. Wouldn't you, Colonel?"

The Colonel pretended to wipe a spot off the counter.

"Thanks, but I'm not hungry," Starr said after a long silence. He looked around the café. "Is it unusual for Mr. Jesse to miss supper? Has he seemed worried lately?"

"Oh, for heaven's sake," Grandmother Miss Lacy Thornton sputtered, standing up at the end of the counter. Her blue-white hair glowed and her powdered face was stern. "Jesse's like the rest of us. He eats here when he wants to and stays home when he wants to. And Jesse was so peculiar no one would know whether he was

worried or not. Excuse me for saying so, young man,"
she said to Starr, "but we've answered a number of your
questions. I think it's time for you to answer ours."

Starr stared at her for a moment, his glare downshift-
ing to neutral. "Yes, ma'am," he said, his voice going
softer. "What would you like to know?"

She studied him, her hair shimmering in the café's
harsh light. "I hear the Tyson brothers found Jesse's
body at Fool's Bridge. And——"

"Who told you that?" Starr asked, his voice sharp.

"Everybody. It's all over town."

Starr sighed. "All right," he said, flipping back through
his notes. "I'd want information too, if I were you. Here's
what I've got. The Tyson boys hauled Jesse Tatum's boat
out of the creek around six o'clock this evening, and found
his body inside. His wallet was in his pocket, with no cash
in it. His death is being investigated as a homicide."

"Well, who killed him?" she demanded.

"I don't know yet, but I intend to find out," Starr said,
snapping his notepad closed.

"Excuse me, sir," Skeeter said in a pre-law voice of
steel. "Aren't we outside your jurisdiction?"

The Colonel cleared his throat and pointed to the No
LAWYERS sign.

"Sorry," she mumbled.

"Understandable," the Colonel said. "These are trying times." He looked at Starr. "Her question is a good one."

"Technically this isn't inside my jurisdiction, but your mayor's asked me to investigate and I've agreed," he said. "Besides, I have a hunch this may tie in with the murder I'm investigating in Winston-Salem. Does anyone have a problem with that?"

The Colonel swiped at a spot on the counter. The room barely breathed. "No? Good. My team's coming from Winston-Salem in the morning. Meanwhile, avoid strangers. Travel in pairs. I don't want any children leaving without an adult. Questions?"

I raised my hand, and Starr sighed. "Mo?"

"They found Mr. Jesse in a boat?" I asked. "I'm wondering if maybe he just up and died. Maybe there ain't no murder. Like the fish weren't biting and he died of boredom. It happens. Boredom kills. I've had close brushes myself, during math."

"Jesse Tatum didn't die of boredom," he said. "The back of his head . . . That is, he suffered a blunt force trauma."

An Azalea Woman moaned.

"Are we safe?" Grandmother Miss Lacy Thornton asked.

Starr looked at her a moment, like he was weighing his words. "Keep your doors and windows locked," he replied. Then he turned to me. "Where were you tonight?"

"Me?" I asked, surprised. "I was at the racetrack. You didn't see me? I sure saw you. You need an alibi for me, ask your girlfriend. How long you known her, anyway?"

"His *girlfriend?*" Attila Celeste said, looking Starr up and down. "What kind of girlfriend does *he* have?"

"Guess," I said. "Too slow. It's Miss Retzyl."

She staggered back. "*Our* Miss Retzyl?"

"That's not all," I said. "She was wearing shorts."

"*Miss Retzyl?* Wearing shorts?"

Starr clicked his pen. "She did mention running into you. You were with that spooky kid. Dale." I glanced at Attila. Dale was the last name I wanted tickling her memory.

The Colonel's words drifted back to me: "The best defense is a good offense."

"So, Detective," I said, "what have you done with Miss Retzyl? As representatives of the sixth grade, Anna and me are hoping you didn't throw her in jail or leave her standing by the creek with a crazed killer on the prowl. Go ahead, Anna, tell him," I said.

Attila nodded uncertainly.

"Exactly what are your intentions?" I asked. "The sixth grade has a right to know."

Grandmother Miss Lacy Thornton raised her hand. "I'm wondering too."

"Your Miss Retzyl is perfectly safe," Starr said. He looked around the café. "Did anyone else see Jesse Tatum tonight?" he asked. "Anyone see anything suspicious?" He sauntered to the bulletin board and stabbed his business card through the heart with a thumbtack. "Please call me if you think of anything that might help."

"Goodness, I hope you're not counting on your cell phone," Mayor Little said.

"Why wouldn't I?" Starr asked.

"No service to speak of," he said. "Oh, you might get a sputter here or there, but not for long. That's one of the benefits of life in Tupelo Landing: no cell bill. No high-speed Internet charges, either, unless you live on First Street and have cable. I'll gladly relay phone messages for you, though, if you'd like to use my landline. I'm sure Mother won't mind."

"I'll get back to you on that," Starr said, looking doubtful. He glanced at Grandmother Miss Lacy Thornton. "Does Jesse Tatum have family here?" he asked. "Is there someone I should notify?"

"Jesse did have a cousin somewhere in the Piedmont," she said. "A security guard. He died years ago—in Jesse's arms, as I recall. Jesse was alone in life."

Starr plucked Mr. Jesse's notice of a finder's fee from the bulletin board and folded it into his pocket. "I think you'll find my team easy to work with, Mayor." He looked around the room. "Thank you, Sensei. Everyone's free to go."

Mr. Li bowed, and the Colonel unplugged the coffee urn. "Everybody out," the Colonel said. "Don't let these kids walk home alone."

I worked my way over to Skeeter. "I'd like to make an appointment," I whispered as we put our kick pads away. "First thing in the morning."

She nodded as Mr. Li walked by. "Mo," he said, his voice hushed, "I'm going to Durham tomorrow. If you'd like for me to take one of your messages along . . ."

"Thanks, Mr. Li." I grabbed a bottle from beneath the counter, and he tucked it under his arm.

Starr watched our customers pay up and step gingerly into the night. "A couple more questions," he said as the Colonel closed out the cash register. "Did Jesse Tatum have any enemies? Did anyone here tonight have a grudge against him?"

"Here?" I asked. "You think the killer comes to the café?"

"Murderers usually know their victims."

The Colonel folded his apron and tossed it on the counter. "As far as I know, Jesse Tatum was a harmless old coot living out his life on a backwater creek without family or friends," he said. "Nobody much liked him. But kill him? Why? Time was Jesse's assassin, and it was closing in on him fast. Murdering Jesse Tatum doesn't make sense."

"You're wrong," Starr said. "Murder always makes sense—to the murderer. By the way," he said, picking up his hat, "where's Miss Lana?"

"Away on business," the Colonel said. "In Charleston."

Starr narrowed his eyes. "Please tell her I'd like to talk with her when she gets in. If I don't hear from her soon, I'll find her." He started toward the door. "One last thing," he said. "I ran that Thunderbird's plates. You bought that car two weeks ago, not two years ago."

The Colonel glanced at me. "You're right. It was a lie, and I apologize," he said. "I should have told the truth. Which is that I don't think law enforcement should meddle in people's lives. That I don't believe my purchases are any of your business. That the only thing as dangerous as an arrogant attorney is an overzealous lawman. Again, I apologize. I bought that car legally and I should have just said so. Now, if there's nothing else?"

I stepped near the Colonel.

Starr studied us for one cold, flat minute. "Don't leave

town," he told the Colonel. Then he nodded to me and headed for the door.

We watched him climb into his Impala. "He's going to be trouble," the Colonel said, unplugging the jukebox.

"Yes, sir," I said, thinking of Dale. "If you ask me, he already is."

Chapter 7
Desperados

The Colonel and I trudged toward home—the flip side of the café. "Been thinking of installing a safety light back here," he muttered as we followed the gravel walkway through Miss Lana's dogwoods and daylilies.

"No you haven't," I said, slipping my hand in his. "*Miss Lana* wants a safety light. You said you'd be fricasseed in hell before you'd drown out the stars."

We marched up the rounded steps, to the porch. "Didn't you leave your night-light on, Soldier?" he asked, stopping by Miss Lana's potted geraniums.

I gulped. "I always leave my Elvis light on, sir," I said. "It's an eternal flame."

"Stay back," he replied, stiff-arming me against the wall.

He eased my screen door open, its voice rising like a rusty hymn. In one motion he flipped my light on and sprang inside. He yanked open my mahogany chifforobe, dropped to his belly to peer under my bed, and then leaped into my bathroom. "All clear," he barked, latching my windows. He grabbed my night-light and thumped Elvis's head. "Burned out," he muttered, tossing it aside. "How fitting."

He waved me in and dead-bolted my porch door behind me.

I followed him into our living room. As he checked for intruders, my eyes wandered to the photograph of Miss Lana and me during my baby days. In it, she sits on a perfect lawn, her skirt spread around her like a paper parasol as I present her with a dandelion. She is young and beautiful, and I am plump and adorable.

The Colonel locked the front door. "Good thing Lana isn't here," he said. "She was fond of Jesse." I could smell the garlic on his shirt. "Are you scared, Soldier?"

I took a shaky breath. I *was* scared, but not for the reason he thought. I slid my hand in my pocket, to the reward money, and felt dizzy. If Attila Celeste remembered who she saw by Mr. Jesse's house, or if Skeeter blabbed, Dale could be in trouble. Big trouble. I had to warn him. "I'm not scared," I lied. "Are you?"

"A little," he said.

"Me too." I hesitated, staring toward my dark bedroom. "I can leave my door open tonight if you'd like. That way I can hear you, if you need me."

I caught the flicker of a smile in his dark eyes. "That might make me feel better," he said. "Perhaps I'll sleep on the sofa. That way it will be easy to find me if I call."

"Excellent, sir," I said, giving him a hug.

In my room, I slipped into my night gear: black karate pants and an old T-shirt. I glanced at my phone and considered calling Miss Lana. I wanted her to come home. Now. On the other hand, I didn't want to tell her about Mr. Jesse. I picked up a pen and Volume 6 instead:

Dear Upstream Mother,

> *Mr. Jesse is dead. Even the Colonel is scared.*

> *I wish you were here. We could make some tea, and chat about Joe Starr, and Dale, and poor dead Mr. Jesse. We'd make a plan, and you'd sit and work a crossword until I fell asleep. Everything would be normal for me.*

> *Sometimes I wish Miss Lana and the Colonel were normal, but Lavender says normal is a relative term. "Right," I said. "What does that mean, exactly?" He said, "It means you think your relatives are normal right up until you notice they're not."*

> *I even mentioned it to Miss Lana once, out in the flower garden. "I wish I had a normal family," I said, very casual, pulling a handful of weeds.*

> *"Normal means ordinary, Mo. The Drab among us have that covered."*

"I don't mean drab, I mean normal," I said. "You know. Parents that go to a regular job, come home to an actual house, maybe cart me around to soccer games. I wish the Colonel was maybe a dentist, like Anna Celeste's dad."

She looked up from her iris. "You want the Colonel to put his hands in other people's mouths?" she said, like I'd suggested him sticking his head in a lion's mouth.

"That's just an example. I'm saying we could be like people who live on a cul-de-sac. Just to try it, and see if it fits."

She sat back on her heels, her face smudged with dirt. "I suppose we could live on a dead end if you really want to, sugar," she said, "but consider this: If the Colonel and I were Anna Celeste's parents, you would be Anna Celeste. I would still love you, but I wouldn't like you nearly so much."

"Right," I sighed. "Being Anna Celeste would be a definite downside."

There is a peculiar spin to Miss Lana's universe, but I admit it's a spin I miss.

Please come find me.

Love, Mo

The instant I heard the drum of the Colonel's shower, I closed my notebook and called Dale. He answered, his sleepy hello muffled by shouts in the background. "Hey, what's going on?" I demanded. "Why's Miss Rose yelling? Is Starr over there?"

"Ain't nothing going on," he said. "Daddy woke up mean as a snake is all, and Lavender stomped out mad. Why would Starr be here?"

"He's investigating Mr. Jesse's murder," I said, easing into my bad news.

"So?"

"So you'll never guess who the prime suspect is."

"Who?" Dale yawned.

"You."

"WHAT?"

"It's all over town. Attila Celeste saw you with Mr. Jesse's boat this afternoon, but she ain't identified you by name. Not yet. Don't say anything incriminating," I added. "My line may be tapped. Stay out of town until I tell you different."

I hung up as the Colonel knocked at my door. "Fan, Soldier," he said, swinging a heavy black fan onto my desk. "Haven't made machinery this elegant since World War II." He clicked it on. "I'm sorry Lana isn't here to comfort you, but perhaps the murmur of a breeze will help."

"She's a beauty," I told him. I meant it too. Her heart-shaped feet rested on a pad of green felt, and her metal blades curved graceful as angel wings. Her patient back-and-forth hum sent a gentle breeze through my curtains, across my wrinkled sheets.

"Good night, Soldier," the Colonel said, resting his hand on my head. And he slipped from the room, leaving our door carefully ajar.

Bump.

The sound grabbed me by the scruff of my neck and shook me like a kitten, waking me from a deep sleep.

What was that? A killer on the porch?

Crack.

A phone line being cut?

Thud.

It came from the window!

Breathe, I told myself, breathe.

Snap-snap-snap.

I squinted at my clock. Three a.m.? Already?

I grabbed my baseball bat and tiptoed to the window. The shrubs swayed crazily.

Tap-tap-tap. The killer?

"Mo," the killer rasped. "It's me. Open the door."

I pushed my curtain aside with the bat. Dale had chinned himself on my windowsill, revealing bloodless knuckles and the top half of his strained face. "Open . . . the . . . door," he panted as his grip gave way and he fell into Miss Lana's gardenias.

I flipped my lamp on, marched to my porch door, and pushed the dead bolt aside. Dale shot in, his face drawn. "What am I going to do?" he demanded, scrambling past me. "They'll try me as an adult. I know they will," he said, his voice bitter. "I'll get twenty years at least. I'll be . . ." His eyes glazed over as he tried to add.

"Thirty-one?" I guessed, locking the door behind him.

"Thirty-one," he wailed, sinking to the floor. "That's almost dead."

"Calm down," I told him. "Attila Celeste only remembers a boy with light hair and a dark shirt, maybe black. She didn't say it was you."

"A black shirt? What am I going to do? Everybody knows I'm still mourning the crash at Daytona." He grabbed the hem of his Dale Earnhardt memorial T-shirt and yanked it over his head, turning to hide the angry red smears across his rib cage.

I used to think Dale was clumsy. Then I realized he only got clumsy when Mr. Macon took drunk.

"Black's all I got," he said. I scooped a white T-shirt off my chair and threw it to him. "Thanks," he muttered, slipping it on and smoothing his hair. "Mo, I swear I didn't kill Mr. Jesse," he said, his voice cracking.

"Of course not," I said, sitting cross-legged on the bed.

"What am I going to do? You're the smart one. Think of something."

I took a deep breath. "Calm down. We'll both think." He settled into my rocking chair, the one Miss Lana used to rock me to sleep in when I was a baby. "We'll do like in science with Miss Retzyl," I told him.

"Science," he moaned. "I'm sunk."

"Remember what she told us. Define the problem, then solve it."

"Right," he said. "So. The problem is . . . the electric chair?" Dale goes dense when scared. He can't help it.

I shook my head. "The problem is, Starr's headed down the wrong path and you're standing at the end of it." I drummed my fingers against my knee. "We could tell the Colonel or Miss Rose about Mr. Jesse's boat. They could talk to Starr."

"No," he said. "Starr don't trust the Colonel, and Mama would kill me." That was true. "Maybe Starr will find the real murderer, and get me off the hook."

"Possible but not likely," I said. "The Colonel says cops can't figure out much of anything. And that's pretty much a quote."

He frowned. "Then how come my folks practically got a guest suite at the jail?"

I decided to let that one go by. "We only got one

option," I said, leaning forward. "We'll find Mr. Jesse's killer ourselves."

"Right," he said, his voice going sullen. "Like we can out-detective Joe Starr. That's nuts, Mo. I'm doomed."

"It's not nuts, and you're not doomed. You're desperate, is all. And it's like Miss Lana says: Desperation is the mother of invention."

He looked at me, his face thoughtful. "Who's the daddy?"

If Dale ever starts thinking in a straight line, he'll be a genius. "We'll call ourselves the Desperado Detective Agency," I continued. "I already got The Case of the Upstream Mother in progress. We'll add on Mr. Jesse's Murder. If there's a reward involved, we'll rent an office. Until then, we'll set up at the café."

He nodded. "Desperado Detectives," he said, trying on the words. "I like it."

I grabbed Volume 6 and an old putt-putt pencil from my nightstand. "We'll need clues," I said. "What do we know about Mr. Jesse?"

"He's dead," he said promptly. Dale has a nose for the obvious.

"Last person to see him alive?"

"The killer."

"Before that?"

"Oh," Dale said, his face falling. "That would be me. Only . . . only . . ."

I looked up. Dale had gone a ghastly shade of pale. "Are you all right?" I asked.

"The window," he whispered, not moving his eyes.

The hair on my arms stood up. I let my gaze drift to the right—from Dale's terrified face, to my window, into the ice-cold eyes of a stranger.

I screamed. Dale screamed.

I grabbed my Charleston snow globe and hurled it at the window. The man—round face, bald—jumped back as the globe bounced off the wall. I leaped to the center of my bed, and went into my karate fighting stance. "Dale!" I shouted. "Up here!"

"Why?" he bellowed, galloping across the sheets to stand by my side.

"We'll go down fighting."

"Not me," he said, backing away.

Dale exasperates me to tears. He hates fighting. I figure it's because of his daddy. Fortunately, I'm a good enough scrapper for both of us, most days. "Hands up!" I shouted. Dale raised his fists, looking awkward and scared.

I peered at the window. Nothing. The wind rustled and Miss Lana's gardenias scraped against my window. "Where's the Colonel?" Dale asked, his voice shaking.

"Asleep on the settee," I said, glancing at the door the Colonel had left open for me. It was closed tight. My heart pounded so hard, I went dizzy. Where was he? The Colonel sleeps like a gnat. "COLONEL!" I yelled. "HELP!"

Silence.

I grabbed Dale's arm. "Are you thinking what I'm thinking?"

"Probably not," he said, pulling away. "I hardly ever am."

"The Colonel must be wounded. Or dead. Let's get in there."

"See?" he said, his eyes going glassy with fear. "I'm not thinking anything like that. I'm thinking 'Run.'"

"He needs us," I said, leaping to the floor. I grabbed my Little League bat and opened the door, slicing the living room's dark with my room's soft glow. "There he is," I whispered, pointing to the sheet-covered lump on the sofa. "Colonel?"

I reached for the light switch. "No," Dale whispered, knocking my hand away. "With a killer outside, we're safer with it off. Everybody knows that."

"Colonel?" He lay still as death. My mouth went Sahara dry. "Wake him up," I whispered.

"Me?" Dale gasped. "I'm not good with the dead. *You* do it. Use the bat."

I crept forward, my pulse pounding. I lifted the bat and bounced it off the arm of the sofa. The effect was electric. The body spun to face us, the moonlight playing on high cheekbones, penciled-in eyebrows, a wide-open mouth set in a creamy white face.

"Clown!" Dale shrieked. He ran squarely into the wall and crashed to the floor.

"Get up!" I shouted as the body wheeled to point at us.

"Dale Earnhardt Johnson III, get up off of that floor right this minute. Moses LoBeau, drop that bat. Both of you settle down! You're enough to wake the dead."

"Miss Lana?" I gasped.

"Yes, dear?" She reached beneath her pillow, pulled out a flimsy gray scarf, and deftly flipped it over her head. She switched on the lamp. "Dang these curlers," she muttered, tucking strands of red hair beneath her scarf and patting them into place. "The things I do to make myself beautiful for you people," she teased. "And you don't even act like you're glad to see me."

"Miss Lana!" I cried, hurling myself into her warm, Noxzema-scented arms. "There's a killer at my window! Thank heavens you've come home!"

Chapter 8
Miss Lana

"Mo, for heaven's sake," she said, squeezing me tight. "What's wrong?"

"Where's the Colonel?" I pushed free, ran across the living room, and threw open the Colonel's door. "Colonel?" His closet stood open, his shirts exactly three inches apart on the clothes bar, his shoes snapped to attention underneath. Olive-drab blankets stretched tight across his empty bunk. "Where is he?"

"Gone," she said, dabbing cold cream from her face. "Again."

"*Now?*" I said. "Gone where?"

"I'm not sure," she said. "I'd barely walked in before he rushed out, muttering something about offense and defense and taking the fight to the enemy. That man makes me so angry I can't hear half of what he says. Some days I can barely see his lips move."

"Miss Lana," I said, "there's a man at my window."

"I saw him too," Dale said.

She looked from Dale to me. "You're serious," she

gasped. She shrugged into her robe as she rushed to my room. She checked my dead bolt and then hurried through the house, checking doors and windows. Dale and I trailed her like puppies. "Everything's secure," she said, grabbing the phone. "But better safe than sorry."

"Who are you calling?" Dale asked. "Not Starr, I hope," he whispered to me.

"Tinks Williams," she said. "We have an agreement. I just hope . . . Hello? Tinks? It's Lana. I'm sorry to wake you, but we've seen someone at our window and I wonder if you could . . . Thank you, dear," she said. "Yes, I promise not to shoot."

That's another rumor the Colonel started: that Miss Lana can shoot.

"He's on his way," she said. "So, let's settle down." She crossed to a large suitcase at the front door. "Dale?" she said, slipping her hand through the handle. "Would you help me? Mo," she said, "grab my valise and makeup case. We'll move me into my suite while we wait. Then I'll make some hot chocolate."

Dale leaned against his end of the bag, his legs churning as he plowed it across the living room to Miss Lana's door. She clicked on a lamp, sending soft light across a large room overlooking the creek. I swung her valise onto the bench by her dresser.

"Thank heavens Cher travels well," she said, lifting her

glossy black Cher wig from her bag and giving it a gentle shake. She opened her closet door. On the shelf sat four stark, white mannequin heads, one wearing a Marilyn Monroe wig. "Can you grab Ava Gardner and Jean Harlow, sugar?" she asked. I passed the wigs to Miss Lana, completing her Hollywood Through the Ages collection.

Miss Lana has a flair for drama.

Now she gave Dale a puzzled glance. "Dale," she said, "I'm glad to see you, but may I ask what you're doing in Mo's room at three forty-five a.m.?"

"Nothing," he said, going shifty. "Whatever you're thinking, I'm innocent." As I may have noted, Dale doesn't think well on his feet.

"Dale just now dropped by," I said quickly. "We've started a small business—Desperado Detective Agency. Dale's here to sort clues. Since school's out, we thought it would be okay. Plus, that's the kind of work ethic we got." I changed tack. "I'm sorry you and the Colonel had a fight. And Miss Lana, I missed you."

She kissed my face. Her kisses are soft as rose petals. "I missed you too, sugar," she said. "And for future reference, your summer curfew is eight p.m. Sharp. And the Colonel and I didn't have a fight, exactly." She sighed. "What *is* it with that man?"

Dale perched on the edge of her bed. "What is it with the Colonel," he said. "That's a tough one." Dale's a sucker for rhetorical questions, especially Miss Lana's.

"Dale," I said sharply. "We've worked on this."

"Oh," he said, his face falling. "Rhetorical?"

I nodded and glanced outside. "Where's Tinks?"

"He'll be here, sugar," she said, eyeing her dresser. "Where are my hairbrushes?"

Dale looked at me. "Rhetorical?" he whispered.

"No," I said, pointing to her makeup case.

As Dale plundered the luggage, Miss Lana prattled on—a nervous habit. "You were sleeping like a baby when I closed your door," she told me. "The Colonel asked me to sleep on the settee, in case you needed me." That explained why nobody came when we screamed: Miss Lana sleeps like a sack of concrete. "He didn't mention that you'd attack me with a bat," she added.

"I'm sorry, I thought you were dead," I explained. "Miss Lana, did the Colonel take the Underbird?"

"No, he left it here. For me."

"Why?" I asked. "You can't drive."

Her smile flatlined.

Miss Lana's the only adult in the county who can't drive. Maybe on the entire planet. It's been a sore point with me since third grade, when my teacher asked her to help carpool my class to the NC Aquarium, near Morehead. Regular mothers drove. Miss Lana borrowed Grandmother Miss Lacy Thornton's Buick and hired a driver—Tinks Williams, in his navy-blue Sunday suit.

"The Colonel's on foot, then," I said. "Tracking the killer. Maybe."

She frowned. "Tracking the killer? Surely Jesse's in custody. Isn't he?"

Mr. Jesse? In custody?

"Miss Lana," I said, "what, exactly, did the Colonel tell you about Mr. Jesse?"

She sailed a wide-brimmed hat toward her closet. "Actually, he left a message with Cousin Gideon—who sends his love, by the way. Gideon said Jesse was involved in a murder, and you needed me. I hopped on the nearest Greyhound. The Colonel didn't say who Jesse killed, but my money's on a certain heavy-set beauty who visits him every Tuesday. Or her jealous husband." She looked at me. "Selma Foster, of Kinston? Jesse's girlfriend? It must be all over town by now."

Mr. Jesse had a girlfriend? I stared at Dale, stunned.

"Gross," Dale said. "Only thing is, Mr. Jesse's not the . . . ah . . ." He stopped, panic spreading across his face like butter across warm toast.

I sighed. "Miss Lana, Mr. Jesse ain't the killer. He's the killee. Mr. Jesse's probably over in Greenville right now, getting himself autopsied. Or funeralized."

"Someone killed Jesse?" she said, the blood leaving her face. "Why?"

"We don't know yet," I said as a car pulled into the café parking lot.

Miss Lana pushed the curtain aside. Two flashlight beams darted along our walk. "Good. Tinks brought someone with him. You two stay put," she said, tying her robe. "I'll talk with them. Then you can fill me in on the details of Jesse's . . . on the details."

For a half hour, Tinks and Sam flooded our yard with light and checked for footprints. Nothing.

As they drove away, Dale and I came clean: about borrowing Mr. Jesse's boat, the reward, the murder, the Underbird, and Detective Joe Starr.

"Miss Lana, that could have been the killer at my window," I said. "Shouldn't we call Joe Starr?"

She shook her head. "Starr doesn't need to know the Colonel's gone. Besides, Tinks looked for footprints. There are none. I don't know what else anyone can do." She stretched, patted her curlers, and began carefully freeing her curls. Her hair looked sleepy and warm, like copper at sunset. "Mo," she said, "has anyone mentioned a memorial service for Jesse?"

"No, ma'am. Mr. Jesse didn't go to church, and didn't have a family. Well, he used to have a cousin, but he died. I guess you were his only friend. It looks like he's on his own, in the eternal sense of things."

"No one's on their own in the eternal sense of things,

Mo," she said. "If no one else volunteers, we'll have a service at the café."

"A funeral? For Mr. Jesse?" I said. "Do you think anybody will come?"

"Murder's always standing room only," she said. "Everybody will come—including, probably, the murderer. Hopefully Joe Starr will be grateful enough to ease up on the Colonel. He can't seriously think Dale's a suspect," she said, "but you may want to talk with Skeeter in the morning, before she mentions her suspicions to Starr."

"Yes, ma'am," I said. "I already made the appointment and I already got a plan."

"Wonderful," she said, glancing at her watch. "You two need to sleep. Dale, you're welcome to the Colonel's bunk."

I hugged her, my head fitting neatly just beneath her chin. Her heart beat strong and sure, steadying my own. "Thank you for coming home so quick," I said.

"I'll always come home to you, Mo," she said. "You know that."

"Yes ma'am." And I headed for bed, leaving my door ajar in case she needed me.

Dear Upstream Mother,
How are you? I'm fine except Mr. Jesse's killer

is on the loose, and the Colonel's out there stalking him like a Borderline Ninja. If you see the Colonel please ask him to call me, so I know he's okay.

We're throwing a funeral for Mr. Jesse. You're invited. I'll look for you there, just like I look for you everywhere. Last week, in Kinston, a woman stared back at me and I thought it might be you.

That night I dreamed my old dream again.

In it, I'm standing by the creek. As I look across the black water, a flash catches my eye. A bottle bobs along at a slant, its cap glistening in the sun. "Finally," my heart says. I splash into the creek and scoop it up. I open it and peer inside. A piece of paper curls there. I know it's a message from you.

I shake the message out and unroll it, the dark water lapping against my knees. But the words blur, and I wake up before I can read it.

It's a long shot, I know, but it could come true.

Love, Mo

PS: Do you have hair like mine? If so, I offer my condolences.

Chapter 9
The Cousin Information Network

Humidity rolled off our slow, black-water creek as Dale and I pedaled past the Piggly Wiggly just a few hours later and dropped our bikes on Skeeter McMillan's lawn. I smoothed my hair—which had gone feral in the heat—and tapped on the open door. "Morning, Skeeter," I said.

"Hey," she said, looking up from her law book. Skeeter opened her Pre-Law Office here in the storage room of her mama's hair salon last summer. It's nice, except for the smell of hairspray. "I've been expecting you," she said, nodding to two lawn chairs. "Let me start by assuring you anything you say here is confidential."

Actually, I thought, I'm counting on it.

"Dale and me would like to retain your services," I said as we sat down.

As if on cue a thin, dark-haired girl appeared at the door. "I believe you know my partner and accountant-in-waiting, Sally Amanda Jones," Skeeter said.

"Hey, Salamander. You've grown," Dale said, and Sal blushed.

Sal, the smallest kid in our class, is shaped like a tube of lipstick. She wears Strategic Ruffles and curls her short brown hair to create the illusion of shape. She also possesses a calculator brain and a love for Dale that will go epic, if he ever notices.

"In addition to standard services," Skeeter said, "we offer unlimited access to the Cousin Information Network." I nodded. Between them, Skeeter and Sal are related to half the county. Maybe the entire state.

Sal hopped onto the edge of the desk and smoothed her skirt. "Let's talk turkey," she said, very professional. "Cash or trade?"

Dale sat up straight. "Trade. I got a heirloom lava lamp, circa 1984."

She wrinkled her nose and shook her head, her tight curls glinting.

"Plus an Elvis night-light," I offered. She shuddered.

Dale shifted and peered into her eyes. He'd borrowed my Carolina blue T-shirt, which made his eyes blue as a July sky. "An original *metal* model of Dale Earnhardt Sr.'s first race car," he said. "Worth seventy dollars, easy."

She knocked the stapler to the floor. "Deal," she breathed.

"Excellent." I ripped a page from my notebook. "We

need background on these persons of interest: Selma and Albert Foster, of Kinston. Friends of Mr. Jesse's."

"My cousin reads meters in Kinston," Skeeter said, taking the paper. "I'll see what we can do. And to fill us in on the case?"

"We're totally confidential?" They both nodded. "Okay. Dale is the boy Anna Celeste saw the day of the murder. He'd borrowed Mr. Jesse's boat, and was returning it for the reward money. Dale? You got anything to add?"

"I didn't know you were going to confess me," he gasped. "I'm innocent," he added, looking from Sal to Skeeter. "I didn't kill Mr. Jesse."

"We believe you," Sal said.

Skeeter hid a smile. "Mo, you all haven't told me anything I hadn't figured out."

"Exactly," I told her. "Dale and me want this *kept* confidential until we clear Dale's name, which should be soon. We've gone professional."

"Detectives," Dale said modestly, handing Sal his card.

She read the hand-lettered card aloud: "*Desperado Detectives. Murders solved cheap, lost pets found for free. Dale, Chief of Lost Pets.* Impressive," she said.

He smiled. "I'd like to have that back when you're through with it," he said. "We just opened this morning, and I only had time to make one card."

Sal handed it back. Then she tapped her knuckle against her chin, the way she does when confronted with Diabolical-Level Math. "What about Anna Celeste?"

"What about her?" Dale asked.

"She knows." My stomach dropped like I was on a Ferris wheel. "She called me last night, about her party," she explained, fluffing a ruffle. She looked at Dale. "Are you going? I am."

Dale's eyes had glazed over. "Party? What party?" he replied. "And what do you mean, Anna knows? Is she turning me in?"

"I . . . don't think so. She didn't say. Actually, I think the fact that it was you she saw kind of slipped out."

Sal was right. Attila wouldn't give away that information for the same reason a trained assassin wouldn't give away bullets. Dale closed his eyes. I knew he was picturing himself in an orange jumpsuit and trying not to cry.

"Sal," I said, "could you call her back, maybe ask her to keep this quiet until—"

"No, I don't ask Anna Celeste for things. Her parents either. Family rule," she said.

Sal is what's known as a Poor Relation of Anna's, meaning she gets invited to Attila's parties, but not to riding lessons. Sal's daddy stocks shelves at the Piggly Wiggly and her mother stays home with Sal's little brother, a confirmed biter. They ain't Money, but somehow Sal still manages to dress like a fashion plate out of JCPenney.

"Thanks for the heads-up," I told her. I tugged Dale to his feet. "Don't worry, Desperado," I told him. "We'll think of something. Sal? Skeeter? We'll be in touch. Right now we got to get to the café before the breakfast rush sucks Miss Lana under."

The breakfast rush had just begun to fade when we finally taped our sign near the cash register:

Desperado Detectives.
Murders Solved Cheap.
Lost Pets Found For Free.

"You're doing great," I whispered to Dale. "Just act calm and look innocent. And stay away from Attila and Joe Starr."

As he headed for the kitchen, Grandmother Miss Lacy Thornton bustled in, lugging a funeral wreath. She took a seat at the counter, swinging the wreath onto the stool beside her. "Good morning, dear," she said. "I hear Lana's home. I'm glad."

"Yes, ma'am," I said. "She's whipped up a pancake special. Nice wreath," I added, sliding a glass of water across the counter. "Is it for Mr. Jesse?"

"Gracious, no," she said. "It's for me. I'm driving over

to Tarboro today, to visit my burial site. I'm prepaid, you know."

"Congratulations," I told her. "You like some bacon with your pancakes?"

"No, thank you," she said, straightening the wreath's bow. "Care to come along? It's a lovely cemetery. We could make a day of it."

"Normally I'd say yes, but I got detective work to do," I said.

She glanced at our sign. "Lovely," she said. "May I launch a bottle for you, then? The cemetery practically overlooks the Tar River."

I reached under the counter and selected a vinegar bottle with my standard Upstream Mother message inside. "Thanks," I said. "And if you think of any murder clues, keep us in mind. There may be a reward involved."

She tucked the bottle in her bag. "You'll be the first to know, dear."

Thes bellied up to the counter with his father, Reverend Thompson. "Have you seen the weather? We got a storm forming in the tropics."

Attila breezed in and Dale ducked behind the counter.

"There's always a storm forming in the tropics," Attila snipped as she claimed a window table. "I'll have two poached eggs and a diet soda, Mo. And I'm in a hurry. I'm picking out my party decorations today." She flounced her hair and sat down, my anti-invitation hanging in the air like eau de skunk.

"Be nice," Dale hissed from somewhere near my feet.

I squinted at her, trying to cripple her with my Karate Death Chi. She smiled and put her napkin in her lap. I sighed. "Coming up, Anna," I said.

Miss Lana came to the kitchen door moments later. "Friends," she said. "Mo and I are hosting a memorial service for Jesse Tatum here at the café, Sunday afternoon. You're all invited. Please help spread the word."

Attila looked up from her soda. "A funeral? *Here?*"

Reverend Thompson tugged his napkin from his collar. "Lana, a service for Jesse is a wonderful idea. This is a great venue, but I wish you'd consider having it at Creekside Church. We have a large sanctuary, and I'm sure Rose would play for the service." Miss Rose is Creekside's pianist. Sometimes Dale solos while she plays. "It would mean a lot to me," Reverend Thompson added.

I looked around the café, into a sea of baffled faces. Mr. Jesse had never set foot in Creekside Church, as far as I knew. But Miss Lana's Go with the Flow kicked into overdrive. "Wonderful," she said. "Shall we say Sunday at two p.m.?"

"Perfect," Reverend Thompson said, and Miss Lana returned to her griddle.

To my surprise, the breakfast crowd headed out early. To my horror, Attila stuck me with her check. On the back, she'd scribbled a message: *Thanks for breakfast, Mo-ron. Say hi to Dale for me.*

As Dale and I finally sat down to eat, around 9:30, Thes darted back in. "I didn't want to mention it with Daddy here, but Spitz is missing. The case is yours."

"Your cat? Again?" Dale said. "Spitz runs away every time the wind changes. He's a repeat offender, Thes. We ain't looking for him."

"You advertised," he said, pointing to our sign. "That's like giving your word."

I sighed and opened my order pad. "We'll need an official description."

"Cat," Thes said. "Orange hair, green eyes, chunky body."

Spitz, I wrote. *Looks like Thes.*

"Last known whereabouts?"

"The churchyard," he said. "Yesterday. About the same time Mr. Jesse turned up dead." He swallowed hard. "You don't think . . ."

"Nobody's thinking serial killer," Dale said, his blue eyes serious. "Not yet."

Reverend Thompson honked his horn, and Thes bolted. "We need to hurry too," I told Dale. "We gotta get to the crime scene."

"Us?" he said. "The crime scene?"

"Of course," I said, ignoring the syrup on his chin. "We're professionals."

"Okay, but I better check in with Mama first," he said. He folded his last pancake into his mouth.

One thing about Miss Rose: She likes to keep track of her baby.

Chapter 10
At the Tobacco Barn

Twenty minutes later, we pounded up Miss Rose's steps. "Mama," Dale called as the screen door slapped shut behind us. "I'm home." Silence. "Must be out in the garden," he muttered. "Come on. She'll want to say hello."

We were halfway down the hall when a door opened behind us. "Hold it right there, young man," Miss Rose said, sticking her head out of her bedroom. "Where do you think you're going?" I knew from the panic on Dale's face that he'd forgotten he'd snuck out last night to come to my house.

How he forgets these things remains a mystery to me.

"Morning, Miss Rose," I said. "Nice morning to sleep in, ain't it?"

"I imagine it would be, if I had the wherewithal to live that way," she said, the frost in her voice nipping my ears.

Her green eyes settled on Dale. "What do you have to say for yourself?"

"Morning, Mama," Dale said, offering a weak smile.

"Did you find my note? I left one so you wouldn't worry."

"A note," she said, fishing through her skirt pocket. "A note. Let me see if I can lay my hand on a note. Oh! That's right. I found something on your bed when I went in to wake you for breakfast. Here it is. What a happy circumstance."

Somehow I doubted the circumstance was going to be happy much longer.

She held out a crumpled scrap of paper and adjusted her reading glasses. "'Mama,'" she read. "'I am a murder suspect over at Mo's if you need me. Please do not worry. Your loving son, Dale.'" She glanced up. "Is *that* the note you're referring to?"

Dale shifted. "It sounded better when I first wrote it."

"A *murder suspect?*" she said, her voice rising.

"I'm innocent," he said.

"You know, Miss Rose, you could say this is my fault, in an odd way," I said, easing into the situation. "You'll probably be surprised to learn I'm the one that called Dale last night about the murder suspect situation. As it turns out, Dale ain't actually been named. So it's a false alarm, in a way."

"*You* had a hand in this, Mo?" she said in a voice shaved from ice. "Really?"

"Yes, ma'am. I probably shouldn't have called so late."

"No, you shouldn't have," she said. "And Dale shouldn't

have left without asking. What do you have to say about that, Dale? Why didn't you ask? Did you think I'd want to tag along?"

"No, ma'am," he sighed.

"Then why . . ." She stopped and tears flooded her eyes.

Miss Rose's tears are like truth serum to Dale. He blurted out his answer: "I didn't ask because I knew you wouldn't want me to go."

I winced.

"I wouldn't want you to go? Because?" she said.

Dale looked like a condemned man tying his own noose. "Because it was past my nine o'clock curfew." She waited while he studied the linoleum's faded yellow peonies. "And because it wasn't safe," he said.

"You got a nine o'clock curfew?" I asked. "Miss Lana gave me eight o'clock." Neither of them looked at me. "Not that my curfew matters right now," I added.

"You could have been killed," she said. If her voice went any higher, Queen Elizabeth would need ear plugs. "Thank heavens Lana called me this morning to let me know where you were. I would have been worried to death if . . ." She took a shaky breath. "What am I going to do with you?"

Fear clouded his eyes. "You ain't telling Daddy, are you?"

"Your daddy isn't in this anymore," she snapped. "You're grounded. No races, no trips to the café, no bicycle riding."

"Grounded?" he wailed. "For how long?"

"For until I say you're not grounded, that's how long," she said, snatching another paper from her pocket. "And as long as you're staying home for the foreseeable future, I have a few chores for you. First of all, I'd like you to clean out the tobacco barn."

"The *tobacco* barn?" Dale said, surprise ringing in his voice. "I thought you'd make me weed the garden or cut the grass."

"Hush," I whispered.

"Why clean out the tobacco barn?" he said. "Nobody's used it in years."

"I'd also like you to repair the things under the shelter."

"What things?"

"Things I've had put there. And I want the stable cleaned out. The manure behind the stable should be composted by now," she said. "I'd like for you to take it to the garden. You can use my wheelbarrow."

"Miss Rose," I said. "I hate to interrupt, but the truth is Dale and me got plans. We just opened a detective agency. Maybe you've heard of us? Desperado Detectives? We got a murder to solve."

She didn't even look up. "In that case, Mo, I suggest you open a branch office in the tobacco barn. Because that's where Dale's going to be for a long time to come."

"Ah, Mama," he said.

"Don't 'ah, Mama' me," she replied, her hands going to her hips.

We froze until she turned and headed for the kitchen. "Dale, that barn's not cleaning itself. You see any snakes, sing out and I'll come running," she said, nodding toward the shotgun by the door. Miss Rose shoots better than anybody in the county, save the Colonel. "I'll be out in a little while to see how you're doing. And," she said, "you had *better* be there, and you'd better be busy."

"Yes, ma'am."

She glanced at me. "What are your plans today, Mo?"

"I figured me and Dale would look into Mr. Jesse's murder today, maybe crack the case," I said. "If there's a reward, we're hoping to share the money with you."

"Isn't someone else working on that?" she asked. "An adult, perhaps?"

"Yes ma'am, Detective Joe Starr," I said as she turned on the tap at the sink and grabbed a bottle of Joy. Dale's daddy refuses to buy a dishwasher. He says if he bought a dishwasher, he wouldn't need a wife. "The thing is, Dale and me are privy to information Joe Starr ain't. Like, Mr. Jesse had a girlfriend. Starr doesn't know that."

Miss Rose just stood there.

"And the girlfriend has a husband," Dale said. "Starr doesn't know that either."

Nothing! The gossip of the century, and she didn't even flinch!

"Dale?" she said, without looking up. "Are you still standing there?"

"No, ma'am," he sighed, and shuffled toward the door.

Queen Elizabeth II joined us halfway across the back-yard. Dale side-armed a stick into a field of deep green, knee-high tobacco plants. "Fetch it, Liz," he said. Sweat trickled down my back and heat monkeys shimmied like ghosts between the rows as she brought it back and spit it at his feet. "Good dog," he said, ruffling her ears. "She's smart, ain't she, Mo?"

"She's brilliant," I lied.

"Practice me," he said, flipping me a pinecone and setting up to my left as we cleared the stable. But I froze, horrified, staring at the tobacco barn dead ahead.

"Holy moly," I whispered. "Your mama's lost her mind."

The barn stood tall and windowless, its tin sides draped in rust. Beneath its lean-to shelter lay a terrifying jumble of wood and metal. A wooden cart lay on its side, its axle busted, boards sprawling like pick-up sticks over the cart's tongue. Rusting chains and worn leather cord decorated a heap of broken chairs and old-timey plows.

Dale's shoulders sagged. "You're going to have to work the murder scene by yourself, Mo. In fact," he sighed, "you may have to go to high school by yourself, because that's how long it's going to take me to finish these chores."

"It might," Miss Rose said cheerily, walking up behind us. "Come on, Mo," she said. "We'll give you a ride home."

I settled into the Pinto, mourning Dale's cruel fate and thinking of the crime scene just two impossible-to-get-to miles down the road.

Chapter 11
Murder Weapon to Go

Within minutes I was reduced to begging. "But Miss Lana, I *got* to get to the crime scene. Please."

"Sorry, sugar," she said, lining up the saltshakers. "It's not safe for you to go out alone." She reached beneath the counter and dangled a gold shopping bag from her fingertips. "I forgot this last night," she said, smiling. "Go ahead, open it."

If Miss Lana doesn't take me to Charleston with her, she always brings me something when she comes back. "Is it a T-shirt from Rainbow Row?" I asked. "Because my old one's down to its last sleeve, thanks to Miss Blalock's barbed-wire fence."

"You tore it on Lucy Blalock's fence?" she asked, opening the salt.

"Last March, remember?" I said, steadying a salt-shaker as she poured. "Dale and me picked you some narcissus from under that squeaky old water tower of hers. You know the one: *ScreeeEEEk. ScreeeEEEk.*"

"That's right," she said absently. "I remember." She

glanced at the bag. "Go ahead, open it. I can't wait to see your face." I tugged the bag's corner and a green scrapbook spun across the counter. "For your autobiography," she said, flipping it open. "I slapped it together in Charleston. This page is blank, for your Coming Ashore Announcement. You do still have it, don't you? A girl should keep her publicity."

I nodded and she turned the page. "This is the story of the Colonel's crash. And these articles are from the old *Tupelo Times*: the café's grand opening, our housewarming, your kindergarten graduation.

"Here's Cousin Gideon, going to court."

"He's handsome," I said, "even in handcuffs."

"And here's the Colonel." I leaned over the book. A young Colonel sat at a table, camo-clad and scrawny. He bounced an unusually good-looking baby on his knee. Behind them, an open suitcase spewed baby things across the table. "Is that the suitcase that started the rumors about the Colonel's money?" I asked.

She laughed. "I suppose so," she said. "Macon started that lie. There's no limit to what some people will say, and what others will believe."

She uncapped the pepper shakers. "Who's this?" I asked, peering at a photo of a thin-faced girl about my age. She stood barefoot, in knee-pants and a trim white blouse, heat curls framing her solemn face.

Miss Lana sneezed. "That's me prior to blossoming," she said. "I was just about your age." I turned the page. "And these are my parents sitting in the shade of our oak tree. There's no telling how many Sunday afternoons we spent there. This was before we had air-conditioning—a hundred degrees, a hundred and three . . ." Her quiet laugh sounded the way she looks without her makeup. "All of us sitting and talking, and moving with the sun."

I studied her parents' faces: strong faces, with eyes that peered straight into my heart. I wondered if my own people would look into my heart too. "Your people have kind faces," I said. "I wish I'd known them."

"I do too, sugar," she said. "They would have loved you."

She flipped the page. "And here's where I discovered the drama club, and came into my own." It was the girl from the first photo, only shinier: putting on makeup. Standing in a spotlight. Holding a bouquet of roses. "Always remember Bill's advice," she said.

"Bill Watson? At the hardware store? But the Colonel says he's an idiot."

"Bill *Shakespeare*," she said. "All the world's a stage, sugar, so hop on up there."

She glanced at the clock. "My goodness! The lunch crowd will be here before we know it, and I still have to set the stage and change!"

I closed the scrapbook. "Thanks for this. I love it," I said. I meant it too. "I'll study it tonight. Right now, I need to go to Mr. Jesse's—if you can handle lunch."

She glanced at the 7UP clock. "I suppose I can. We're so slow. . . . If I need some help, I can ask someone. But you are not to go out alone, Mo. I mean it. Be patient," she said. "Someone will drop in for a glass of tea, and offer you a ride." She glanced outside as I picked up a few order pads, to hold my clues. "Where on earth is our mid-morning crowd?"

"Beats me," I said.

It took me about fifteen minutes to find out.

As I unloaded my bike from the back of Redneck Red's truck I saw half the town milling about the top of Mr. Jesse's tree-lined drive. "Hey, Skeeter. Is my competition here yet?" I asked, looking toward Mr. Jesse's house.

Skeeter nodded. "Starr and two plainclothes cops. A young guy and a dark-haired woman of undetermined age." Skeeter has a good eye for detail. "They've been in there about an hour, to the best of my knowledge."

I surveyed the crowd. The café's customers stood in dwindling patches of shade, asking questions, making up answers, and passing them along as fact.

"Starr says he'll arrest anybody that crosses his crime scene tape," Skeeter added.

Sal darted out of the crowd with two bottles of icy

water and handed one to Skeeter. "Hey, Mo." She smiled, her gray eyes shy and hopeful. "Where's Dale?"

"Grounded," I said. "Maybe for life."

"May be just as well," Skeeter said, cutting her eyes toward Attila and her mother, who had set up chairs by a crepe myrtle. Attila had crossed her arms and slouched in her chair, scowling. I zeroed in on Mrs. Simpson— pinch-faced, shrill, beige—as she closed their cooler. "I don't care whether you want to or not, Anna," she was saying. "Our family sings, and you will too. You just need to get over being self-conscious." I smiled at Attila, who turned an unflattering shade of red.

"I'll try, Mother," she said, her voice loud. "At least I know who our family is, and what we do." Her mother glanced at me and hid a smile.

I hate Anna Celeste.

"Hey Mo," Thes said, wandering by. "Have you found Spitz yet? Because he's mostly an inside cat, and we got eighty percent chance of rain tonight. Plus he's a very finicky eater. He only likes canned."

"We're on it, Thes," I said. "But you're right: The first twenty-four hours are critical." He nodded and wandered back into the crowd.

I scanned the rambling drive. Mr. Jesse's old Tahoe had crushed the gravel to silvery gray dust; grass crept hungry and thin along the path's ragged center line. Starr's stark yellow crime scene tape looked out of place, stretching across the drive and meandering through the pines. "How far does that tape go?" I asked.

"All the way around Mr. Jesse's, down to the creek. That's alleged," Skeeter said quickly. "I ain't seen it myself. In North Carolina, waterways belong to the people. Which is probably why they stopped at the creek." I nodded, but it was news to me.

"It's almost dinner time," Sal said, easing into the shade. "Are y'all gonna cater out here? Folks won't want to leave until Starr heads out."

"That's right," Skeeter said. "They'll be hungrier for information than for Miss Lana's special."

An idea sat down before me, fat and sassy as Thes's brainless cat. "Sure. We can cater a crowd this big." I grinned. "You two want a free lunch?"

Skeeter's eyes became guarded. "I don't know. I'm not personally hungry." Skeeter's negotiation skills are legendary.

"It's not so much a free lunch I'm offering as it is a Wonder Bread retainer of sorts," I said, and she perked up. I handed them order pads from my bike's basket. "Canned drinks and burgers only. Fries if they beg. One dollar per item. Take the orders to Miss Lana and I'll handle it from there. If I ain't back with the eats by twelve thirty, tell them the cater's been canceled and they have to go to the café."

"Deal," Sal said as an orange cat slunk out of the underbrush, pale gray feathers stuck to his round face. Somehow, he didn't look like such a finicky eater to me.

"Hey Thes, here's your cat," I called. "Courtesy of Desperado Detectives." I pushed off and pedaled down the highway, zigzagging to keep in the shade as I raced the length of Mr. Jesse's property.

I ditched my bike in a ramble of honeysuckle, by the creek, tucked my last order pad into my pocket, double-tied my plaid sneakers, and scanned the bank for water moccasins. The warm water crept to my knee as my foot sank into the soft creek bed and I stepped forward, mud slurping at my shoes.

Slipping past the bay tree where Starr had tied his crime tape, I headed for the bend just below Mr. Jesse's. I froze as Starr's voice sliced through the honeysuckle: "Ben, try over here."

I peered between tupelo branches. Starr's deputy stood in chest-deep water. Even in a wet suit he looked strong. I took out my pad. *Deputy Ben,* I wrote. *Muscles.*

Ben sloshed toward Starr, on the pier. "Water's awful muddy," he said. "But if the murder weapon's here, I'll find it." As he adjusted his mask and slipped beneath the water's dark surface, a woman stepped out of the shade thirty yards downstream.

"Hey," she shouted. "I got another set of footprints over here!"

"Good, Marla," Starr called. "Which way are they headed?"

I wrote, *Deputy Marla. Loud.*

"Into the woods. Looks like they might be a boy's," she said. "Size five. Nike sole." My heart tilted. Dale's prints.

"Make a mold," Starr shouted. "Then see where they lead."

Ben surfaced. "More trash," he said, slinging an old reel up on the dock.

"A couple more dives and we'll trailer Jesse Tatum's boat," Starr said. "It's going to rain, and I don't want to lose the blood evidence on the gunnels."

Blood evidence? I eased forward, bending a branch out of the way.

"Narrow your search. For the blood to spatter this way, he would have been hit like this," Starr said, swinging his fist. "If the weapon flew out of his hand, it should be over there."

Where? I couldn't see. I eased forward. *Snap!* The branch broke.

Starr reached for his pistol. "You," he barked, aiming

about ten feet to my left. "Put your hands where I can see them and come out. Now."

I turned to run, and my foot snagged. I staggered and splashed sideways. Out of the corner of my eye, I saw Starr adjust his aim. "Don't shoot!" I screamed. I threw my arms wide, for balance. My order pad flew out of my hand as I fell into a perfect back flop. The creek closed around me, swallowing the sun. I reached back to the thick creek bottom and pushed off. "Don't shoot," I wheezed, raising one hand. "It's Mo!" I cried, wiping the mud from my eyes. "I'm a possible orphan. Don't shoot!"

"Hold your fire!" Starr bellowed. "It's the kid from the diner."

I yanked at the root that tripped me. That's when I made the find of the century.

That was no root: It was Mr. Jesse's oar. And was that water glistening on its splintered blade? Or were those bloodstains?

Starr splashed to me. "Mo LoBeau, what are you doing at my crime scene?"

I smoothed my shirt and grabbed my soggy clue pad as it drifted by. "Good day, Detective," I said, keeping my voice professional as I pushed the oar toward him. "Here's your murder weapon."

He grabbed the oar. "What the . . . ?"

"Mr. Jesse's oar," I said. "He carved the handle last winter, to fit his hands."

I stood up straight, pen poised, the way Miss Lana taught me. "Welcome to the café's cater division," I said. "Have you made your luncheon selection, or do you need more time?"

Chapter 12
Stay Away from My Crime Scene

"I knew I'd end up cruising in an unmarked patrol car one day, but I always figured I'd be the one driving it," I told Starr as we purred down Mr. Jesse's drive in Starr's dirt-colored Impala. Briars crowded the path, squeaking down the sides of the car.

"Driving? You're lucky you're not in handcuffs," he growled. "It's illegal to disturb a crime scene."

"I didn't cross your tape," I said, brushing my wet hair back from my face. "I came in on the creek, perfectly legal. You don't believe me, ask Skeeter, my attorney-in-training."

Starr grinned. "Funny name for an attorney."

I thought so too, but I didn't like him saying it. "The Colonel says *all* attorneys should be named for blood-sucking insects so we know up front who we're dealing with," I said. Starr's grin widened. He looks younger when he smiles. His eyes crinkle, and the side of his mouth dimples. I could almost see why Miss Retzyl might like him.

"You can't interfere with an investigation. No matter what your friend says."

"I wasn't interfering, I was finding the murder weapon," I said as we rounded a bend. "Hey, you'd better slow down. Most of the town is at the end of this drive, waiting for word on the murder. Besides," I added, "folks are gonna want to see who's riding with you."

Starr tapped the brakes as the crowd came into view. I rolled down my window.

"Hey, Mr. Li," I shouted. "I found the murder weapon!"

Mr. Li waved. "Very good, Mo. Ask Miss Lana to double my fries. I'm starving!"

"Me too," Thes shouted.

Sal darted to the window. "Mo, Anna Celeste said she and her mom are eating free of charge today," she said. "I didn't know what to do . . ."

Blackmail. Attila had enough on Dale and his whereabouts the night of the murder to shake me down for eternity—another reason to clear Dale's name.

"I'll handle it, Sal," I said. "Thanks."

Starr sped up, and the crowd parted. "Buckle up," he said, his voice like gunmetal.

"Pretty snazzy ride," I said, clicking my seat belt and waving to a clump of high school kids. "You get to drive this over to Miss Retzyl's, for dating? How long you known her, anyway? As a rising sixth grader, I got a right to know."

"You ask too many questions."

"Occupational hazard. Detective," I added before he could ask.

He snorted. "It takes years of training to become a detective."

"Lucky I didn't know that earlier," I said, lifting the radio from its hook. "You wouldn't have a murder weapon. Speaking of which, you sending my oar to the lab?"

"We don't know if it *is* the murder weapon," he said, putting the radio back on its hook. "But yes, my deputy bagged it for the lab."

"You find any other clues out there? One investigator to another."

"Nothing comes to mind," he said. He shot me a cool look. "How about you? You know this town. What's your take? One investigator to another."

So *that* was why he was being nice. He wanted my clues. "Beats me. You can let me out at the head of that path," I added, pointing. "I got to pick up my bike."

He didn't even slow down. "I don't mind giving you a lift to the café," he said. "I don't want you out by yourself. Besides, I'd like to have a word with the Colonel."

My confidence wobbled like a bike in heavy sand. "The Colonel?" I said.

"Yeah. That's not a problem, is it?"

I shrugged. "Not for me," I said, hoping I was right.

A few minutes later Starr parked beside the Colonel's Underbird and followed me into the café. "Come in," Miss Lana sang from the kitchen. "I'll be with you in a minute!"

Starr swept off his hat. "Things have changed a little since I was here," he said.

That was an understatement.

You can tell who's running the café the instant you walk through the door. The Colonel keeps the café military crisp; Miss Lana prefers a theme. Glancing around, I pegged today's theme as 1930s Paris—her favorite. A miniature Eiffel Tower graced the counter, and scratchy accordion music crackled from the ancient Victrola she'd placed near the jukebox. The red Formica tables sported white lace cloths, which she'd turned catty-corner, lending the café a bohemian flair. The blackboard behind the counter read: *Le Menu*.

"Bonjour," Miss Lana said, backing through the kitchen's swinging doors. Her calf-length, pale pink dress clung to her body like a fine, shimmering mold. "Welcome to la café." She wheeled gracefully, placed a tray of sparkling glasses on the counter, and beamed at Joe

Starr. "Mo, where are your manners? Take the gentleman's hat," she said, picking up her fan and, with a practiced flick of her wrist, snapping it open. "Welcome, *mon capitán.*"

When Miss Lana goes into character, she goes into character.

I popped Starr's hat onto the counter. "He ain't a captain, he's a detective," I said, wiggling my eyebrows in the universally recognized sign for Be Quiet. "He's here about the murder."

She ignored me. "Wine, sir? Unless you're on duty . . ."

"Iced tea," Starr said, his eyes traveling past Miss Lana's Jean Harlow wig to the 1930s black-and-white Hollywood photos on the wall.

I elbowed back into the conversation. "Detective Joe Starr, this is Miss Lana. Miss Lana, DETECTIVE Joe Starr," I said. "The one I told you about. The one investigating Mr. Jesse's murder. Are those our lunches over there?"

"Yes, sugar," she said, glancing at the neat row of brown paper bags lining the counter. "All packed up and ready to go. Sal brought me the takeout list. She said Anna's lunch was prepaid . . . ?"

"Right," I said, cutting her short. "I got her money right here. You want to carry some of these lunches out for me?" I asked Starr. "Maybe give me a ride back to the driveway? Folks are hungry, and you are a public servant, after all."

Now *he* ignored me. "It's slow for lunchtime," he said to Miss Lana.

"Naturally," she said. "No one's thinking of the café today. All eyes are on you."

Starr glanced at the café's one occupied table. Miss Lana's lone customer had slumped forward, cradling his head in his arms. "Too much wine?" Starr asked, nodding toward the man.

She sighed. "Too much drink well before he arrived at my door." She picked up the coffeepot, swayed across the room, and carefully topped off the man's cup. He sat up and focused blearily in our direction.

Crud. Dale's daddy. Could my day get any worse?

"Hey, Mo," Mr. Macon mumbled. He looked horrible—like time had grabbed his face with both hands and stretched the life right out of him.

"Hey," I muttered, heading for the jukebox. Maybe if I stood here long enough, he'd go back to sleep. Dale's was the last name I wanted to come up with Starr in the room.

"Where's the Colonel?" Starr asked. "I'd like a word with him, if you don't mind."

"The Colonel?" Miss Lana hesitated. "Why, I don't

believe he's here. Then again, he's so hard to keep up with . . . Such a mercurial personality." She smiled. "Is his car out front?"

"Yes, ma'am," he said.

"Go to the kitchen and call him, sugar," she told me. "Maybe he's out back, fishing."

If he is, he ain't the only one, I thought.

I shot Dale's daddy a quick look. Out cold again, thank heavens. I tromped through the kitchen to the side door and cupped my hands around my mouth. "Colonel?" I called, so Starr could hear me. "Miss Lana wants you." I waited a minute, and came back inside.

"Very well, Detective," Miss Lana was saying. "Two hamburgers to go. Pity you're not staying for lunch. We could get better acquainted."

"The Colonel didn't answer me," I said. "I guess he couldn't hear me."

"That man will be the death of me." She sighed, giving Starr a baleful look. "Oh, he'll come slipping back in when I least expect it with some ridiculous story about a bass or a . . . What are those other things he talks about, sugar?"

"Catfish?" I suggested. It was all bunk, the idea of the Colonel fishing. The Colonel's only fishing story involves a stick of dynamite and a bushel basket.

"Catfish," she said, beaming. "Of course."

She smiled her most leisurely smile, but moved like lightning as she slapped Starr's hamburgers together, folded them in crisp tissue, and put them in a bag. She wanted Starr gone as bad as I did. "There you are. On the house," she said, sliding the bag toward him.

"Thanks anyway," he said, putting a ten on the counter. "Keep the change."

"*Très bien*," she sang. "*Au revoir!*"

"*Merci*," Starr muttered, heading for the door. "Oh," he said, turning. "You haven't mentioned the murder, which I find odd. That's the first thing most folks ask about."

"Well, *pardonez-moi*," she said. "How is your investigation going, Detective?"

"Fine. And don't worry about not asking. After all, there are a few things I haven't asked *you*," he said. "For instance, any idea who might want Jesse Tatum dead?"

I stood behind Starr, waving my arms, mouthing the words *No! No!* as Miss Lana studied me.

She shrugged delicately. "Well," she said, "his girlfriend may have wanted him dead. Or her jealous husband. I'm sure you know about them. Selma and Albert Foster, from Kinston?"

I went dizzy. Those were my best clues!

"You know them, then?" Starr said, taking out his pad.

"No," she said. "But you hear things when you run a café."

Starr nodded. "And where were you the night Jesse Tatum died?"

"On a Greyhound, coming home from Charleston."

"Alone?"

She smiled. "In the existential sense, we all travel alone, don't we?" she said. "At times I feel it like a dull, aching pain, right here," she said, bringing her hand to her heart. "Don't you? Like a child yearning to go home."

Starr frowned. "Right," he said. "I had the same thing last Thursday. But I'm asking more in the alibi sense of things. Were you alone physically?"

"I was on a *bus*," she said, her smile slipping. "I'm sure that's easy to confirm."

Starr nodded and snapped his pad shut. "Probably so. I'll find out for you. You want a ride back to Jesse Tatum's driveway, Mo?"

Before I could say yes, Miss Lana's hand fell on my shoulder. "No, thank you, Detective," she said. "I'll drive her back."

Now what? Miss Lana can't drive.

"One more question," Starr said. "Somebody mentioned seeing a boy near Mr. Jesse's the day he died. Scrawny kid, blond hair, black T-shirt. Any idea who that was?"

"My goodness," she said. "Surely you don't suspect a child."

"I've seen murders done by kids younger than Mo, there," Starr said. "Shrinks say bad parenting's to blame, but who knows?"

"Yes, they can be such mad dogs, the poor dears," she said, patting my head.

Behind me, Dale's daddy's chair scrubbed against the floor. "Hold it right there, you slick-talking son of a gun," he slurred.

"Macon!" Miss Lana cried.

Mr. Macon rose unsteadily, his face twisted in rage. "There ain't nothing wrong with the way I'm raising my boy," he said, his voice thick. "If anybody's to blame for the way he's turned out, it's his mama. Ain't that right, Mo? Who does she think she is, telling me to get out of my own house?"

"Miss Rose threw you out?" I said. "Does Dale know? Because it's news to me."

"Mo," Miss Lana said. "Hush."

Mr. Macon glared at Starr. "Dale don't need nothing he ain't getting from me."

"Tell me, sir, your kid got blond hair?" Starr asked. "Like to wear black T-shirts?"

Mr. Macon lurched across the room. "So what if he does? Leave my boy alone," he said, jabbing a finger into

Starr's chest. Starr stepped back lightly, like a cat. "Don't nobody tell Dale what to do except me. He's a good boy. Ain't he a good boy, Mo?"

"Dale?" Starr kept his eyes on Mr. Macon, but I knew he was talking to me. "That's your friend, isn't it, Mo? The spooky kid I met the first time I came in here?"

I didn't answer.

He turned back to Mr. Macon. "Where's your son now?"

"Probably home with that no-good mother of his," he said. "Throw me out of my own house after I treated her like gold all these years . . ."

"Oh for heaven's sake," Miss Lana said, her hands going to her hips. "That house is Rose's, not yours. Her father left it to her. If it wasn't for her good name and good graces, you'd have been locked up years ago. You never gave her anything except a couple of good-looking kids, a mountain of bills, and a heart turned to stone with grief."

She turned to Starr. "I've known Dale since he was a baby, and I've never known a gentler soul. I can't even *pay* him to kill a garden snake. The idea that he murdered Jesse is ludicrous. Please stop wasting time on him and find the killer. We're all worried to death."

Starr stared at her a moment. "Miss Lana, I need to talk to Dale and his mother. If you see them, please tell them I'll be at Jesse Tatum's place all afternoon. If I don't see them by the end of the day, I'll come looking for them. And when the Colonel gets in, let him know I'd like to talk to him too. You," he said, looking at me. "Stay away from my crime scene. And you, sir," he said, looking at Dale's daddy. "If you ever jab your finger in my chest again, you'll wake up in handcuffs. Are we all clear?"

When we didn't answer, he smiled. "I thought so," he said, and headed for the door.

Chapter 13
Don't Call Me Baby

Miss Lana shoved the bagged lunches into the Underbird's backseat, tossed her fan beside them, and opened the driver's door. *"You're really driving?"* I said, backing away from the car. "Couldn't we call Miss Rose? Or hire a driver?"

"Bad news is best delivered in person, and I have no driver at the moment," she said, sliding behind the wheel. "Everybody's either working or at Jesse's. Besides, I've already called Rose once this morning, to update her on Macon's condition. That bulletin sent her to the garden for the rest of the day. Dale will be in shackles before I can reach her again by phone," she said, squinting at the dashboard. "That garden has saved Rose a fortune in therapy over the years," she muttered.

"It's cranked out some good tomatoes too," I said. "But you still can't—"

"Mo, please get in the car." She tugged the rearview mirror down and applied a fresh coat of lipstick. "We'll drop the lunches off on our way."

I slid in. "Miss Lana?" I said.

"Yes, sugar?"

"I think maybe I better drive."

She glared at me, her wig glistening gold in the sun. "How old are you?"

"Eleven," I said.

"And *why* should you drive?"

I looked away. "Because, Miss Lana," I said. "You don't know how." She graced me with a stony silence, the chill rolling off her in the noonday heat. "Everybody in town knows you can't drive," I said. "It's common knowledge."

"There is nothing common about knowledge," she replied. "The fact that I haven't driven doesn't mean I can't. Now," she said, tilting her head. "This vehicle is new to me. Where is the ignition?"

I slumped in my seat, fastened my seat belt, and prepared to die. "Right there," I muttered, pointing. I closed my eyes as she turned the key.

"I am ready to back up now, if common knowledge will allow," she said, studying the gear shift.

I sighed. "The Underbird is an automatic. Just put that pointer on *R*."

"*R?*" she said, placing her foot on the accelerator and pressing it toward the floor.

"It means 'reverse,'" I shouted over the engine's roar. "You don't give it gas until after—"

She yanked the gearshift to *R*. The Underbird lunged backward and we skidded across the parking lot in a spray of gray gravel and dust. Only our collision with the sycamore kept us from careening around the building, down into the backyard.

"See?" she said, taking her foot from the gas.

"*D* means 'drive.' This time, shift before you give it gas. That way—" Spinning wheels and flying gravel chewed up the end of my sentence, spitting it across the parking lot like a fighter spitting teeth, and we were on our way.

To my relief, Miss Lana had the Underbird somewhat under control by the time we swerved into Mr. Jesse's drive. I thought so, anyway, until she took dead aim at a throng of our neighbors. "Use the brake!" I cried, diving into the foot of the car and slamming both hands onto the brake.

"Lunch, dears!" she called as a pine branch whipped across our windshield. "Mo," she said, "get up. People will think you're daft."

"Yes, ma'am," I muttered, wiping the grit from my hands.

Ten minutes later we headed for Miss Rose's. "Dale's house is around this curve," I said. "I mention that be—cause you might want to slow down. By using the brake," I added.

She hunched over the wheel. "Rose is already depressed, so we'll present our news gently," she said, easing up on the gas. "Be positive. Follow my lead."

She gave the steering wheel a tug to the left. The tires screamed as we skidded across the asphalt, bounced off the drive, and crunched across Miss Rose's petunia bed. As we lurched to a halt with our front left tire on the porch step, Miss Rose dropped her hoe and sprinted toward us. "*P* for 'park,'" I instructed as the Underbird issued an ominous hiss. I opened my door and stepped out.

"Remember," Miss Lana said. "Be positive."

"Hey, Miss Rose," I said, smiling. "I'm sorry Mr. Macon took drunk again, but at least there ain't nobody in jail yet. That's positive."

"Mama," Dale cried, pounding around the corner of the house. "I heard tires. Is Lavender here? Oh!" he said, spotting me and Miss Lana. He stared at the pine branch trapped beneath the Underbird's windshield wiper, his mouth falling open.

"Hello, dear friends," Miss Lana said, opening her door as far as the front porch would allow. She slithered out sideways, wiggling her butt along the porch until she reached the back of the car.

"Gosh," Dale said. "I didn't know you could drive."

"She can't," Miss Rose said, her voice flat as her petunias. Like Dale, Miss Rose has a firm grasp of the obvious.

"Rose," Miss Lana said, "if you don't mind, we need to talk. You don't have any tea, do you? I'm parched."

A half glass of iced tea later, the four of us roared back toward Mr. Jesse's place, with Miss Rose at the wheel. Dale and me huddled in the backseat. I could feel him trembling. I pressed my shoulder against his, trying to will my calm into his body. "I just know I'm going to jail," he whispered.

"No you ain't," I told him. "You're a juvenile. Besides, even if you do, it won't be so bad. You can bond with the incarcerated side of your family. And I'll bring you your homework assignments so you don't fall behind in school."

"Great," he muttered. "Jail time and math. My life can't get no worse than this."

He was wrong.

Dale's life got a lot worse just about the time Detective Starr started asking questions.

"So, you admit to stealing the boat?" Starr asked, taking his notepad from his pocket and sitting on Mr. Jesse's porch rail. I tugged my clue pad out of my pocket and settled in the porch swing beside Dale.

"Dale didn't steal nothing," I said.

"Stealing is such a harsh concept," Miss Lana agreed, popping her fan open. "Dale didn't say he stole Jesse's boat, he said he returned it."

"That's right," I said.

"Dale?" Starr said. "I'm talking to you, son."

"I . . . I guess it might look like I stole it, but I didn't," Dale stammered. "I just borrowed it good and strong. Me and a friend wanted to go fishing is all."

"Fishing ain't no crime," I added quickly.

"Depends on what kind of license you got," Starr said, and the blood ran from Dale's face. It's just like Dale to worry about getting caught without a fishing license after he admitted to stealing a boat.

"Who were you going fishing with?" Starr asked.

"Me," I said, saving Dale having to rat me out.

"Dale?" Starr said. "I'm talking to you."

"I was gonna take it back." Dale looked at Miss Rose. "I *did* take it back," he pleaded.

Miss Rose nodded. She sat in Mr. Jesse's rickety old rocking chair, her hands folded calm as prayers in her lap. To me, she looked worried.

"When did you return it?" Starr asked.

"Right after my brother invited me and Mo to time laps at Carolina Raceway," Dale said. "Yesterday. Same day we saw you at the speedway with Miss Retzyl."

"Such a good boy," Miss Lana said, beaming at him. "You took that boat back out of the goodness of your heart, didn't you, Dale?"

"No, ma'am," Dale said. "I took it back because we needed the reward money for fried baloney sandwiches."

I winced. Dale is not cut out for a life of crime.

"Tell me about the boat," Starr said.

"Well, Mr. Jesse hardly ever used it, and I only hid it a ways down from his place. He coulda found it if he really wanted to."

Starr looked at Dale, his eyes hard. "Tell me about taking it back."

Dale shoved his hands in his pockets. It made him look smaller, somehow. "Well," he said, "I walked the boat up the creek. Then I went over to Mr. Jesse's house and knocked on his door. And Mr. Jesse, he come to the door and he said, 'Afternoon Dale, how's your mother?'

"And I said, 'She's fine, Mr. Jesse. I sure hope you are. I got exciting news for you: I found your boat. I hope it wasn't a hardship, not having it.'

"And he said, 'Not at all. Thank you, son. Here's your reward money,' and I left."

Starr looked up from his notes. "No kidding," he said. "That was real cordial."

"Sure," Dale said. "Mr. Jesse was a real cordial man."

Starr scratched an eyebrow. "Well, I guess I'm a little

surprised," he said. "From what folks have told me, I didn't think Jesse Tatum was a particularly cordial kind of guy. Did you find him cordial, Miss Rose?"

"Of course not," she snapped. "Dale Earnhardt Johnson III, you stop this foolishness," she said, cracking her words like a whip. "You tell Detective Starr the truth and you tell it now."

"Yes, ma'am," Dale said. His chin quivered, and he looked at Starr. "Maybe just you and me could talk," he said. "Man to man."

"Dale, whatever it is, just say it," Miss Rose said, her voice gentler now.

He looked across the yard, fixing on Starr's car like he could stare the shine right off of it. "All right," he said. "I walked the boat up the creek to Mr. Jesse's dock, and I knocked on the door, like I said. Mr. Jesse come to the door in his pants and his undershirt, and he unlatched the door and pushed it open, and . . ." Dale took a deep breath. "And he said, 'What are you doing on my door stoop, you no-good son of a white trash drunk.'"

Miss Rose gasped, but Miss Lana nodded. "That's the Jesse I knew," she said.

Dale's voice was low. "Then Mr. Jesse said, 'You get your scrawny good-for-nothing self off my land before I call the law. And you tell your daddy if I see him on my land again I'll call the law on him too, no warning given.'

"Then I said, 'I'll be glad to get off your filthy scrap of swamp soon as you pay the reward you owe me for getting your boat back, you ugly old waste of human skin. And if you got a message for my daddy, you can deliver it yourself, if you ain't scared.'

"Then he said, 'You think I'm shelling out ten bucks on the word of Macon Johnson's leftovers? You show me my boat if you got it.' So we walked down to the creek and he saw his boat. He gave me ten dollars and no thank you, and I skedaddled."

Starr nodded. "Which way did you go?"

"Through the woods."

"Who was with you?"

"Nobody."

I raised my hand. "Even if somebody was with him, which there wasn't, it wasn't me," I said. "I can tell you an alibi, if needed."

Starr didn't take his eyes off Dale. "Don't lie to me, son," he said. "There were two sets of footprints where you hid the boat, and there were two sets on the creek bed, by the dock. Yours, and an adult's."

Two sets of footprints?

"I'll ask you again," Starr said. "Who was with you?"

"Nobody," Dale said, looking scared. "I got the boat and walked it up the creek. I tied it right about where I found it."

"Where it was when you stole it?" Starr asked.

"I object," I said. "We've already established this wasn't a technical steal. This was more like a surprise borrowing between neighbors. Don't say nothing, Dale," I warned.

Starr turned to Miss Rose. "Doesn't sound like Mr. Jesse thought much of your husband."

She looked suddenly tired. "Nobody thinks much of my husband," she said. "Can't say that I blame them."

"Where was he last night?"

"He came home around eight. He left maybe three hours later. I'm not sure where he came from, or where he went."

"Had he been drinking?"

"He's always been drinking," Dale said. "You leave Mama out of this."

Starr ignored him. "What size shoe does your husband wear?"

"Nine, nine and a half."

"Well, here's the situation," Starr said. "I've got Dale's footprints and an adult's footprints at the scene of a crime. Dale admits stealing Jesse Tatum's boat. Your husband was drinking and his whereabouts at the time of the murder are unknown. So, I need you to fill in some blanks for me—unless you really *do* want to call a lawyer."

Now Miss Rose looked scared. "I don't know that I can fill in many blanks," she said, "but I *can* tell you Dale is no murderer." She gave Dale a look that would break a stone. "A thief, maybe, but not a murderer."

"I promise," Dale said, his eyes filling with tears. "I didn't steal nothing. And I don't know whose footprints got tangled up with mine."

I thought back, to Dale returning the boat, and then farther back, to the day he took it. "I know," I said quietly. I studied my notes until everyone was looking. There's no need to waste a dramatic pause—that's what Miss Lana says. "Those prints you found were from Lavender's shoes."

"Lavender's?" Miss Rose cried, grabbing Miss Lana's arm for support.

Dale blinked, and then smacked himself on the forehead. "Right," he said. "Lavender's shoes made those prints, only he wasn't in them. See, when I decided to borrow Mr. Jesse's boat, I borrowed Lavender's sandals too. They're huge. That way if Mr. Jesse saw my footprints, he'd think somebody else took his boat."

Starr blinked, startled. "Hold on," he said. "Lavender is . . ."

"My brother," Dale said. "The racecar driver."

"What size shoes does he . . ."

"Twelve," Miss Rose said.

Starr stared at Dale, his face thoughtful. "That would

explain why the footprints are so shallow," he said. "You can't weigh more than, what, seventy pounds?"

"Seventy-two," Dale muttered. Like I say, Dale is the second-smallest in our class, behind Salamander. He's sensitive.

"Dale and me been busy," I told Starr. "He ain't had time to grow. The important thing is, Dale didn't have no accomplice except a pair of sandals."

"And where are those sandals now?"

"In the café," I told him. "By the drink machine."

"I'll need them," he said. He studied Dale, looking friendlier now. "Dale, I'd like for you to ride out of here in the back of my car. In fact, come here." Dale stepped forward uncertainly as Starr produced a pair of hand-cuffs. "Hold out your hands."

"Now *I* object!" Miss Lana cried.

"We want an attorney," Miss Rose said, stepping in front of Dale.

"I'm not charging Dale with anything," Starr said. "If you let him ride out in cuffs I'll take them off of him as soon as we get to the café. Dale's no killer, I know that. But there's a chance the killer's watching this investigation, and if he thinks Dale's our suspect, he might get sloppy."

"Sexist," Miss Lana hissed. "The killer could be a woman."

"Could be," Starr said. "In fact, it could be a woman

in a bad wig, for all I know." Miss Lana's hand flew to her wig. "Rose, it's a lot to ask, but it could really help," he said. "I'd want people to think I've released Dale into your custody. Dale, I'd need you to let people see the handcuffs when we drive out."

"A setup," I breathed. "Excellent."

"Rose, I'm not going to lie. We don't have many leads. If you'll agree to this, we'll watch Dale like he's our own until this case is closed," he said. "And we'll hope Mr. Jesse's real killer makes a mistake—either because he thinks he's in the clear, or because he doesn't like someone else taking credit for his work. Either way, mistakes work in our favor."

Dale looked at me, his blue eyes full of questions.

"If you're in, I'm in," I said.

"What . . . what would we have to do?" Dale asked.

Starr gave him a quick smile. "Do whatever it is you do when you're not conning cantankerous old men out of pocket change and interfering with my investigation. We'll do the rest." Starr glanced at Miss Rose. "My deputy is renting a room from Priscilla Retzyl, and I'm staying in Greenville. Between us, we're here twenty-four/seven. What do you say?"

Miss Rose looked at Dale. "Baby?"

Dale squared his shoulders. "Don't call me baby," he said, and held out his hands.

Chapter 14
Deputy Marla

Dale went instantly famous. In fact, he's all people talked about: Dale waving from Starr's Impala, his handcuffs glinting. Dale being followed out by Miss Rose, Miss Lana, and me in the Pinto. Dale being released to Miss Rose with a warning not to leave the county. As if he had anywhere to go.

Fame changed him. He got in the Impala a terrified kid. He stepped out a rock star. If Miss Rose hadn't already grounded him, he probably would have thrown himself a parade.

His faux-suspect status had another benefit: Attila lost her power over us. With Dale in fake custody, she couldn't turn him in.

I dropped the lunch bill she'd stuck me with in the mail.

Meanwhile, Miss Lana grew quiet. On Saturday she closed the café and hung a wreath by the door.

"I don't like it," I told her, polishing off my cereal. "If the Colonel comes home and sees that wreath, it will scare him crazy."

She looked up from the papers spread across our kitchen table. NPR hummed in the background. "There's nothing wrong with the world taking note when a person dies, sugar," she said. "Besides, I can't write a eulogy while I'm feeding everybody in town. And I need my beauty rest. We'll be center stage at the funeral tomorrow."

"How's the eulogy going?" I asked, peeking at her paper. It looked like my autobiography: false starts, scribble-throughs, cross-outs.

"Slow," she admitted. "At the moment I'm listing things Jesse taught me. You might like to do the same."

"Sounds . . . good," I said. "I'll be sure to do that." I hovered until she looked up again. She laid her pen down, glanced at the clock, and took a deep breath. Her face was drawn, and her hands shook slightly. I recognized the symptoms: homework anxiety. Next she would crave salty foods. Then chocolate.

"Miss Lana, have you heard from the Colonel?"

"No, I haven't heard from him yet, Mo," she said, ironing the sharp out of her voice. "But today's just his second day away."

"But you'd think with a killer on the loose . . ."

"Let's not worry unless there's something to worry about." She smiled. "I wonder if you'd do me a favor. Priscilla Retzyl has offered to arrange flowers for Jesse's service, and I told her we'd drop some glads by."

My mouth went dry. Please, God, not another road trip.

"The Underbird hasn't recovered from our last drive," I told her. "Lavender's still got it. Besides, Joe Starr hangs around Miss Retzyl like a fly around sugar. If he sees you driving, you'll be living with Dale's people, in the slammer."

She laughed. "I've sworn off driving, Mo," she said. "I have no flair. But I cut a basket of glads for Priscilla this morning. Could you take them to her? They're on the porch."

Me? Visit a teacher? The tips of my fingers and toes tingled.

"Miss Lacy Thornton will be by in a few minutes, on her morning walk," she said. "You could walk with her."

That's another thing about a small town: Everybody knows everybody's schedule. We spin around each other like planets around an invisible sun.

"Yes ma'am," I sighed.

"Great. I'll let Priscilla know you're coming."

I rinsed my cereal bowl as the radio announcer's voice whispered across the airwaves. "The first hurricane of the season's barreling across the Atlantic. Amy, they're calling her. Let's hope she spins herself out at sea. And now, Beethoven's Moonlight Sonata, written when Ludwig was thirty-one years old."

"Turn that radio off, would you, sugar?" she said. "NPR's too chatty this morning." I clicked it off and headed for the door.

A short time later Miss Retzyl stepped out on her front porch. A trellis dappled the soft light. "Morning, Mo," she said. "I hope you're well. Aren't those gladiolas beautiful," she continued, smiling. "Let's get them in some water."

I stepped into the Teacher's Lair and waited for my eyes to adjust.

To my surprise, her living room looked nothing at all like homeroom. Wicker chairs and a love seat sat angled around a quiet Oriental carpet, and a ceiling fan swiped lazily from her high, white ceiling. As she took my basket, something stirred in the corner, by a large fern. "Mo, this is Deputy Marla Everette," Miss Retzyl said, heading for the kitchen. "Marla, this is one of my best students, Mo LoBeau."

One of her best students? I felt a surge of confidence.

Deputy Marla leaned into the light, her gray eyes flickering over me. She'd swept her short, dark hair up. "*Detective* Mo LoBeau, I believe," she said, a smile softening her broad face. "How are you today?"

"Fine," I said, giving her a sophisticated nod. "I hope you are." She sat forward to take a coffee cup from the table. A forsythia swayed outside the window, sending a mosaic of faint shadows across her face and coarse linen blouse.

"Can I get you something, Mo?" Miss Retzyl called from the kitchen. "A glass of lemonade? I just made a pitcher."

"Thank you," I said, taking a seat. "It's hotter than the devil's curling iron out there." Deputy Marla sipped her coffee. "Joe says you bagged the murder weapon for me," I told her. "Thanks."

"*Who* said that?" Miss Retzyl said, strolling in with two tall glasses of lemonade.

"Detective Joe Starr," I said quickly. "That's what I meant to say, anyway." She handed me a napkin and sat down. I hesitated, and then draped the napkin over my knee. When Miss Retzyl put hers on a side table and set her glass on it, I smoothly followed suit. I looked around the room. "Nice house," I told Miss Retzyl. "Dale's not going to believe you let me in here."

She smiled. "I'm glad you like it, Mo," she said.

"I see you got cable." I leaned slightly, trying to look down the hall. "Where are your encyclopedias? I know you got some."

"Upstairs," she said. "Mo, Deputy Marla was telling me about her work. You might find it interesting. She handles Detective Starr's communications and does fieldwork too."

The deputy sipped her coffee. "As I was saying, I primarily help with homicides," she said. "But we handle other cases. Robberies, forgeries, abductions. Even missing persons now and then, if things are super-slow."

"Missing persons?" The words jumped me like a bobcat.

"Really?" Miss Retzyl said, tilting her head. "Joe never mentioned that."

"It's rare," she said. "We're usually busy with other things. It's great when a missing person case works out, and you can reunite a family. But it can be tough when things don't go well, especially when a kid's involved."

I spit an ice cube back into my glass. "You ever look into cold cases?"

She smiled, her eyes glinting. "I'm afraid not," she said. She rose up, tall and slender. "I wish we had time for them." Her sandals whispered across the floor. "Pris, I've got to go, but I should be back before dark."

Miss Retzyl nodded. "Must be tough, working weekends."

She shrugged. "I might as well, there's nobody waiting at home." She glanced at me. "Mo, would you like a ride?"

Before I could answer, Miss Retzyl stood up. "Don't worry about it, Marla. I'm going by Mo's on my way to the church," she said. "I'll give her a lift."

"See you at the funeral, then," Deputy Marla told me, and disappeared.

Poor Miss Retzyl, I thought as the deputy drove away. Only two roads in town, and she doesn't know which one leads to the café, and which one leads to the church.

She's direction-impaired, I thought. Wait until I tell Dale.

Chapter 15
A Spiritual Curveball

As it turned out, Mr. Jesse was way more popular dead than alive.

Lavender, Dale, and me showed up for his service early, only to find the church parking lot packed. People streamed toward the glistening white church in busy, crooked lines, like ants heading for a sugar cube. The church's windows arched like praying hands, and a graveyard meandered to the creek.

Lavender adjusted his blue tie in his truck's rearview mirror as Dale peered in the side mirror and raked his fingers through his hair. "That tie looks good with what's left of your black eye, Lavender," I said.

"Thanks, Mo," he said. "You look pretty too."

I smoothed my dress—black, with pockets in the skirt—and ignored Attila Celeste, who nudged open the door of her mother's white Cadillac and looked our way. "Hey Dale," she said, drawing out the words. "You look nice."

It was true. Dale had selected his Outlaw Funeral Ensemble: black pants, black shirt, black flip-flops, black tie. She swung her legs out of the car like her knees and ankles were glued together, and pushed her blond hair back. Dale veered toward her like a compass needle toward magnetic north and grabbed her door. "Aren't *you* sweet," she said. "Sorry you couldn't come to my party last night."

"Me too," he said.

She invited him? And he didn't tell me? My stomach rolled like a dead carp.

She smiled. "And Dale, I'm sorry about . . . before."

Before? Like when she tried to scam me out of my life's savings and scared Dale half to death? Like before he was the most famous kid in Tupelo Landing?

Dale blushed. "That's okay. This is the church me and Mama go to," he told her, like she didn't know. "Mama plays piano, and I'm singing today. I hope you enjoy it."

She dropped her honey-pie expression. "I don't see how you stand up there and do that," she said, her voice going frank. "It's so hard."

He rocked up on his toes. "Singing is like racing," he said. "You get as ready as you can, step up to the starting line, and let it roll until you get the checkered flag."

Attila's mother minced toward them. "Straighten your

skirt, Anna," she said, looking switchblades at Dale. She led Attila away, and Dale stumbled toward us like a sleepwalker. I punched his arm.

"Hey!" He winced, rubbing his arm. "What was that for?"

There was no point in explaining. "Are you really singing today?" I asked.

He nodded, looking pleased. "As far as I know, this is the first time an alleged suspect has soloed at the funeral of the Dearly Departed. Besides, Mama didn't have time to get anybody else," he added as the big-haired twins roared by in a red Mustang.

Lavender waved. As they swerved away from him, he shoved his hand in his pocket. Poor Lavender. First a wrecked car. Now this. "They probably didn't recognize you," I lied. "I'm pretty sure they can't drive and think at the same time."

He gave me a halfhearted wink and then looked at Dale. "I still can't believe Mama let you ride out of Mr. Jesse's in handcuffs," he said, shaking his head.

"Dale's got a bodyguard, that's why," I said.

"Yeah," Dale said. "I got some short guy that sweats a lot. Mo spotted him behind an azalea. We call him Plainclothes Phil."

"A bodyguard? You're a regular celebrity. No wonder the girls are after you. I envy you, little brother," Lavender said, watching the twins link arms with Tinks Williams and stroll toward the church. "I couldn't get a date right now if my life depended on it."

"Yes you could," I said. "I'll go out with you in just seven more years."

He smiled. "Thanks. Hey, I'd better go talk to Sam, to see what's going on with the car," he said. "I'll see you two after the service."

As he threaded his way through the crowd, Skeeter and Sal drifted by. "Mr. Jesse's friend and her hubby just pulled up," Skeeter said, nodding at a dark sedan.

"Good work," I said, pretending not to watch as a dumpy woman in a flowered dress climbed out of the car. "Thanks."

Dale and I entered the church to find most of the pews full. Miss Rose sat at the piano, playing old hymns. "Mama looks like an angel," Dale whispered. She sounded like one too, playing prayers for Mr. Jesse.

We slid into the front pew, beside Miss Lana. The huge mirror behind the piano gave me a view of everyone behind me—the whole town, and then some. My eyes lingered on the strangers as I performed my Upstream Mother scan. No one looked like me. I scanned a second time, wishing the Colonel would stroll in wearing his dress uniform, his hat tucked beneath his arm.

Why would he stay away now? Why didn't he call?

"The murderer has to be here," Dale whispered.

"Starr thinks so too," I said. Starr, dressed in an iron-gray suit, crisp white shirt, and black tie, sat on the very last row, Miss Retzyl by his side.

We rustled to silence and Reverend Thompson strode to the pulpit, black robe billowing. I slipped my pad from my pocket as he prayed. "Amen," he said.

Miss Lana took the pulpit, looking stately in black. She stood strong and sad as she waited for our eyes to find hers. "Jesse Tatum was our neighbor," she said. "He shared his life with us, he shared his meals with us, he left without saying good-bye."

Then came the spiritual curveball.

"This is our chance to say good-bye, and to tell each other what we learned from Jesse," she said. "The Good Book says a child shall lead us, so we'll start with Mo."

What?

When Miss Lana told me to think about what I'd learned from Mr. Jesse, I thought it was just something people say, like "Walk facing traffic," or "Don't put your elbows on the table."

She smiled benevolently. "Say whatever's in your heart, sugar."

Sometimes I could kill Miss Lana. But then who would I have?

I faced the congregation. Lavender sat on the back

pew. Attila sat to my left; Mr. Jesse's girlfriend to my right. Grandmother Miss Lacy Thornton shared a pew with Skeeter and Salamander. A gaggle of strangers, including Plainclothes Phil, crowded the door. "I'm Mo LoBeau of Desperado Detectives. I was used to Mr. Jesse and I'll miss him," I said. "I'm sorry he's dead, but I'm glad I found the murder weapon."

"Nice," Dale whispered.

"One thing I learned from him was even if you're stingy, tip good. Finally, I'd like to say if you are the murderer," I said, looking around the church, "Desperado Detectives will hunt you down like the dog you are. Thank you."

"Straight from the heart," Miss Lana said. "Now you may call on someone."

"Not me," Dale whispered. "Pick a suspect."

A suspect? Brilliant. "The double-chinned lady with the jealous husband," I said, pointing to Mr. Jesse's girlfriend. I winked at Lavender and sat down.

"Me?" she sputtered. The crowd turned. "I barely knew Jesse Tatum, and my husband doesn't have a jealous bone in his body," she said. "We were at a shag contest in Myrtle Beach the day Jesse died. Anything else you've heard is a lie."

I scribbled a note on my pad: *Ask Skeeter to check her alibi.*

She pointed to Anna Celeste, who rose, smoothing

her blue sundress. "Mr. Jesse taught me to dress neatly because people talk, bless his heart. Sally Amanda?"

Sal stood, her face framed by a halo of tight curls. "I hardly knew him. I call on Dale," she said, blushing.

He gulped. *"Me?"*

"Sorry, Dale," she said. "I forgot you might be the murderer." She looked at Miss Lana. "May I have a do-over? I call on Thes."

Thes popped to his feet, his round face red and glistening. He loosened his bow tie. "Everybody thinks Mr. Jesse was cheap," he said. "But he wasn't. Every Saturday night he slid a hundred dollars under the church door. He did it for eleven years that I know of. Even in hazardous weather."

The church erupted like a hive of startled bees.

I looked in the mirror to see Joe Starr lean forward, his hand on the pew before him, to study the crowd. "What?" Mayor Little cried. "Jesse Tatum made donations?"

"It's true," Thes said. "I saw him."

"Thank you, Thes," Reverend Thompson cried, jumping to his feet and throwing his arms open. "Let us pray," he boomed over the hubbub.

I looked in the mirror. Everybody in the room bowed their heads.

Everybody except me, and Joe Starr.

* * * * *

At prayer's end, Dale strolled to the piano, closed his eyes, and began to sing.

Amazing Grace is right. When Dale sings, even the wind stops to listen.

As his last crystal sound died away, the congregation rose and headed for the door, murmuring like doves. I, on the other hand, trailed Thes. At the choir loft, a hand snaked out of the shadows. "Pssssst," Deputy Marla hissed. "Over here."

"Hey, Deputy," I said, watching Starr slip inside Reverend Thompson's office. Her grip was cold against my skin. I twisted my arm against her thumb, the way Mr. Li taught me, and pulled away. "You scared me."

"Sorry." She smiled as Starr closed the door behind him.

The pattern of her close-fitting summer suit blended with the diamond shadows of the choir loft's small windows. She's good at surveillance, I thought. Good at hiding. "Look, I had a feeling you wanted to tell me something yesterday, at Priscilla's," she said. "I'm sorry I had to rush off, but my work is like that. Is everything okay with you? Kids don't usually ask about cold cases, even if they are detectives."

Don't tell her, a voice inside me whispered.

But why not? Everybody in town knows about me.

"I was thinking about my Upstream Mother," I said. "She went missing eleven years ago and I been tracking her ever since. That's how I got into the detective business."

"So that's your cold case," she said. "Your mother." Her eyes went soft. "That's tough." She studied me a moment. "I'm sorry, Mo, we really don't handle cold cases. But . . ."

I shrugged. "That's okay, I got it covered."

"You didn't let me finish," she said. "We don't handle cold cases, but if there's ever a *specific* piece of information I can help with, or if you need a sounding board, come see me. I'll do what I can. As a professional courtesy." Then she grinned, and winked. "Just don't tell my boss," she whispered.

A professional courtesy? For me? "Thanks," I said.

She faded back into the shadows, and I headed for Reverend Thompson's office. "Good afternoon," I said, pushing the door open. "Sorry I'm late."

Before Starr could react, Reverend Thompson waved me in. "Come in, Mo," he said. "We're just answering some questions for Detective Starr."

"About Mr. Jesse's contributions," Thes added.

"Thanks, Reverend," I said, taking my place beside my fellow detective.

Starr cleared his throat. "You say all of Jesse's contributions were in cash?"

"Hundred-dollar bills," Reverend Thompson said. "I didn't know who they were from until recently, and I never tried to find out. The first one came with a note."

I opened my clue pad. "A note? Do you still have it?"

Starr snapped his pen and glared at me. He looked sharp in a suit—starched, pressed, and shined. Some people look like they were born on a clothes hanger. Not me. I look more like I was born in a dryer.

"Mo," Starr said, "you can stand in on my interview, but be quiet. Otherwise I'll clear the room. Got it?" I nodded. "Do you still have Jesse Tatum's note?" he asked the reverend. I rolled my eyes. That was *my* question.

"No," Reverend Thompson said. "But I can tell you what it said: 'Keep this money quiet or the rest goes to the Episcopalians.'"

Episcopalians? I wrote.

"Did that strike you as odd? Jesse Tatum leaving money here?"

"Yes. Jesse never attended our church, even as a visitor."

"Not even when there was free food," Thes added.

"But, Grace happens," the reverend said. "Jesse could have been a believer, but not a church-goer. Or he could have felt guilty about something, and felt better sliding a little just-in-case money under the door."

"Tell me about seeing him the first time, Thes," Starr said.

Thes glanced at his father, who nodded. "It was an accident. My cat Spitz had got out again, and I was looking for him. As usual."

"And you saw Jesse Tatum . . . ?"

"I saw him sneak up in the moonlight, and slide a white envelope under the door. After that, I staked out the door for a couple of weeks. It was him, all right."

"What did you do with the money?" Starr asked Reverend Thompson.

The reverend smiled. "First I thanked God for it. Then I put it in the bank. We bought paint for the sanctuary, updated the baptistery, mended the roof. You're welcome to look at our books."

"That won't be necessary. How much money are we talking about? Total."

Reverend Thompson reached for a calculator, punched in some numbers, and whistled. "Let's say eleven years . . . roughly fifty-seven thousand two hundred dollars."

I gasped. "Where did Mr. Jesse get that kind of money?"

Joe Starr snapped his pad shut. "Good question," he said. "Where, indeed?"

That night I grabbed my pen and notebook.

Dear Upstream Mother,

Death makes you think. Everybody has a way of believing.

The Colonel says God took Sunday off, so he does too. He walks in the woods or lies on his bunk. He says if God needs him, He knows where to find him. Miss Lana believes in treating people right. She mostly hits Church Festivities—Easter, when she wears a new hat, and Christmas Eve, to cry while Dale sings "Silent Night."

Dale goes to church because Miss Rose likes him to. I sometimes go to keep him company, and hear stories of the Original Moses. Miss Rose plays the piano. I sit with Dale and Grandmother Miss Lacy Thornton, whose alto runs true as a rusty fence. My voice is like a turkey gobble crammed in a corset, but nobody's told me to stop singing, and I ain't shy.

Lavender, who I will one day marry,

believes in NASCAR Zen, which I suspect
he made up. "The car is the body," he says.
"The driver is awareness zipping in and out
of traffic. And the Zen is the Everything of
it—track, car, self, other drivers. You focus
without thinking to win," he says. "You feel it.
It's one reason I love racing."

What do you believe? Please let me know.

If you're wondering about me, like Miss
Lana I believe in treating people good. And
like the Colonel, I think God can find me.
Love,
Mo
PS: The Colonel still hasn't called, and today
made three days. Miss Lana says not to worry,
that she will handle it. I'm worried anyway.
Where is he? Why would he leave us when
there's a killer on the prowl? He has to have a
good reason, but what reason trumps keeping
us safe? If you see him, please ask him to call
home.

Chapter 16
Lavender Blues

By Monday morning, the Colonel still hadn't called. "We have to do something," I told Miss Lana as we walked up the gravel path to the café.

"I'll handle it, Mo," she said—again. "You don't need to worry." She kept her voice easy, but I knew from the thin of her smile that she was worried too.

At the café, where Mr. Jesse's church donations were the topic du jour, rumors ran rampant: Mr. Jesse had won a lottery Up North; Mr. Jesse had millions in a Swiss bank; the Baptists had somehow snookered the Episcopalians.

Miss Rose and Dale came in mid-morning, glistening from time in the garden. "Mama's giving me time off for good behavior," Dale told me, toting a bucket of cucumbers to the kitchen. "You want to go to Lavender's, and then look for clues?"

"Only if you don't swagger and mess with your hair," I said. "It's embarrassing." I turned to Miss Lana. "Is it okay? Can I go?"

She nodded, filling three takeout cups with iced tea. "Tell Lavender hello for me, and don't you stay too long. He's working on his car, I imagine."

He wasn't. We found him at his house, sleepy-eyed and tousled. "Hey," I said as he opened the door. "Miss Lana sent you some iced tea."

"Bless her," he said, taking a cup and stepping aside.

His house shocked me. Lavender generally keeps his place neat and full of light. Today the rug lay heavy with dirt, and socks slouched pigeon-toed by the kitchen door. Yesterday's funeral tie dangled from a doorknob, and drawn shades let dusty slices of sunlight into the room. "It's nearly ten o'clock," I said. "You sick?"

He stretched, his arm muscles twisting like cables, and tucked his pale yellow T-shirt into his faded jeans. "I'm just slow starting this morning, Mo. I'm fine."

Dale glanced around. "Did the twins do this?" he asked.

"The twins have been scarce since the crash, little brother."

"I'm not surprised," I said as Lavender sank into a chair. "Those girls are like crows. Probably saw something shinier on the other side of town."

"Yeah," he said, "there's not much to a racecar driver when he's walking." His smile didn't erase the lines beneath his eyes. "How's your life unfolding, Miss LoBeau?"

"Not so good," I admitted. "We ain't heard from the Colonel, and yesterday made three days. We got to do something, I just don't know what to do."

He leaned forward. "What does Miss Lana say?"

"She says not to worry, but I do. We could tell Starr, I guess, but the Colonel don't like Starr. We could tell Deputy Marla," I said, scanning Lavender's face. "She's nice, and she likes me."

He pushed his hair back. "That sounds like a good plan," he said. "It might be worth running by Miss Lana, anyway." I relaxed. I like to have a plan.

Lavender took a sip of his tea. "You sounded great yesterday, Dale," he said.

Dale grinned. "Thanks."

"I was really proud of you. I bet Mama un-grounded you as a reward."

"No," he sighed. "I'm still grounded, just off for good behavior. I never been so sick of fixing things in my life." He looked around. "You ought to clean up in here."

"He can't, Dale," I said. "He's depressed."

Lavender snorted. "I am not."

"Sure you are. This is classic. You ain't shaved, your car's wrecked, your love life's a disaster. Next you'll maybe start eating out of control and have to get hoisted out of here with a crane. Look at those fingernails," I added. "They're filthy."

"Whoa," he said. "Cut me some slack. Sam and I were up until two o'clock this morning, working on my car. I haven't had time for a manicure." He jumped up and scooped some dirty dishes from the floor. Lavender moves like a big, blond cat.

Those twins are idiots. Even depressed, Lavender is melt-down gorgeous.

"Well, if you're working on your car I guess that's a good sign."

He headed for the kitchen. "Maybe," he said, letting the dishes clatter into the sink. "But the Sycamore 200 is just two weeks away. I already paid my entry fee, but it looks like I'll have to drop out. We just can't get the car together in time."

Dale frowned. "But you and Sam are the best mechanics in the county."

"It's not talent we're short on," he said. "It's money for parts. I've fixed every car I can find, including the Underbird—which is ready, Mo, if you want to tell Miss Lana. Even after she pays me, I'm short a thousand bucks, and slam out of credit."

"So?" I said. "Since when did you race for money? You'll run a different race." Silence hung on the air like stale tobacco smoke. I looked from one brother to the other. They both avoided my eyes. "What's wrong?"

"Nothing," Dale said. "It's just Mama's money ain't right lately, with Daddy acting the way he is. And I'm no help," he added.

"You might be," I said. "If we solve Mr. Jesse's murder, and if there's a reward."

"That's a lot of ifs, Mo," he said, slumping in his chair.

Uneasiness ran its fingertips across my shoulders. Dale's people never had much money, but I'd never known them to worry. Lavender grabbed a T-shirt off the floor. "That race is a long shot, but I was hoping it would pay off," he said. "It's good money if you can win it."

"Would that fix things for Miss Rose?" I asked. "If you won, I mean?"

The Colonel says trying to drive your way out of being broke is like trying to starve your way out of being skinny. It takes real money to put a car on the track, and good money to race. You got to buy fuel, tires, and spare parts for every race. A good-running car is worth good money. A wrecked one ain't worth nothing.

"It would help," Lavender said. "But like I said, it's a long shot."

I made a decision. "So? My entire life's a long shot. Dale, we'll come up with the thousand dollars. We might as well," I said as his mouth fell open. "We can't do much detective work with you grounded and with Plainclothes Phil following us."

"Us? Raise a thousand dollars?" he gasped. "How?"

Good question. "I ain't ready to unveil my plan yet," I said.

Dale rolled his eyes. "That means she ain't got one," he told Lavender.

"Naturally I got to hone the particulars," I replied. "But I'm thinking we'll strike at this year's Mimosa Festival." Actually, it was a no-brainer. The festival opened in just a few days. Normally Dale and me hit the rides and food booths, and avoid the crafts and raffles. "A town full of folks with spending money seems like a good place to start."

Lavender laughed. "Thanks for offering, Mo. You're a true friend. But don't worry your pretty head. Sam and I will come up with the cash for the car. All you got to do is keep my desperado brother here out of trouble."

A pretty head? Me?

"Nope," I said, heading for the door. "We'll raise the money. You fix the car."

He tossed his dirty socks toward the hall. "If you do I'll pay you back every penny," he said. "Twice. But there's one thing."

"A contract?" I guessed.

"A loophole. If you don't come up with the cash, it's no big deal. Agreed?"

"Agreed." I grabbed the ring on a dusty window shade. It snapped up, rolling itself dizzy at the top of the window. "We'll be in touch," I said, and we stepped outside, the heat slamming into me like a steamy sponge as he closed the door behind us.

"Hey, Dale," I whispered, peering across the street. "There's your bodyguard. Act like you don't see him."

"I didn't until you pointed him out," he muttered. He hesitated, and then waved. "He's not very friendly," Dale said as Plainclothes Phil darted behind an azalea.

I jumped off the porch.

"Let's stop by the church and see if we missed any clues. Thes will let us in," I said. "He owes us for finding his halfwit cat."

"Yeah," Dale said. "He owes us big."

Chapter 17
Mr. Jesse's Final Contribution

Thes sat on the church steps, dangling a toy mouse in front of his cat.

From beyond the church door, a weak voice followed a plink-plink piano tune like a tired dog trailing a rabbit. Lots of kids come to the church for Miss Currie's music lessons. Happily, I'm not one of them. "Hey Thes," I said. "How's the weather?"

"Hot," he said. "Thunderstorms tonight. Hurricane Amy's turned in the Atlantic. She's going to miss us."

"Great," I said, settling in beside him. "Any word on Mr. Jesse?"

"Nothing much. Except it turns out Daddy hadn't deposited Mr. Jesse's last hundred-dollar bill after all. He thought he had, but he found his bank bag under his front seat this morning. With Mr. Jesse's cash in it."

A clue! "We'd like to take a look at it," I said.

"Can't," he said as Spitz leaped for the mouse. "Daddy gave it to Joe Starr." He reached into his pocket.

"I thought you might want this, though," he said. He handed me a wrinkled photocopy of the hundred-dollar bill, including its serial number.

"Thanks," I said. "We've been hoping for a break like this."

I slid the photocopy into my pocket, trying to look like I knew what to do with it. "As long as we're here," I said, "I thought I might look around the sanctuary, see if I overlooked anything Sunday."

He shrugged. "Okay," he said. "Hey Dale, watch this." Spitz pounced, and Thes and Dale both laughed as Spitz grabbed the toy and rolled across the porch.

As I reached the top of the church steps, the door flew open. Miss Currie swept past hugging an armload of music. "Hey," I said.

"Hello, Mo," she murmured, and hurried by, humming.

I heard the voice when I cracked open the door— a harsh voice, high-pitched and demanding, from the front of the dim church. "Was that the *best* you can do?"

"I'm sorry, Mother," a girl replied. The voice sounded familiar. Like someone I knew talking through Jell-O. "I just don't have a good voice."

"Everyone in our family sings," the woman said. "You have the talent. You just need to apply yourself. Practice."

"I do practice."

"Stand up straight when you sing. Look like you have some confidence."

"But I don't," the girl wailed.

"Then *find* some," the woman snapped. "Your father and I aren't paying for these lessons because we're tired of looking at the money."

That did it. Nobody talks to a kid like that. Not when I'm around.

I swung the door open and stepped into the dim sanctuary. "I don't think you ought to talk to a kid that way," I said, my voice echoing. My eyes adjusted to the light. If I could have un-opened that door, I would have.

"Oh. Hey, Anna Celeste."

Attila looked away, and my eyes traveled to Mrs. Simpson—hard-eyed, unsmiling, beige Mrs. Simpson.

"Oh," Mrs. Simpson said. "It's the girl from the café."

The girl from the café? She knows my name.

My heart pounded like a crack-head chimpanzee with a bongo. For a brief moment, my anger outweighed my hatred of Anna Celeste. I took a deep breath. "I didn't know you took voice, Anna," I said. "That explains a lot."

Mrs. Simpson's eyebrows arched. "Really?"

"Sure," I said. "Anna Celeste has the best girl's voice in our class." It was true-ish. Sort of. We all sing like bullfrogs. "I bet you're proud to have her in your family, Mrs. Sampson. You should be."

"Mrs. *Simp*son," she snarled, and Attila almost smiled.

"Right. Sorry." I glanced around the church. It had been tidied, vacuumed, and polished since Mr. Jesse's funeral. Any clues were long gone. "See you around, Anna," I said as the door swished shut behind me.

I filled Dale in as we walked to the café, sweat trickling down my back. "Mrs. Simpson would make a terrible mother-in-law," he said, looking worried.

I snorted. "Not that it will ever matter to you. Anna Celeste will forget your name the instant your fame wears off."

"Maybe." We walked in silence, the heat rising like ghosts along the blacktop. "You think Miss Lana will call Starr? About the Colonel?" he asked.

My stomach fluttered. "I hope she already has."

She hadn't when we got back to the café at 11:30. She still hadn't when Deputy Marla dropped in for lunch at 12:15.

The Rolling Stones rocked the jukebox, and lava lamps graced the tables as Deputy Marla slipped onto a bar stool and glanced at the Specials Board.

"Hey," I said, pouring her water. "How's your investigation going?"

"Funny you should ask. I just talked to Joe," she said. "Your oar *is* the murder weapon, Mo. But there were no fingerprints. We're following a couple other leads." She looked around. "1960s diner theme?" she guessed as Miss Lana swished by in a tie-dye blouse and Gypsy skirt, the locks of her glossy black Cher wig swinging.

"Café circa 1968," I agreed as Dale darted by with a dish of hot apple pie, his hair combed back in a ducktail. "Dale went retro. Welcome," I said, standing up straight and draping a napkin over my arm. "Today we're featuring the Groovy Chick Trio for four ninety-nine," I said. "Your choice of fried chicken, chicken pastry, or chicken salad. The first two come with two garden vegetables: okra, cucumbers, potato salad, or turnip greens. The chicken salad comes on pale lettuce slivers, with chips or saltines. All dinners come with cheese biscuits and tea. May I take your order?"

"Fried chicken," she said. "With okra and cucumbers. And sweet tea. How's *your* case going?"

I slid her a basket of cheese biscuits. "The murder?"

"Actually, I was thinking of your mother," she said.

I poured her tea and avoided her eyes. "Nothing new."

"Well, I know how *that* feels. Hang in there," she said, squinting at the Desserts Board. "That's probably why I like the police force. It gives me a feeling of family."

I slid her silverware to her. "What do you mean?"

"Is that apple pie homemade?" she asked, and I nodded. "I'll try it," she said. "I just mean I understand what you're going through, Mo. I grew up in a children's home. I know what it's like to wonder. That's just between us. Okay?" She winked. "Put some ice cream on that pie," she said. "You only live once, right?"

"And I'd like some of Lana's chicken salad," Miss Retzyl said, sliding onto the stool beside her. Dale dropped a plate on the other side of the room. He falls apart around teachers, even if he can't see them. It's like radar with him.

"Hey, Miss Retzyl," I said. "What's up? You don't eat here."

"Not usually," she agreed, cool as sherbet. "But I heard Marla was coming by, and thought I'd surprise her. I'll have un-sweet tea with that chicken salad, please."

The lunch crowd swept me away, but as I served lunches and poured tea, I kept my eye on Deputy Marla. No wonder she understood my search for my Upstream Mother. She had searched too. She'd understand about the Colonel being gone too—probably. Miss Lana cruised by. "Miss Lana, can we talk?"

"After lunch, sugar," she said, ringing up a customer. "I'm swamped."

I looked up to see Deputy Marla and Miss Retzyl heading across the parking lot, and made an executive decision. I grabbed the photocopy of Mr. Jesse's Final Contribution, and jotted the C-note's serial number on my order pad. Then I jammed the photocopy in my pocket. "Hey," I called, rushing outside as Miss Retzyl pulled away in her very normal, dark blue convertible. "Deputy Marla, I want to ask you a hypothetical," I said, skidding to a stop in front of her. "One professional to another."

"Shoot, Detective."

I ignored the crumbs on her blouse. Even professionals make mistakes. "Say somebody was supposed to be home or call last night, and he ain't been heard from yet. What would you do, given the current Killer-on-the-Loose Situation and so forth? Hypothetically speaking."

She frowned. "Mo, is everything all right?"

"Yes ma'am. I'm totally theoretical on this."

"Well," she said. "I'd probably give him an extra twenty-four hours. Then I'd call a cop. A friendly one," she said. She pulled out a card. "Detective Starr could help you. Or here's my number at Priscilla's. In case you have any more questions, hypothetically speaking."

"Thanks."

"Sure, kid."

"One more thing." I reached into my pocket. "I know Starr's heard about this, but I got this copy of Mr. Jesse's Final Contribution. *With* serial number. I thought you might like it. I pay my own way. The Colonel and Miss Lana taught me that."

She went pale, stumbled, and reached behind her, for the car.

"Deputy Marla? Are you okay?"

"Must be the heat," she said, shaking her head as she took the paper. "I'm fine. Thanks for this, Mo. I believe Joe's got the info, like you say, but it never hurts to have backup. See you, kid."

And she got in her patrol car and sped away.

That night, as the rain Thes had predicted pattered down, I sat close to Miss Lana, on the settee. "The Colonel's a day late calling," I told her. "It's been nearly twenty-four hours since he should have checked in."

"I know," she sighed. "Every time the phone rang today, I was sure it was him."

I pulled Deputy Marla's card out of my pocket. "Deputy Marla gave me her number," I said. "She's a orphan. She'll help us."

"An orphan?" she said, taking the card. "What does that have to do with anything?"

"We could call Starr," I said. "But I'm pretty sure the Colonel wouldn't like it."

"Starr?" She took a deep breath. "Maybe I'll try Marla first." She strolled to the phone and let her hand rest there, her eyes closed. "Give me a moment to collect my thoughts," she murmured. Just as she opened her eyes, the phone rang.

We both jumped.

"Hello?" she said, and then laughed. "Colonel! Where are you?"

Relief flooded through me. All that worrying, for nothing.

"Are you okay?" she asked. "We've been worried sick." She listened for a moment, and then flinched. "Since when do you call me . . . yes. Yes. Of course. Well, when you broke the Three Day Rule, I . . ." She glanced at me. "No, I'm sure you left before midnight, but . . . Yes, she's right here."

I started for the phone, but she frowned and shook her head.

"I will, I'll tell her. Are you sure everything's all right? You don't sound like . . . Yes. I understand. . . . No, we're fine." She nodded, looking puzzled. "Then we'll hear from you by Thursday, at the latest. I . . . Hello?"

She lowered the phone, looking stunned. "That was the Colonel," she said, as if I didn't already know. "He sends his love."

"You act like that's bad news," I told her.

"No," she said. "It's good news. Of course it's good news. It was just a strange conversation."

Strange? The Colonel? That wasn't exactly a news flash. "Strange, how?" I asked.

"Well, he called me baby, for one thing."

"*Baby?* He never calls you baby."

"And he called you Moses, for another."

"*Moses?* The only time he ever called me Moses was when he named me."

"I know," she said. She stared at the phone's face like she could read its mind. "Well, at least he called, and we know he's safe. He'll be back in a few days, and then we'll find out what's going on."

"Right," I said. I hugged her and went to bed. But I slept restless and dreamed thin. My universe didn't fit together. My world spun wobbly, like a worn-out top.

I woke up once, dreaming my old dream. The one where I'm standing in a creek, and a bottle bobs by. I shake the message out, my heart pounding. But, like always, the words blur before I can read them.

Chapter 18
Miss Lana!

By sundown the next day, Dale and I had developed a genius-level plan to raise money for Lavender's car. We put it into action Wednesday at the grand opening of the Mimosa Festival.

By then, Dale was sick of fame.

"Letting Starr take me out of Mr. Jesse's in handcuffs is the dumbest thing I ever did," he said, dipping his brush into a pint of purple paint.

"No it ain't," I said as I shifted our sign on the table. "You've done plenty of dumber things. Watch out, don't drip. I want Lavender's sign to look professional."

The festival opened at 5:00, giving us just two hours to finish our booth. We'd already set up Miss Lana's red-and-white party tent, and put two lawn chairs underneath. All we needed was a sign. Dale hesitated, brush poised. "What did you want me to write?"

I turned my sketchpad: *Race to Riches with Lavender!* Underneath, I'd drawn Lavender's car, and divided it into ad spaces. "This race is almost big time," I reminded him. "Television, radio. If we can sell twenty ads at fifty bucks each, we'll have the thousand dollars Lavender needs for parts. Here," I said, taking the brush. "Let me do it. At the rate you're going, the race will be over before we get started."

He flung himself in a lawn chair. "I thought Starr would've caught the killer by now, and I'd be a hero," he said, his voice dull with grief. "Instead, people talk about me and my family worse than ever, which I didn't think was possible. Attila's avoiding me. And I'm sick of cops following me. There goes stupid Plainclothes Phil with another funnel cake," he muttered.

"Where?"

"Behind the Baptists' Dunking Booth."

I squinted at the booth, where Sam Quinerly was oiling the springs, just in time to see Phil duck out of sight. "Hey, Sam," I shouted. "Where's Lavender?"

"At the garage. But he'll be here tonight," he said, striding over.

"Good. We need him here to sign autographs and kiss a few babies."

"I don't know about kissing babies, but I'm pretty sure he can sign his name," Sam teased. "Thanks for doing this, you two. Your confidence has lit a fire under him. He's got every part we need lined up and ready to buy. We can have that car together faster than— Hey, nice sign."

I stepped back to admire my handiwork. Crud. The letters skinnied down near the edge of the board. "I made the letters at the edge thinner so they look like they're going fast," I said. "What do you think?"

"Special effects," he said, nodding. "Looks good, doesn't it, Dale?"

Dale frowned. "To me, it looks like you run out of room."

"How about putting this up for us?" I said, nudging the sign toward Sam. "Dale and me are making Lavender famous, and we're doing it tonight."

"Famous?" Sam grinned. "Make us solvent and you'll be a goddess to us both."

By 7:30 I was well on my way to goddess status.

Miss Lana gave me a big boost, buying the entire hood to advertise the café. "Three hundred dollars? I'll take it, sugar," she said, whipping her checkbook out of her kimono sleeve. "Not a word of this to the Colonel," she whispered.

"Stick around and help us, Miss Lana?" I asked.

"I'd love to, but I want to get a couple of turkeys into the oven for tomorrow's special." She leaned close to Dale. "I roast them on low heat, all night long. That's why they're so juicy. Don't tell anyone," she added, popping his arm with her fan.

Dale nodded. "Thank you for buying the ad," he said, blushing. "I know the café don't need it. Everybody in town already eats there."

"Pish." She turned to me. "Mo, I want you home at nine thirty, at the latest. I know Starr's people are keeping an eye on you two, otherwise I'd never agree to this. Using children for bait," she said, smoothing her red kimono. "What has the world come to?"

"Rhetorical?" Dale whispered, and I winked.

Moments later, Tammy of Tammy's Daycare popped by. "I'll take an ad on the driver's door *if* you come up with a slogan for me," she said.

"Tammy's, the We-Care Daycare," I replied. "That will be sixty dollars—fifty for the ad and ten for the slogan. Make it seventy dollars and we'll add your phone number."

She scribbled her number on a slip of pink paper. "How about giving my number to the driver instead?"

"Dale's his brother. He'll do it," I said. Dale moaned, but stuffed the paper in his pocket.

Mr. Li bought a fender panel (Li's Karate for a Kicking Good Time), and Buddha Jackson, owner of Buddha's Bar & Tanning Salon, coughed up sixty bucks for a door panel (Get Toasted at Buddha's). As he left, an Azalea

Woman strolled over to ask about a spot for the Uptown Garden Club. "A panel costs just eighty-five dollars," I said.

"Eighty-five?" she said. "I heard fifty."

"That's for a tacky spot," I said. "I didn't think you'd want it, but okay. Dale, give her the gas tank."

Her hand flashed to her throat. "The gas tank? We'll take the nice one for eighty-five." I winked at Dale. An Azalea Woman would rather be dead than tacky.

Lavender showed up at 8:00, looking devilish handsome. The festival was in full riot by then: hobby horses twirled, the roller coaster rattled, the Tilt-A-Whirl squalled. "You two get yourselves something to eat," he said, handing me a ten-dollar bill. "I'd recommend something wholesome, like the deep-fat-fried Oreos."

When we returned, the stand was swamped. With Lavender signing autographs, we sold the entire car by nine o'clock. "I can't believe it: One thousand ninety-nine dollars and seventy-nine cents," he told me, snapping our cash box shut.

"Ninety-nine dollars and seventy-nine cents? How..."

"Mayor Little said the town was short, so I cut him a deal."

What happened next will live as one of the great moments in history: Lavender smiled, bent down, and kissed my face.

My first kiss! And it was from Lavender!

"Mo," he said, "you really are a goddess of free enterprise."

Me! A goddess of free enterprise!

I shoved Dale into Lavender, and Lavender laughed. "Race you," I shouted at Dale, and bolted from the stand. The crowd slipped by in a blur of lights. I ran faster than any human has ever run, speeding to the edge of town, turning toward the creek, zipping to the café.

My sneakers pounded out *Lavender's kiss, Lavender's kiss* as I ran full-tilt around the corner of the café, down the walk, and up the steps. "Miss Lana!" I cried, the screen door slapping the wall as the soles of Dale's shoes hit the porch behind me. "Miss Lana! Guess what!"

My view of the living room hit me like a fist.

The mahogany bookcase lay facedown. Miss Lana's velvet chairs lay on their sides, their seats slit and torn. Sofa cushions lay helter-skelter across the floor, and the lamp dangled headfirst from the table, hanged by its own cord. The photos from my sixth birthday party tilted haphazardly across the wall, peering blindly through cracked glass. The desk's gaping drawers spewed papers. "Miss Lana?" My voice sounded small and distant as Dale skidded to a halt behind me.

"Find her!" I shouted. We ran across the wrecked living room, calling her name. The other rooms stared back at me, untouched but shocked and vacant and still.

"What's this?" Dale demanded, scooping a note from our kitchen table.

I grabbed it, surprised at how far away my fingers felt, at how difficult it was to focus on the note's block letters:

STARR—WE BOTH NEED SOMETHING. YOU HELP ME AND I'LL HELP YOU.

"What does it mean?" Dale whispered.

"It's the killer. He's got Miss Lana. Run!" I shouted, pushing him toward the door. "Run!"

As we crossed the living room, the front door slammed open and a man stood silhouetted against the stars.

"My room, Dale," I shouted, turning. "Go!"

"Stop!" the man bellowed. "It's Joe Starr! Everybody calm down!"

I grabbed Starr's hand. "This way," I panted. "The killer's got Miss Lana."

For the rest of the night, light flooded our house and yard as Starr's people and our neighbors searched for Miss Lana. Deputy Marla found the double footprints along the café wall. "There was a scuffle. Looks like he dragged her the last few feet," she told Starr, avoiding my eyes.

I tried not to think about the instructions Starr had given his men as he'd sent them to search the woods:

"The killer left his first victim in the creek," Starr had said. "He could go there again. Be careful. Call me if you find anything."

Starr slid the killer's note to his deputy. "What do you make of this, Marla?"

A slow flush burned her face. "'We both need something,'" she read, and scowled. "He's playing us."

"Right," Starr said. "But why?"

"Maybe he's angry," Dale said. "Maybe it's like you said when you took me out of Mr. Jesse's in handcuffs. Maybe he doesn't like me taking credit for his crime."

I glanced out the window. The yellow beams of the search party's flashlights flickered high in the trees and low along the water. "Look like fireflies," I murmured.

"What?" Starr said, studying the road map on the kitchen counter.

"The flashlights," I said. "They look like fireflies."

"Are you sure you didn't see anybody?" he asked again. "An unfamiliar car . . ."

"Nobody," I said. "I told you. Why don't you stop picking on me and go find Miss Lana? She might be . . ." My voice broke up like a radio from too far away.

The shaking started next. "Get a blanket," Starr told Deputy Marla. "Dale, where's your mother? I think Mo might like to spend some time with her."

"I already called her," Dale said. "She's waiting for

Lavender to pick her up. She could have drove her own self, except Daddy swiped her Pinto and brought it back empty."

Deputy Marla settled the Colonel's scratchy green army blanket over my shoulders and gave my arms a squeeze. The blanket smelled like pine and wood smoke, like camping in the backyard.

I closed my eyes and the shaking stopped. My fear melted, and Dale's voice drifted away. I imagined I was camping in the springtime, in the backyard, just the Colonel and me.

"There's nothing like camping out to restore a sense of size, Soldier," the Colonel was saying. "Remember that. When you lose your way, wait under the stars."

I spread out my blanket. "Wait for what?"

"You'll know," he said, and closed his eyes, peaceful as a baby. "What do you hear?"

"Well, I thought I heard a car crank. Might be Lavender. What do you hear?"

"The usual," he murmured. "The swirl of crickets, the whirl of stars. . . .

"Listen to me," he said. "We're born over and over, day by day. When you feel lost, let the stars sing you to sleep. You'll always wake up new." He looked at me, his face fierce and beautiful as a rocky crag in the moonlight. "Do you understand what I'm telling you, Soldier?"

I touched his hand. "I don't know, sir," I said. "But I admire the way it sounds."

He threw back his head and laughed. "Right-o!" he said. "You are honest as granite, my dear. Get the marshmallows, then. Let's build us a roaring good fire."

"Mo?" Starr said, dropping a clumsy paw on my shoulder and shaking me like a bear. "Can you hear me? She's going into shock," he told someone. "Call a doctor."

"That won't be necessary," Miss Rose said from the door.

"Mama!" Dale cried.

Miss Rose sailed across the kitchen, her green eyes worried. "Oh, Mo," she said. "I'm so sorry." Her arms closed around me, and my eyes filled with hot, frightened tears.

I sobbed like a first grader.

"We'll find Miss Lana," she said, smoothing my hair. "Don't worry. We'll find her."

"Mama, where's Lavender?" Dale asked, looking up from Starr's laptop.

"He's searching, like everybody else," she said. Knowing he was near helped. "Dale," she said, "what are you doing?"

"Checking out mug shots," he said, hunching forward to peer at the computer's screen. "Mo and me got here right after the killer. Maybe we saw him and just don't remember. That's why."

"Rose, we're doing everything we can to find your friend," Starr said. "I have people scouring the woods, and we've set up roadblocks on US 264 and I-95. Deputy Marla is preparing to search the area's vacant houses and barns. Rose, has Lana mentioned having difficulty with anyone? At the café, or in Charleston?"

I leaned against Miss Rose. Her blouse smelled like just-cut grass. "Lana came by yesterday," she said, "but she didn't mention anything out of the ordinary. She was worried about Jesse's . . . situation, and when that would be resolved."

"Did she mention the Colonel?"

Miss Rose's hand went still in my hair. "I might as well tell you," she said. "The Colonel's been away since late Thursday night. She said he called Monday, and sounded . . . strange."

"Strange, how?"

"He called her baby. And he called Mo Moses. He never does that."

"*Moses?*" Dale said. "That's weird."

Starr scribbled a note. "Anything else?"

She shrugged. "Not really. She didn't like him leaving, under the circumstances, but those two have always spent more time apart than together."

"Meaning, they fight?"

"No," she said. "Meaning they don't fight, because

they spend time apart. Believe me, Detective, some things that will cure you in a small dose will kill you in a larger one."

Starr clicked his pen. "Rose," he said. "If you know where the Colonel is . . ."

"If I knew," she said, "he'd be on his way home."

"Hey," Dale yelped. "Why is Plainclothes Phil in here?"

I pushed away from Miss Rose to peer at the photo on the computer screen.

"What's your undercover man doing in there?" I demanded, glaring at Starr. "I don't think you should ask Dale to help you, and then try to trick him."

"My undercover man? What are you talking about?" He spun the laptop around and squinted at the mug shot. "That's Robert Slate, a bank robber. He broke out of prison a few weeks ago. He's a wanted man."

"If you wanted him, you should have come to the festival," Dale said.

Starr jumped to his feet. "Slate's here?" He turned to Deputy Marla. "You were watching Dale. Did you see him?"

"No," she said, looking bewildered. "I didn't."

Gooseflesh walked across my arms. "You were watching us? I never saw you."

"That's the idea, Mo," she said. "I was undercover."

"And you didn't see Slate?" I said, my voice rising. "He

was at Mr. Jesse's funeral. At the festival, in the azaleas across from Lavender's . . ."

She studied the photo, and then glanced at Starr. "I don't know what to say, Joe. I could have missed him, I guess, but it doesn't seem likely."

"Are you two sure?" Starr demanded, and we nodded. He ran his finger across his eyebrow. "Better safe than sorry," he said. "Marla, notify the Highway Patrol. Tell them Robert Slate has a hostage and may be headed to Winston," he said. "And tell them he might be driving one of Dolph Andrews's missing cars."

"Dolph Andrews? The dead guy from Winston-Salem?" Dale whispered.

I stood up. "If this guy hurts Miss Lana . . ." My voice crumbled, and Starr put his hand on my arm. His hand was strong, like the Colonel's.

"Mo, Miss Lana's safety is my top priority. Dale? Thanks for your help, son," he said. "Rose? I'd appreciate it if you took these children home so I can get to work. I'll have someone watch your place until morning."

"No," I said. "This is my house and I ain't leaving unless you promise to find Miss Lana."

He took a deep breath. "Mo, I'll do everything I can, and I'll stop by Rose's in the morning, to tell you what I've learned," he said. "I promise."

Miss Rose put her arm across my shoulders. "Thank you, Detective. Come on, Mo," she said. "Let's get your things."

I felt like a stranger in my own room. My unmade bed stared as I dragged my old-timey suitcase from the chifforobe and popped its brass latches. Its navy-blue lining had faded to indigo splotches. I stood there, running my finger along its rough tan stripe, not sure what to do. "Miss Lana says never go anywhere without money to get home," I finally said, checking the suitcase pocket for cash. "This Emergency Five's brought me home every time," I said. "I sure wish Miss Lana had it now."

"Lana's smart," Miss Rose said, folding my karate pants into the suitcase. "She'll find her way home. She'll be proud of the way you're handling this. You'll see."

I tossed Volume 6 into the suitcase as she added a stack of T-shirts. "I won't need those," I said. "Miss Lana will be back before daylight."

"Probably, but Starr will want to work here even after she comes home."

After she comes home. *Please let her come home,* I thought.

I felt like a leaf, falling.

"Mo, can you think of anything else you might need?"

I grabbed my green scrapbook, the one Miss Lana put

together in Charleston. "This is the last thing she gave me before . . ." My words collapsed.

"It's all right, Mo," she whispered, wrapping me in a hug.

"No, it's not," I said, tears rolling hot down my face. "They *have* to find her. Without Miss Lana, nothing will ever be all right again."

Chapter 19
Listening to the Stars

Later that night, Dale's bedroom door creaked open, shooting a dart of light to the bed where I lay, pretending to sleep. I propped up on my elbow, the bedsprings grumbling. "Dale?"

Queen Elizabeth's toenails *tick-tick-ticked* across the floor. "Hey girl," I whispered, putting my hand out. "Come on up." She leaped onto the bed and squirmed in beside me. I ran my hand down her velvety ears and she nudged my wrist, comforting me. I snapped on the lamp—a homemade one, from Miss Rose's wine-bottle-craft phase.

Dale's room is okay unless you're squeamish, which I ain't. It smells rich and clean, like a just-plowed field, thanks to the earthworm farm in his closet—refugees from last summer's get-rich-quick scheme. His sheets smell like wind.

His newt, Sir Isaac, stirred in the terrarium. I leaned down and scooped my scrapbook off the floor. "Here, Liz," I said, opening the book. "Sniff out a clue."

"What's up?" Dale whispered from the door, and Liz and I both jumped.

"We're looking at photographs," I said. "What are you doing up? Your mama's gonna skin you alive if she finds you wandering around this house."

It was true. Once we got to her house, Miss Rose barked out sleeping assignments like the Colonel himself: I got Dale's room. She gave Dale and Lavender, who stayed to protect us, Lavender's old room. She kept hers. "Doors locked, lights out, everyone in bed until morning," she'd ordered.

"Liz got hungry. I got up to make her a peanut butter sandwich," Dale said. "I made us one too. You seen her?"

"She's over here," I said as Liz's tail thumped the mattress.

Dale dragged a cane-bottomed chair to my bedside. "Here, Liz," he said as she jumped to the floor. She gently took the sandwich from his hand and stretched out at his feet. She held the sandwich between her paws and nipped it. "She eats ladylike," Dale said, tossing a sandwich to me. Extra-crunchy—my PB of choice.

"You're not sleepy?" I asked.

He yawned. "It ain't that," he said. "Lavender talks in his sleep."

My heart jumped. "Really? Did he mention me?"

"Not unless you've changed your name to the Sycamore 200. What kind of photographs you got?" he asked, peeping at the scrapbook.

"Some Miss Lana brought from Charleston." Dale munched his sandwich, his hair spiked in a jagged halo, his pale blue pajamas mis-buttoned and lopsided. I looked around his room, at the faded wallpaper, at the NASCAR models his daddy gives him every year for his birthday even though he really wants a guitar, at the small rack of weights. "Since when do you lift weights?" I asked him.

"Since never. Lavender gave them to me. He said to let them collect dust until I hit puberty. Then I can use them or sell them, whichever I want." He stuffed the rest of his sandwich into his mouth and licked his fingertips. "So," he said. "When do we start?"

"Start what?"

"Talking clues," he said, taking my notebook from the nightstand and handing it to me. "About Miss Lana."

He frowned and leaned toward me. "She's—been—kidnapped?" he said slowly, raising his voice at the end, as if I had gone dense. "We—are—detectives?"

"Some detectives," I said. "We can't tell a bank robber from a bodyguard."

"We'll find Miss Lana, Mo," he said. "We'll do like

Miss Retzyl taught us. Remember? Define the problem, then solve it. Problem?" He tilted his head the way Miss Retzyl tilts hers when he gives up in math.

I sighed. "Miss Lana's been kidnapped by Slate."

"Because?"

"How should I know?" I wailed. "Nothing makes sense."

"Shhhhh. You'll wake Mama."

He pulled Miss Lana's scrapbook toward him. "Why would anybody want to take Miss Lana? I mean, she's nice, but she drives the Colonel so crazy he stays away half the time." He glanced up from the scrapbook. "I mean that in a good way," he said. "I love Miss Lana."

"I know. I love her too."

"It could have been accidental," he said. "Maybe Slate thought she was a movie star. Cher, maybe. She does wear wigs. No," he sighed, saving me the trouble of shooting him down. "That's not it."

"Maybe she surprised him," I said. "Maybe she found him ransacking the living room, looking for . . . something. Or for the Colonel. Slate had already been to our house once. Remember? The night Mr. Jesse died."

"That's right," he said, and turned a page in the scrapbook. "Who's this?"

I glanced at the photo. "Miss Lana, prior to blossoming."

He turned to her drama club collage. "Wow," he muttered. "Way to blossom." He yawned. "Why would a bank robber take Miss Lana? What do bank robbers want?"

"Money?" I guessed as he turned to the photo of the young Colonel, with me on his knee. "Only she ain't got none. Neither has the Colonel, unless . . ." I stopped, staring at the photo, at the open suitcase on the table.

Dale looked up. "Unless what?"

"Unless Slate believes that old rumor. About the suit-case full of cash."

He snorted and closed the scrapbook. "He can't be that stupid. Daddy started that rumor so people would be nice to the Colonel when he first came to town."

"Never underestimate the power of stupid, Dale. What if Slate thinks that rumor's true? What if he kid-napped Miss Lana to get money that isn't even real?"

Dale scratched his head. "Even if he did, we still got to find a way to get her back." He stood up and stretched. "Let's sleep on it, Mo," he said, picking up the scrap-book. "Can I take this? I can study it while Lavender mutters." I nodded. "Don't worry. We'll find her." Queen Elizabeth jumped to her feet. "Liz," he said, "you stay with Mo."

A photo fluttered from the scrapbook as he closed the door. In it, a young Colonel and Miss Lana stood arm in arm in front of an old church, smiling at me. The wind whipped Miss Lana's hair around her face. I laid it on the table, clicked off the light, and settled back into bed.

I closed my eyes and tried to sense where Miss Lana was. *Please Miss Lana,* I thought, *think to me. I'm at Miss Rose's house.*

Finally I shoved the sheet away and walked to the window overlooking the barnyard. The night sky stared back at me patient and black, dressed in wide sweeps of stars.

The Colonel's voice found me, steady and clear: *"When you feel lost, let the stars sing you to sleep. You'll always wake up new. Do you understand what I'm telling you, Soldier?"*

"I think I do now, sir," I whispered.

I dragged Dale's beanbag chair to the window and fell asleep listening to the stars.

Chapter 20
A Suitcase Full of Cash

"Miss Rose," I said the next morning, "I want to tell Joe Starr about the Colonel's suitcase of money, and about the night he crashed at the edge of town."

She sat at the kitchen table, stirring cream into her coffee. "That old story?" she said, looking startled. "Why?"

"Because," I said, "Slate might think that old story's true. It's the only reason I can think of that he might have stole Miss Lana. And we can't tell that story without telling about the Colonel's crash."

Lavender ambled in and slid my scrapbook across the table. "Nice photos," he said, taking a basket of eggs from the refrigerator. "You want some eggs, Mama?" She shook her head. "Mo, you think you can make toast?"

Can I make toast? Is he kidding me?

As I popped two slices of Wonder Bread into the toaster, the bathroom door slammed. "Dale's up," I said, taking two more slices from the bag and twisting it shut. I glanced at Lavender, who'd tied a gingham apron over his jeans. "What do you think we should do, Lavender?"

"I think we should get some plates and forks."

I headed for the cupboard. "I mean about Miss Lana."

He studied me, his blue eyes serious. "I think we should do everything we can. If searching will help, I'll search. If talking about the suitcase or the Colonel's crash will help, I'll talk. I'm surprised nobody's already told him, anyway."

Have I mentioned I will marry Lavender one day? We'll adopt six children, some of them twins. He poured the eggs into the pan. "Dale!" he bellowed. "Get a move on!"

The toaster popped up two pieces of burnt toast. "We need to tell it careful," I said. "Starr might not take the Colonel serious once he finds out he can't remember anything."

"Oh, Mo, everybody takes the Colonel seriously," Miss Rose said. "He only missed being mayor by one vote last year, and he wasn't even running."

"Miss Lana voted against him," I said. "Twice."

Lavender shoveled eggs onto three plates. "Dale!" he called. "We're eating."

Miss Rose smiled at him as he sat down beside her. "Macon started that rumor the same day I met Lana. You were such a cute baby," she told me.

"Yeah, except for that diaper thing," Lavender said, wrinkling his nose.

I flipped a fork of eggs at him.

"Don't throw your food," Miss Rose said automatically. "Macon and I went over expecting to find the Colonel with you. But there was Lana sitting on the porch, rocking you and singing a lullaby. I can see her clear as day, wearing that light blue dress, the one with the little flowers and the pearl buttons down the back.

"We introduced ourselves, and suddenly Lana and I were best friends. After a while we went inside, and there was that old, striped suitcase lying open, full of baby things. And beside the suitcase was a stack of cash. The Colonel scooped the cash into the suitcase and closed it, and then he and Macon laughed about the Colonel's suitcase full of cash."

She glanced at Lavender, her eyes dancing. "You know how your daddy used to be, before . . . Well, before. Soon it was all over town—how Lana and the Colonel were living out of a suitcase of cash, buying whatever they needed to get the café up and running." She shrugged. "I don't see much reason to tell Starr about it, Mo, but I don't see any harm in it either, if you want to."

"Tell me what?" a voice said from the hallway, and we jumped. I whipped around, my mouth full of eggs. Starr stood in the door, hat in hand. His clothes were wrinkled and tired, and his chin wore a dark sheen.

"Did you find Miss Lana?" I asked.

"Not yet."

Suddenly my eggs didn't look fit to eat.

"Come in," Miss Rose said. "I'll pour you some coffee."

He tossed his hat on the counter and sank into a chair. "Thanks." His eyes found mine. "Well, I'm reporting, as promised. We've searched all the deserted buildings in the area. We didn't find her, but we also didn't find any sign of foul play. Second, we suspect Slate's driving a black Malibu—the last unaccounted-for car that belonged to Dolph Andrews. It helps to know that. And third, my people are searching Slate's old hangouts in Winston-Salem. Also good."

"Winston-Salem? But that's so far away!"

"But it's my territory—which gives me the advantage," he said. "Now we wait. Waiting's tough, but every detective knows that's part of the job, right?"

I nodded, blinking back tears.

"That's my report. Now, what did you want to tell me?"

I pushed my plate away as Dale slipped into the room. "I wanted to tell you about a suitcase," I said, still trying not to cry.

"Actually," Miss Rose said, "it's an old *rumor* about the Colonel and a suitcase of cash."

Starr frowned. "Cash?"

Dale inched around Starr and plucked a piece of toast from my plate. You could tell Dale the world had ended and he wouldn't lose his appetite.

"It was a lie," I said, finding my voice again. "Dale's daddy told it after the car crash that brought the Colonel to town and made him forget his life." Somehow, it didn't sound so good out loud. "The point is, Slate might think that rumor about the money is true. I'm thinking that's why he kidnapped Miss Lana."

Starr nodded. "I've heard the Colonel has memory problems," he said. "How about filling me in?"

I opened the scrapbook and slipped the Colonel's story out. "Here's the story in his own words," I said. "You can skip the first part. It's about me. The second part's about him." To my surprise, he read the whole thing out loud:

Dear Soldier,

I know you wonder how we came to be here, in Tupelo Landing.

You were born during a hurricane. I imagine your mother did what people do on hurricane days: She bought food, tied the porch furniture down, fell asleep listening to the wind. No one expected a flood.

Like others, she awakened in darkness, startled by the bump of furniture against her walls. She swung her legs over the side of the bed and screamed. The floodwater lapped against her knees. She splashed across the porch and scaled the trellis as bits of other people's lives drifted by: an easy chair, an oil drum, a chicken coop with a drenched rooster perched on one side. You were born as the water crept up the roof and her world shrank smaller and smaller.

In the distance, I believe, she caught a glimmer of hope: a broken billboard spinning crazily on the tide. She wrapped you in her gown as the sign skidded across the roof. Gently, she placed you there, then cried out as the makeshift raft slipped from her hands. You spun away, my dear. And you were not afraid.

I, on the other hand, was scared out of my mind.

"This next part is more about the Colonel," I said. Starr turned the page:

I awakened in a wrecked car, in a raging storm, my head howling. Winds roared. Trees fell. Worlds drowned.

Who was I? I couldn't remember. Where had I come from? I didn't know.

I slid down the bluff by the creek, grabbing great hands full of kudzu to break my fall, and crouched by the creek. My leather shoes sank into the mud. I locked my arms around my knees and rocked to keep from screaming.

I didn't know there was a dike upstream. I didn't know it would break.

"Why, God?" I cried. "What do you want from me? Give me a sign."

In that instant, your billboard careened ashore on a wall of water, cracking the back of my head. I reached for balance and touched what I thought was a puppy. Then you grabbed my finger. My God, I thought. It's a baby. I fainted dead away. That's how Macon found us the next day—me unconscious on half a billboard, you nestled in my arms, nursing on the pocket of my uniform. The half billboard said: ". . . Café . . . Proprietor." Our path seemed clear.

I will always love your mother for letting you go, Soldier, and I will always love you for holding on.

Love, the Colonel.

PS: I apologize for naming you Moses. I didn't know you were a girl until it was too late.

I slid my plate to Starr. "Try the blackened toast. I made it special. I hope you ain't taking any of this about the Colonel the wrong way," I added.

"I'm trying not to. How much money is in this rumor?"

"Oh," Miss Rose said, brushing imaginary crumbs from the table. "Thirty thousand dollars or so." The phone rang. "Dale, do you mind getting that?" Dale trotted off down the hall, toward the living room.

"Thirty thousand dollars?" Starr sputtered, going red at the collar.

"It's just a rumor," I said.

"Really? That's a good trick, building a real café with rumored money," he said.

I hadn't thought of that. I looked at Miss Rose. "The Colonel had *some* cash when he came to town," she said. "Lana brought some. . . . Macon liked the Colonel. He might have loaned him money, for all I know. Things were better for us then."

Starr ran his finger along his eyebrow. "Is any of that money left?"

I pictured the dollar bill over the café's kitchen door, and the Emergency Five in my suitcase.

"I doubt it," Miss Rose said. "As far as I know, their money was gone before Mo could walk. Except . . . there is the dollar bill over the kitchen door." She laughed like a wind chime on a shady porch. "Lana bought the first lunch special at the Colonel's café, and if memory serves, she paid for it with *his* money. He hung it up the same day."

"Great. I'll run the serial number," Starr said. "See if it's connected to Slate."

"What? The Colonel ain't no robber," I said, my voice rising. "I didn't tell you this so you could run the blooming serial number."

"Calm down, Mo," Lavender said. "Detective Starr's trying to help."

"Mo, everything I learn gets me closer to finding Lana," Starr said. He leaned forward, putting his elbows on the table—something Miss Rose don't allow. "I'm working every angle I can find. Right?" He glanced at my plate. "Anybody gonna eat that last piece of toast?"

"Help yourself," Miss Rose said as Dale trudged back into the kitchen. "Who was on the phone, baby?" she asked.

"Slate."

Lavender and Starr leaped to their feet.

"Don't bother getting up," Dale added. "He said he'll call back later."

Chapter 21
Ransom

Around eleven o'clock, Grandmother Miss Lacy Thornton rapped on the door. "Rose?" she called. "Is Mo here? I'm nibblish, and with the café draped in crime scene tape, I thought I might dine here today—if she's available."

Starr looked up from his phone-tracing gizmo. "She dropped by for lunch?" he whispered to Deputy Marla. "During an investigation? Is she insane?"

I handed the screwdriver to Deputy Marla. "I'll act like I didn't hear that, as that's practically my grandmother you're talking about," I said. "It wouldn't hurt you to show some respect." I turned to the door. "I'm in here, Grandma Miss Lacy," I called. "Miss Rose is in the garden and Lavender's in town, working on his car. Come in and I'll make you a sandwich. Miss Rose has Wonder Bread."

The screen door squeaked open. "Please don't call me Grandma, dear," she said. "You know I prefer Grandmother." She smiled at Starr and extended her hand, which is as fragile and blue-veined as a baby bird. "Detective Starr," she said.

"Ma'am," he said, giving her hand a gentle pump.

"Would you like a PB and J?" I asked her.

"Don't trouble yourself, dear," she replied. "I have a basket of fried chicken in the Buick. Let's spread a tablecloth on the porch. Detective? Deputy?" She fastened her smile on Deputy Marla. "You are a full deputy, aren't you, dear?"

"Yes, ma'am," Deputy Marla said, standing up straight.

Grandmother Miss Lacy Thornton beamed at her. "That's wonderful," she said. "Won't you two join us for a picnic dinner?"

"I will," Dale said, trotting down the hall. "I'll get us some iced tea."

"Thank you, Dale. That would be wonderful."

I followed Grandmother Miss Lacy Thornton to the porch and helped spread her yellow gingham tablecloth. She'd brought a feast: fried chicken, deviled eggs, coleslaw, potato salad, and rolls. As she passed out the plates, Mayor Little drove up in his dinged Jeep. "Mind if I join you?" he asked, pulling a paper sack from his front seat.

"Make yourself at home," I said. He tiptoed across the porch, shrugged off his blue seersucker jacket, and folded it over the back of the swing.

"Sorry to hear of the recent unpleasantness, Mo," he

said. "I'd have dropped by sooner, but I'm monitoring the hurricane. I doubt she'll turn this way, but if she does, your civil servants stand ready. I may open the school to refugees."

"They can have my desk," Dale offered.

Mayor Little settled in the swing and smoothed his napkin over his tie as Lavender and Sam roared up in Lavender's GMC. Sam took the steps two at a time and handed me a fistful of orange daylilies.

"I do admire daylilies," Grandmother Miss Lacy Thornton murmured. "They're as pretty as they are tough."

Sam smiled. "Yes ma'am," he said. "Just like Mo."

"Gag me," Dale muttered as I headed to the kitchen for a jar of water.

By noon, half the town draped themselves over Miss Rose's yard, chatting and eating lunches they'd brought over themselves. Thes and Reverend Thompson nudged in among the Azalea Women, who'd claimed the garden table. Attila Celeste and her mother sat by their Cadillac, eating grapes and carrot sticks. Skeeter's folks spread a blanket on the lawn.

When Skeeter headed for her family's van, I followed. "Skeeter, I need you to check a couple of serial numbers for me. One off a hundred-dollar bill from Mr. Jesse's." I swallowed hard. "And one off a five. Here, I wrote them down for you," I said, handing her a page from my notebook.

"I don't know, Mo," she said, looking doubtful. "My cousin works drive-thru at the bank in Kinston but I don't think . . . Well . . . Let me see what we can do."

The first time Miss Rose's phone rang, everybody froze. "Starr's in there," I called out. "They got a trace on the line. Go ahead with your lunches."

They nodded. I moved to the door and pretended not to eavesdrop as Miss Rose took the call: "Oh, hello . . . No, no, it's dreadful, my tomatoes have it too. . . ."

Dale cupped his hands around his mouth. "Wilt!" he bellowed.

"Pity," Mayor Little sighed.

Lavender balanced his Pepsi on the porch rail. "They have a trace on the phone line? What kind of trace?"

Dale shrugged. "Beats me. Involves wires is all I know."

"It's the latest equipment from Winston-Salem," I said, grabbing a deviled egg. "I held the screwdrivers, so I got a good look. Headphones, dials, everything. Deputy Marla set it up. She's a genius. Wouldn't surprise me if she went FBI someday."

Sam slit open a honey bun with his pocketknife. "Mo, if I could I'd go over there and snatch a knot in whoever's taken Miss Lana. If you ask me—"

"Have a Nab," Lavender interrupted, holding out a pack of orange crackers. "Starr's got this under control, Sam. All we got to do is keep cool. Right, Mo?"

I nodded, wishing I felt as sure as he sounded.

The phone jangled a second time a half hour later, as the lunch crowd packed up. Again, everyone froze. It looked like Miss Rose's yard was full of picnicking mannequins. My heart pounded as Dale leaned against the door frame, listening. "Telemarketer trying to sell Mama a free vacation somewhere she wouldn't go if they paid her!" he shouted, and folks headed for their vehicles.

Out of the corner of my eye I saw Attila Celeste heading for us. Now what? "Hey," she said, placing two tall, blue bottles on the porch. It looked like she'd regained her composure since we crossed paths at the church.

"What are those?" I asked.

"Nice bottles. With attractive corks."

"Right," Dale said, giving her a daredevil smile. "Very nice bottles."

She gave him a quick smile and looked away. "Actually, I've had these in my window, catching sun. They made me think of you, Mo, because the ones you send out are ugly. Vinegar bottles, hot sauce bottles. They look trashy. Who would pick them up? Not me. Maybe not your mother." She looked at me. "I thought you might have better luck with these."

I hesitated. Was Attila actually being nice?

She blushed. "Anyway, I'm tired of them and the idea's stupid enough to appeal to you, so I brought them by." She glanced at Dale as he smoothed his hair. "You know, Mo, I've always thought you were lucky to have two mothers," she said. "Miss Lana, plus a fantasy one."

The word hit me like a splash of cold water. "A fantasy one?"

"Well, maybe *fantasy*'s not the right word . . ."

"Anna Celeste!" Mrs. Simpson shrilled. She glared, her hands on her bony hips.

"Coming, Mother."

"Attila?" I said as she started toward her mother. "Thanks. For the bottles. They're nice."

"No problem, Mo-ron," she said. And she was gone.

Grandmother Miss Lacy Thornton was among the last to finish lunch, primarily because she'd brought slices of her famous homemade coconut cake, which she kept concealed to prevent a riot. "Your family is odd, but well loved," she said, sliding a piece of cake toward me.

I nodded, feeling shy. "Lunch was delicious. Thank you for coming."

"Of course, dear," she said, touching my face. "I thank you for having me."

The third phone call came just as she drove away.

"Mo," Miss Rose called, her voice strained. "It's for you."

As I walked in, Starr whispered, "It's Slate, asking for you. Normally I wouldn't ask a kid to do this, but . . ."

"No problem," I said. "I'm a professional."

He hesitated. "Just be polite. Stay calm and keep him talking so we can trace the call. That's all. Don't tell him I'm here, and don't tell him we've identified him."

"Act natural," Dale whispered, crowding into me.

"I *am* natural," I growled, taking the receiver. It felt like my heart would rip through my shirt, I was so scared. "Back up, Dale. Give me room to work. You're breathing on me."

Deputy Marla held up her hand, halting my words as she adjusted a dial. "Now," she whispered, pointing to me like I was on TV.

"Mo LoBeau speaking," I said, my voice like glass. "You better not hurt Miss Lana, or you'll have me to deal with."

The voice on the phone was faint and scratchy. "Is this the Colonel's kid?"

"Of course it's me, reptile brain," I snapped. "What do you want? What have you done with Miss Lana? Is the Colonel over there?"

"Are you alone?"

"You just spoke to Miss Rose. How could I be alone?" I looked around the room. Starr and Deputy Marla hunched over their equipment, Miss Rose stood by the bookcase with her arm across Dale's shoulders, Lavender and Sam slouched in the door like hounds. "Yeah," I said. "Except for Miss Rose, I'm alone. Who's this?"

Starr gave me a thumbs-up.

"I'll ask the questions."

"Who made up that rule?" When he didn't answer, I pressed on. "You some kind of pervert, calling up little girls and asking if they're alone? Because I'm not allowed to talk to perverts. That's a rule. Miss Lana made it for me. If you don't believe me, ask her. She's there, right? In fact, put her on the phone and I'll double-check it myself."

No answer.

"You do have her over there, don't you?" I demanded, my voice getting louder. Starr grabbed for the phone. I turned my back, ducking away from him. "Where are you?" I shouted. "Where's Miss Lana?"

The phone went quiet save a distant crackling and, in the background, an odd sound: *screeEEeek,* like a swing on a rusty chain. Slate's voice came back cold and mean. "Do you want to see the Colonel and Miss Lana alive again?"

"Of course I do, you idiot," I shouted. "Bring them back right now!"

Starr snatched the phone away from me. "Hello? This is Detective Joe Starr. Who's this?" His eyes narrowed.

"Well, I just walked in," he said. "Which is fortunate, since I'm the one you need to talk to." He listened. "All right," he said. "I'll see what I can do, but I need to speak to Lana first. Or the Colonel. You choose."

"Give me that! I got more to say," I shouted, leaping for the phone. Lavender grabbed me around the waist, dragged me onto the porch, and pushed me into the swing.

"Calm down, Soldier," he said.

He'd never called me Soldier before. My temper settled like ashes around a fire.

"Let Starr handle this," he said, sitting beside me. "It's his job. You did great, but Starr knows the psychological mumbo jumbo."

"Could you tell anything?" Dale asked. "Was it really Slate?"

I shrugged, awash in misery. Why can't I ever keep my mouth shut? Why didn't I do what Starr told me? "I guess so. The line was too scratchy and far away. It sounded like . . . I don't know. Like something metal. Something creaking . . ."

"Well, don't worry," Lavender said. "They'll trace the call."

Turned out, they couldn't.

"It was Slate, all right," Starr said a few minutes later as he came out onto the porch. "Marla says he hung up before she could trace him. I thought we had him," he said, looking puzzled. "But he's smart," he said, pulling up a chair to face me.

"Did you talk to Miss Lana?"

"Not yet," he said. "Could you hear her?"

I shook my head.

"It's okay. Slate needs her there, for some reason. We'll talk to her next time."

"I'm sorry," I told him as Miss Rose came onto the porch. "I've been working on my temper, but sometimes it feels like my brain's straight-wired to my mouth."

"You did fine," Starr said. He hesitated. "Mo, what do you know about the Colonel's finances? Or Miss Lana's?"

"Their money?" I shrugged. "Well, far as I know, Miss Lana ain't got any. The Colonel, he's got the café. I reckon that's probably worth a fortune," I said. "I mean, it's creek-front. What do you think, Miss Rose?"

"The café?" She waggled her head. "Probably worth about eighty thousand."

Dale whistled between his teeth. "I didn't know you were rich," he said.

"Eighty thousand? Is that all?" Starr asked.

She nodded. "Look around you, Detective. This isn't Winston-Salem. Dirt's still worth dirt around here."

Starr rubbed his eyebrow, like he could coax an idea

out of it. "Eighty thousand dollars," he muttered. "Does the Colonel have other assets? Real estate? Stocks?"

I shook my head. "He mostly pays cash from the Crisco can."

"Slate's asking for a ransom," he said, watching my face. "When a kidnapper asks for a ransom, he thinks the family can pay it. But in this case . . ."

"A ransom?" Dale gasped. "How much?"

"A half-million dollars," he said, and Miss Rose sat down hard beside me.

Lavender gulped. "A half-million dollars? The Colonel ain't got that kind of money. Shoot, everybody in town together ain't got that kind of money."

"I know," Starr said. "But Slate thinks he does, and he seems to think Mo knows how to get her hands on it."

"Me?" I cried. "I'm on allowance and tips, which I get docked almost every week for sloppy room keeping. I'm lucky to get five bucks!"

Dale's face went pale. "What . . . what if she can't come up with it?" he said. "Slate already killed Mr. Jesse. He won't . . . I mean, he wouldn't kill . . ."

I felt it coming like you feel a storm before it hits.

"Mo?" Starr said again. "Can you can think of *anything* that might help me?"

I meant to say no.

Instead, I threw up Grandmother Miss Lacy Thornton's fried chicken and deviled eggs all over the porch, all over my daylilies, all over Starr's perfectly shined black leather shoes.

Chapter 22
A Town Full of Nobodies

I woke up snuggled deep in Miss Rose's feather bed, sunlight filtering through her lace-trimmed curtains and playing along her faded wallpaper. "Mo," Dale whispered, rapping softly on the door. "You up?"

"Yeah," I called. "Come on in."

He peeked around the door. "You through barfing?"

Dale can't tolerate other people throwing up. He gets what's known as the Synchronized Heaves. Lavender says if they ever make it an Olympic sport, Dale's an automatic for the gold. He placed a paper-towel-covered plate on the bed beside me. "Tomato sandwich," he said. "I made it the way you like it: fat homegrown tomatoes, double mayo, salt and pepper."

Dale and Miss Rose eat a lot of homegrown. They start their seeds early, in a hotbox around back. "Thanks," I said. "I'm starving."

I polished off the sandwich in record time, wiped my mouth, and settled back against the pillows. "It's quiet," I said. "Where is everybody?"

"Mama went to Snow Hill to see a lawyer," he said.

"A lawyer? Who's in jail this time?"

"Nobody. It's about getting Daddy moved out. For good, I mean," he said, not meeting my eyes. "She said not to worry, so I ain't."

Dale can choose not to worry like he chooses not to wear socks. Miss Lana says I have more of a Jack Russell brain. I think things apart for sport.

I glanced at the clock on the mantel. "Miss Rose needs to wind her clock."

"No," he said. "Eight o'clock tomorrow morning is right."

I sat bolt upright. "It's Friday morning?"

"Yep. You slept all Thursday afternoon, and all night too. Mama says you were worn slam out from worry."

"Friday?" My life settled around me like a net of bad dreams. I couldn't breathe. "Have they found Miss Lana?"

"Not yet," he said, looking away.

"The Colonel?"

He shook his head.

I stared at the embroidery on Miss Rose's bedspread until I was sure I wouldn't cry. "Where's Starr? Where's Deputy Marla?"

"He's in town, and she's in the living room. Starr says Marla can handle Slate if he calls," he said. He perched gingerly on the side of my bed, leaving himself a shot at the door. I tried to settle down.

It's a pretty room, Miss Rose's, with no sign of Dale's daddy. An old-time clock on the mantel, a soft-bottomed chair by the open window, a desk against the wall. A gust of wind sent papers fluttering from desk to floor. "I got it," I said, rising and padding across the worn wool rug. I scooped up the pamphlets, glad to have something new to focus on. "Hey, you all going on vacation?"

His face lit up. "Are we?"

"Looks like it," I said, scanning the brochures. "Farm Life Museum, a Tobacco Museum . . . Sounds boring."

"So don't come with us," he said, taking them from my hands. "Come on, Mo. Mama didn't take your barfing self into her room so you could rummage through her desk," he said, pulling the desk top down. "I got to water Cleo and fix that broke-down stuff at the barn," he said. "You want to watch? We can discuss Miss Lana's case."

"I'm not much for watching," I said, sliding my feet into my sneakers. "But I'll help." I opened the door—and ran square into Deputy Marla. "What are you doing here?" I asked, an uneasiness tickling the back of my neck.

"Me?" She grinned, tucking her hair behind her ear. "I was coming to check on you. How are you feeling, Mo?"

"Better," I said. "Jumpy, I guess. Has Slate called?"

"No," she said calmly, "but he will. We're ready for him. And we still have people searching. No news is good news, right?"

It sure didn't feel that way. "Slate wants money. Why hasn't he called?" I asked.

She slid her arm across my shoulders. "Come have a glass of tea with me," she said, herding me toward the kitchen. "Both of you." She flowed around the kitchen like it was her own, filling glasses with ice as Dale and I sat at the table. She slid each of us a glass of tea and sat beside me. "Mo," she said, "I've been thinking. Slate believes the Colonel has a ton of money." Her eyes searched my face. "That means a safe, a lockbox, a bank book. If you have any idea . . ."

"I ain't ever even heard of it," I told her. "A half-million dollars is crazy. Why would the Colonel have that much money?"

"Yeah," Dale said, and spit an ice cube back into his glass. "The only way he could get that much money would be to rob a . . . Oh."

"Only the Colonel ain't a thief," I said.

Deputy Marla tilted her head, watching me. "I don't think he is either," she said. "But Slate's asking for a half-million dollars—exactly what he and an accomplice stole in Winston-Salem, twelve years ago. An odd coincidence, wouldn't you say? I would, since the money from Slate's heist was never recovered." I didn't answer. "Mo," she said, "it's hard, being alone. I know. I want to find the Colonel and Miss Lana for you. So, please. Try to remember anything the Colonel's said or done that might help us. A bank account, a hiding place. It's important."

Dale leaned away from her. "She already said she don't know," he said. "Plus, Mo's a kid. If somebody's thinking, I think it should be you and Starr."

She hesitated. "Of course," she said softly. She slid her hand to mine. "I'm sorry, sweetie," she said. "Sometimes I go overboard, trying to help. Tell me what you two have planned for today."

I pulled my hand away. "We got chores."

"You want to come?" Dale offered. He pointed out the window at his mule, Cleopatra, who stood in the pasture, munching grass. "Cleo's a great mule. She's half Tennessee Walker. You can water her if you like."

Deputy Marla's grin made her look younger. "I just might take you up on that one day. Where are you two working?"

"At the tobacco barn," he said.

She poured herself another glass of tea. "Well, stay where I can see you. And if anything happens, call me. Understand? I'm stuck by the phone until Slate calls."

We headed for the door.

"That was weird," Dale said as Queen Elizabeth slunk out of hiding and fell in beside us. "What's all that about her knowing what it's like to be alone?"

"She's an orphan," I said. "She told me."

He frowned. "Why would she tell *you* that?"

"Because I told her about Upstream Mother, and how I ain't yet found her," I said. "Deputy Marla and I got a lot in common."

He snorted. "No you don't. She's playing you."

"Playing me? Why would she? There ain't nothing to win."

"Yes there is, you just can't name it yet," he said. "Believe me. She's as much a con as my uncle Mike, and he's doing three to five."

"You just don't trust her because she's law enforcement."

He shrugged. "Suit yourself." He slung a stick into the tobacco field. "Fetch it, Liz," he said. "Good girl!" We walked the rest of the way in silence.

Skeeter showed up a half hour later, swinging a battered attaché case. "Hey," she said. "I caught a ride with Mama so I wouldn't mess up your phone tap. She brought y'all a broccoli casserole."

I gasped.

"Broccoli casserole? Your mama's Death Dish?" Dale said, looking up from the tangle of worn plow lines at his feet. "Who died? What have you heard?"

"Nobody," she said quickly. "Gosh, I'm sorry, Mo. Everything's fine. We just didn't know what to bring for a kidnapping, but that seems to comfort people when somebody . . . goes away. Anyway, hope you like it."

"Thanks," I said, my heart finding its usual pace. "That's nice of you all."

She opened her attaché. "Anyway, I wanted to report. We checked those serial numbers, Mo. The C-note from the church *is* hold-up money."

Dale whistled. "So Mr. Jesse *was* in on the heist."

"He was at least in on the loot," she said. "But the five-dollar bill was clean."

"It was?" Suddenly I felt like a half-million dollars, even if I couldn't lay my hands on it. "Great."

"Five-dollar bill?" Dale asked. "What five?"

"Tell you later," I said. "Thanks, Skeeter."

"Don't thank me," she said. "My cousin at the bank's drive-thru couldn't do a thing. Thank Anna Celeste. Her great-aunt on her mother's side runs a bank in Wilmington. Sal talked to her for you." She glanced at the house. Deputy Marla and Skeeter's mother were walking to the van, chatting like old friends. "See you, Desperados."

As Skeeter strolled away, Dale picked up a snarl of old

reins and began teasing the knots apart. I could feel the anger rolling off his silence. *Now what?*

Oh yeah. Right. The five-dollar bill.

"I guess you're wondering about that five spot," I said. He didn't look up. "It's the Emergency Five from my suitcase. The one that's always been there. I kind of thought it might be a clue."

"And you didn't tell me because . . . ?"

"I don't know," I said. Even to me it sounded like a lie.

"You thought maybe the Colonel was in on the heist, so you had the number run without telling me," he said, his voice flat. "What if it had come back the other way? What if it was part of the loot? Were you going to tell me then?" When I didn't answer, he shook his head. "I thought we were partners," he said.

"We are. I didn't tell you because . . . I don't know. I should have," I said. His fingers worked at the knot, pulling, tugging. "Give me a break, Dale. Deputy Marla's right. If I can't figure this out, I'm alone. I got nobody except an Upstream Mother I can't find."

"Nobody?" He dropped the reins and stared at me so angry, his lips went pale. "You got people driving out here to sit with you, bringing you food. You got Skeeter helping. You got Sal breaking her family rules for you. You got Anna Celeste helping, and she can't stand you. You got me, and Mama, and Lavender. You got a town

full of nobodies, in case you haven't noticed," he said, his voice picking up steam.

"And I'm sick of hearing about your Upstream Mother. You think you're the only person that ever got thrown away?" he said. "You think Anna Celeste doesn't get thrown away every time her mother looks razor blades at her? You think I don't get thrown away every time Daddy . . ."

He clamped his mouth shut. He sat there looking like a tired, angry old man. Then he jumped to his feet and brushed past me, heading for the house.

An hour later I tapped on the door of Lavender's old room. "Dale?" I turned the porcelain knob and pushed the door open a whisper. "Can I come in?"

"If you want to," he said, his voice like frost.

He sat sideways in an overstuffed chair by the window, his legs over the chair arm, leafing through a back issue of *NASCAR Illustrated* magazine. Liz curled by his chair. "I'm sorry," I said.

"Really?" he said, squinting at a photograph.

I sighed. Dale can be stubborn.

"I know how much you and Miss Rose and Lavender do for me," I said. "I appreciate it. I know this ain't a great time for you all, with your daddy acting the way he is." He turned a page. "I hate him for hitting you, Dale."

He shrugged. "Nobody said anything about—"

"I've seen the marks. If he tries it around me, I'll take him down." He cocked an eyebrow. "I'm a born scrapper, plus I have karate skills," I reminded him.

He looked up. Finally. "He's twice as big as you are, Mo. And he ain't like Mr. Li, at Karate Night. When Daddy hits, he means it. And he's getting worse. That's why Mama's thrown him out."

"Mr. Li says no matter how big the enemy—"

"Don't hit him unless you aim to kill him, Mo," he said, looking me full in the face. "I mean it." I could hear myself swallow. "Hey, I got an idea," he said, his voice flat. "Let's talk about something you actually know about. Like that five-dollar bill."

I sat on the edge of Lavender's old bed and looked around. It was a used-to-be room full of kid stuff left behind. "When Starr said he'd run the serial number on that dollar bill over the café's door, that five was the only other old piece of money I could think of. I didn't tell you because . . ." I stared at the rag rug. "I was ashamed."

He closed his magazine. "Of the Colonel?"

"Of me, for not being sure. I'm sorry," I said. "I hope you'll forgive me." I looked out the window. A bedsheet flapped on Miss Rose's wash-line.

He propped his chin on his hand and studied me, his blue eyes serious in his freckled face. Then, like sunlight after rain: "Okay," he said. "I forgive you."

Dale kills me. "Just like that?" I never forgive. I like revenge too much.

"Yeah," he said. "I'm Baptist. So far, Fast or Never is the only speeds I got with forgiving. But from here on, Mo, if we're partners, we're partners. If we're not, we're not. You decide, and decide it now."

"Partners."

He jumped up. "Good. Let's give Queen Elizabeth a bath. Lavender's coming for supper, and I want her to smell good."

"Dale," I said, "you're the best friend I got."

"I know." He grinned. "Come on, Desperado. You wash and I'll dry."

Dear Upstream Mother,

It's night. Everybody's asleep. Still no word from the Colonel or Miss Lana. I feel like a sky without stars.

Dale and I had a fight today. Then we made up and gave QE-II a bath.

Lavender came for supper. He wore jeans and his chambray shirt with the sleeves rolled up. Lavender and Sam drive to Sycamore tomorrow, almost to the mountains, to race in the Sycamore 200. He says his car runs great and looks like a million bucks with our ads painted on it.

Deputy Marla came too. In fact, she mashed the potatoes. "Congratulations on achieving your dream," she told Lavender. "That must feel great."

Lavender spooned green onions onto his turnip greens. "It does, but dreams are shape-shifters. Get close, and before you can lay a hand on them, they change." She smiled the way women smile at Lavender, but I can tell she secretly thinks he's crazy.

The hurricane's turned toward Charleston. I hope Cousin Gideon will be okay.

I got three bottles ready for launch: two blue ones, and a clear one.

Lavender's dropping my bottles on his way west. You might at least see one drift by. I hope you won't mind, but the messages say: "Lost: Miss Lana. 36 years old, 5'6", red hair, 130 pounds. Last seen wearing a black wig and red kimono. Contact Mo in Tupelo Landing. 252-555-4663."

If you see Miss Lana, please help her. I'm pretty sure the Colonel can take care of himself.

Mo

Chapter 23
Creative Chaos

By the next morning, Hurricane Amy had hit the warm Gulf Stream waters and swerved north. "She's coming," Miss Rose said, clicking the television off. "You three get the house ready. I'm going to head into town for supplies—batteries, candles, drinking water. Dale, find the transistor radio, honey, and make sure it's working. Then tie down the stable and the yard. Mo, could you give him a hand?"

I nodded, trying not to think of the Colonel and Miss Lana. It didn't work.

She grabbed her keys and gave me a quick hug. "Mo, you know why Starr hasn't found Lana, don't you?"

"Because Slate is a reptile, making it impossible to guess where he is or when he's going to strike?" I guessed.

"Because he's greedy and he's smart," she said. "Slate believes Lana's worth a half-million dollars. Believe me, he'll keep her safe so he can cash in. We'll find her, Mo. We just need some faith. All right?"

"Yes, ma'am," I said, hoping she was right.

I looked across the barnyard as she drove away. To the east, the clouds gathered like an invading army.

Dale and I tied down the porch furniture and headed for the stable. The wind had picked up. It rolled across the fields in waves, tearing the brittle tobacco leaves. As I watched the clouds boil toward us, I made a decision. "If Slate calls again, I'm paying the ransom," I told Dale.

"With what?" he asked, scurrying up the rough wood ladder to the stable loft. "We ain't got ten dollars between us."

"Slate don't know that."

"You're nuts. Stand back," he called, dropping a bale of hay. I cut the rough baling twine with his pocketknife and carried an armload of prickly, sweet-smelling hay to Cleo's stall. "She'll be extra-hungry," he said, looking at the sky. "She always is in a hurricane. Same thing happens to me."

He led Cleo into the stall and removed her bridle. "You'll be okay," he told her, running his hand along her flank. "You'll do just fine."

We spent the rest of the morning putting up or tying down anything the wind could throw or steal. Liz stuck close as the clouds rolled in dark and sullen. "She's clingy," Dale said, nudging her out of the way with his knee. "She feels the storm."

By lunchtime, the storm had claimed half the sky.

The tops of limber young pines swayed in the wind as giant oaks and pecan trees groaned and creaked. "Hey Deputy," Dale yelled as we slammed the back door and swarmed the kitchen. "You want a cucumber sandwich?"

Silence.

We found her stretched out on the settee, asleep with her mouth open, her hand curled over her pistol. "How can she sleep with a hurricane coming?" I asked.

"Shhhhh," Dale said. "She got in late."

"She left us? Why? She's supposed to be waiting for Slate's call."

He shrugged. "Let's eat."

We tiptoed back to the kitchen. Halfway through our sandwiches the phone jangled, and we both jumped. "Slate!" I cried, reaching for the phone.

He knocked my hand away. "No. We got to trace the call. I'll get Deputy Marla." He sprinted across the room. As he cleared the doorway, I grabbed the phone.

"Slate? Mo LoBeau. You win, dirtbag. I know where your half-million dollars is. I'll take you to it as soon as you give the Colonel and Miss Lana back. I get them, you get the money. Deal?"

The voice on the end of the line came through scratchy and thin. "Soldier?"

My heart exploded like fireworks. "Colonel?"

"Listen to me," he said. "I've escaped. . . ." The call faded, then popped back in. ". . . Slate's after me. As soon . . . I lose Slate . . . return . . . free Lana." The call faded again.

"Colonel?"

". . . my closet . . . shelf . . . packet. . . . to Rose's. . . . Don't trust anyone . . ."

"But Starr says—"

"Don't trust . . . Starr. Don't trust . . ."

"Why not?" I heard a hollow click. Deputy Marla had cut into our line.

"Go . . ." he said, his voice full of urgency.

"I don't have to, moron," I snapped, hoping he would play along. "I already told you, I don't want your stupid all-expense-paid vacation. Neither does Deputy Marla. Ask her yourself, jerk brain. She just came on the line."

It worked.

The Colonel hung up. I stood in the kitchen, my heart turning handsprings. The Colonel was free! Soon Miss Lana would be too. I wanted to laugh out loud. *He's free, he's free, he's free,* my heart pumped.

As Deputy Marla charged down the hall I smoothed the grin off my face. *Think. Tell her the Colonel's free, and Starr will be her first call. And Starr can't be trusted.* I chewed my lip, trying to remember if she had met the Colonel, if she might have recognized his voice. She answered the question for me. "Telemarketer?" she asked, stepping into the room.

I nodded, trying to look miserable. I had to go home, find that packet and get back before the storm hit. "Yeah," I said. "False alarm. You can go back to sleep."

"I'm caught up with my rest," she said, stretching.

"Why weren't you here last night?" I asked. "Slate might have called."

"Joe said he needed my help with some reports," she said, reaching for the mayonnaise. "It was a calculated risk. What was your telemarketer selling?"

"A cruise." I grinned. "Into a hurricane. Come on, Dale. We still got to tie things down at the tobacco shelter."

"Maybe we can let that stuff blow away," he muttered.

Deputy Marla stifled a yawn. "Stay where I can see you," she called as the screen door slapped shut behind us.

It took me ten seconds flat to clue Dale in. "We got to go to my place. I'm swearing you to secrecy," I told him. "Fink me out on this and your life won't be worth goose spit."

"I don't think you should threaten a partner. Plus, geese don't spit," he said. He grabbed my arm. "And your house is a crime scene!" he cried as if he'd just thought of it. Which, maybe he had. "I could get grounded for the rest of my life."

"At least we'll be grounded together."

"Great," he mumbled.

"You in or you out?" I demanded.

"I'm in," he said miserably. "But you owe me, Mo LoBeau."

We grabbed Dale's faded red bike and sprinted across the yard. At the edge of the asphalt, he swung into the saddle. "Hurry," he said. "Hop on." I landed neatly on the handlebars. Within moments we flew along the road, Dale standing and pumping the pedals while I leaned back, holding my legs away from the spokes.

We met just one truck on the way to town.

"That was Daddy," Dale panted. I nodded, trying to ignore the heat of his breath against the back of my neck.

"He wasn't weaving," I said comfortingly.

The scorn in Dale's voice could have curled my hair. "Don't mean nothing," he said. "He mostly drives straighter drunk than he does sober."

Five minutes later, we passed the WELCOME TO TUPELO LANDING sign. The wind gusted, shaking dead limbs from the trees and perfuming the air with their scent. "Steer clear of the Piggly Wiggly," I told Dale. "We don't want nobody to see us." Instead of swerving left, as I expected, Dale rocked back hard on the pedals. We skidded to a halt and the bicycle spit me forward. I landed on my feet, running.

"If you want to decide where we're going, you pedal," he said, his face flushed. "What have you been eating, lead?"

"I been eating your mama's cooking," I said, trotting back to him. "Hop on."

I pedaled the rest of the way to the café. "Shhhhh," I told Dale, lifting the yellow crime scene tape. It was spooky inside, dark and gloomy—partly from the thickening clouds, and partly because the furniture lay sprawled across the room. "This way," I whispered, heading for the Colonel's quarters. The door swung open. "The closet's over here," I said, grabbing a chair and dragging it across the pine floor.

Dale looked at the jump boots standing at attention by the Colonel's footlocker. "The Colonel sure is neat," he said.

"The Colonel says keeping your interior space neat lets you practice creative chaos in your exterior life. Without this sanctuary, he says he'd have to shoot Miss Lana and leave her for dead. Hold my chair, Dale."

"Creative chaos," Dale murmured. "That explains a lot."

I stepped up into the chair and rummaged along the Colonel's shelf, pushing aside a shoe box, an old checker set, and a fruitcake left over from Miss Lana's baking binge three Christmases back. I stretched to my tiptoes. "Ah-ha," I said, pulling a packet from the back corner. I blew the dust off. "Sorry," I said as Dale coughed. I rubbed my arm across the dark brown packet. The word scrawled across its front flap stopped my breath. "What on earth . . . ?" I handed the folder to Dale.

"Slate," he read. "How come the Colonel has something with Slate's name on it?"

"I don't know." I hopped down and peeked inside. Newspaper clippings? I scanned the headlines: *Slate Found Guilty. Slate Gets Life.* Underneath lay a legal pad of notes—all of them in the Colonel's scrawl. My mouth went dry. Why would the Colonel have notes on Slate?

I stuffed the folder under my shirt and tucked my shirttail in, the packet making me swell-chested, like an umpire. "We'll check this stuff out at your house," I told him, wiggling the packet into place. "Let's go."

As we sprinted across the living room, something clunked on the front porch. Someone swore softly.

"Hide!" We bolted to Miss Lana's suite and slid under her bed like sliding into home.

I held my breath as dusty boots clomped past us, and Miss Lana's closet door scricked open. "Wigs? This must be the lunatic's room," a man muttered. He backtracked, and headed for the Colonel's quarters. I closed my eyes as he tore through the Colonel's closet, cursed, and finally headed for the front door.

"Had to be Slate," Dale whispered, squirming forward.

"Wait," I said, grabbing his arm. Was that a second voice? A woman's voice? I lay still, trying to pan human sounds from the wind. "Let's go," I said. We crept into the living room.

I felt the shadow in the doorway more than saw it. I wheeled to find Deputy Marla standing behind us, pistol drawn. "Well, well, what have we here?" she asked.

"Don't shoot," Dale yelped, raising his hands.

The pistol didn't budge.

"Deputy Marla," I said, crossing my arms over my chest—and the Colonel's packet. "What are you doing here?"

"I have a better question. What are *you* doing here?"

"Don't say nothing, Dale," I warned. He stood quiet and still. Dale hates guns. "We ain't a danger to you," I told her. "Ain't no reason to pull a gun."

She blinked slowly. "No," she said, lowering the weapon. "Of course not. I just . . . didn't know who I'd find," she said, her eyes moving to the Colonel's quarters.

"It's just us," Dale said, breathless.

"Rising sixth graders," I added, staring at the pistol. "Unarmed kids."

She holstered the gun. "Well? What are you two doing at my crime scene?"

Surely she'd seen Slate—hadn't she?

I faked a smile. "We're looking for clues, like any detectives worth their salt. If we found anything, which we didn't, we thought we'd turn it over to you. You could get a promotion out of it. We hope so."

She stepped forward, her eyes hard. Dale and I backed up, into the Colonel's quarters. "Starr might have missed something," I continued. Her eyes flickered to the Colonel's bunk and boots. "Plus I miss my family," I continued. "I'm homesick."

"I told you to stay where I could see you," she replied.

Who did she think she was, using that teacher voice on us?

She kept herself between me and the door, her hand close to her pistol. I looked up into her eyes. It was like looking into the eyes of a snake. The Colonel had warned me not to trust Starr, but maybe it wasn't Starr I needed to worry about.

Maybe it was Deputy Marla.

"I know it might look like we disobeyed you, but that's black-and-white thinking," I said. "Miss Lana says nothing's really black and white, except zebras and old movies. Even dreams aren't black and white unless you're a dog."

It was a cheap trick, but like most cheap tricks, it worked. I needed to think, and Dale has never, in the eleven years I've known him, passed up a chance to talk about a dog. He didn't disappoint. "Queen Elizabeth II dreams quite a bit, Deputy Marla," he said, relaxing. "You ever watch a dog dream?"

"I don't have a dog," she said, keeping her eyes on me.

"Sometimes Queen Elizabeth prances in her sleep," he said. "Her paws flit. Or she grins and tosses her head like she's in a field of butterflies. One time I think she caught a dream rabbit. I know she caught *something*, because she shook her head back and forth, but it could have been a squirrel. I'd rather not think it was a rat," he said, lowering his voice. "Still," he said, turning to me, "I don't know where you get off saying Liz dreams in black and white. I mean, she didn't actually tell you that, I'm pretty sure." He hesitated. "Did she?"

"No," I said. "I think Miss Lana told me, maybe. She listens to NPR and unless I'm mistaken, NPR is saying black and white for dog dreams."

Deputy Marla interrupted. "Well, Miss Lana's wrong."

"You think dogs dream in color?" Dale asked, his face brightening. "Me too."

"I *mean* Miss Lana's idea of black-and-white thinking is psychobabble poppycock," she snapped. "There are absolutes in life, and the sooner you learn that, the better. Take you, for instance," she said, glaring at me. "I've caught you on the wrong side of the law. That means you absolutely have a problem."

"On the wrong side of what law?" I asked. "All I did was come home."

"All you did was lie to a law officer, escape protective custody, and disturb a crime scene," she said. "That, plus dragging Dale into trouble."

"Dale just came along to keep me company," I said. "He's polite that way."

"He pedaled you over here," she said. "That makes him an accomplice." Her glance raked Dale. "Your daddy told me he saw you on the highway. He's lucky I didn't arrest him for drunk driving."

Dale shifted. "Daddy's home?" he said. "Where's Mama?" He looked at me, his eyes scared. "I got to get back home."

"What's wrong?" she sneered. "You afraid of a storm?"

No, I thought. *I'm afraid of you.*

I took a step toward the door. "Well, this has been real nice, but we got a couple more errands to do."

"I don't think so," she said, grabbing my arm. Her fingers pinched mean as a rusty bicycle chain. She gave me a sharp shake.

"You ain't supposed to shake a kid," I told her, clamping my elbows to my sides to keep the Colonel's packet from sliding loose. "You can cause brain damage."

She put her face close to mine. "Who called you at the house?" she demanded. "What are you doing over here?"

"Nobody called me. We ain't doing nothing," I said, and she shook me again, snapping my head back.

"Hey!" Dale shouted, moving toward her. "Leave her alone!"

Anger raced across her face like fire across a wheat field. "I'm tired of your redneck mouth," she said, pushing Dale with her free hand.

"Calm down, Dale," I said. "She won't hurt me. She ain't stupid enough to get herself a child abuse charge." Doubt flickered across her face, and her grip loosened—barely.

Why so angry? Not because a couple of kids gave her the slip. I wiggled my arm to test her grasp. "How did you know where to find us?"

"I told you. Dale's father."

"Bull," I said. "We didn't tell him where we were going."

"That's right," Dale said. "And I kept the bike on the pavement. So you didn't track us either."

Her eyes narrowed. "What I know is none of your business."

Deputy Marla didn't follow us here. She couldn't have. She came on her own. Either she overheard the Colonel on the phone, or Slate tipped her off. She was mad because we got here first.

She shook me again, and the Colonel's packet slid out from under my shirt. "What the heck?" she muttered, reaching for it.

"Dale!" I shouted. "Set! Down! Hut-hut-hut!"

He sprinted toward the door. I dropped back three paces as Dale did a neat buttonhook. The Colonel's packet sailed up, over Deputy Marla's hands, toward Dale's outstretched arms. She whirled toward him and when she did, I picked up the Colonel's steel-toed boot and swung it with all my might. She threw an arm over her face and ducked as she twisted on the waxed floor. Her feet flew up, and her head cracked against the corner of the bunk. She crashed to the floor like a sack of rotten onions.

"Shoot," Dale gasped, skidding to a stop. "You killed her."

"I did not," I said, hoping it was true. She moaned. "See? She ain't dead. Help me tie her up."

"No," he said, backing away. "You can't hit deputies and tie them up. Even my people know that."

"I didn't hit her, I missed," I said. "She fell down. Help

me, Dale. Miss Lana needs us." I rushed to the closet and plucked out both of the Colonel's neckties. "Here," I said, tossing the one with flamingos to Dale.

"The Colonel wears *this*?" he said, holding it at arm's length.

I grabbed the light-up clip-on featuring Charleston's Rainbow Row and tied it over Deputy Marla's mouth. "Miss Lana, Christmas before last," I told him. "Hurry!" We lashed her hands behind her with the flamingos and knotted her shoe strings together. Finally, I snagged the packet and the Colonel's bayonet. By the time I scampered down the steps, Dale had already rounded the side of the building. "Dale!" I shouted. "You forgot your bike!"

He didn't look back.

A gusty wind rattled the maples and shook the pines as I dropped the packet by Deputy Marla's car. It's harder to flatten a tire than I expected, but by the time I got to the car's fourth tire I had my technique down: Place the point of the bayonet just so, and slam the handle with a landscaping stone. As the car sank to its rims, Joe Starr's voice crackled through the radio: "Marla! Come in."

I stared at it. If no one answered, he'd come to Miss Rose's for sure. I grabbed the radio. "Hey Joe," I said, making my voice low.

"Marla, is everything okay there? Why aren't you by the phone?"

I tried to deepen my voice. "I'm securing the vehicle." In a way, it was true.

Starr's silence crackled. "I'm riding out the storm at Priscilla's. You stay put, and keep those kids safe. Over and out."

I hope she *does* stay put, I thought. I looked for the Colonel's packet. "No," I breathed. The wind had pried it open, and articles skittered toward the creek. I pounced, cramming all I could reach inside the packet, and looked at the sky.

"Hey Dale," I shouted, running for the bike. "Wait for me!"

Chapter 24

Right Under Our Noses

Dale pumped like he could out-pedal the storm, me balanced on his handlebars, the storm's flat, angry hands shoving us along the blacktop. Dale stood up on the pedals, panting as the front wheel began to squeak. There was something about that sound, the sound of metal, the whirring squeak. . . .

"Stop!" I shouted. "I know where Miss Lana is!"

He slammed on brakes, catapulting me off my perch. "Where?" he panted.

"Right under our noses."

Dale looked down, then out across a pitching ocean of corn, its green leaves going silver beneath a rolling sky. "I don't see her," he said. "Get back on."

"The Old Blalock place," I said, pointing to a sandy path etching its way through the corn. "It's the perfect hiding place. Ain't nobody been there since Miss Blalock died last winter—nobody except us hunting daffodils, and maybe Redneck Red to check on the still everybody pretends he ain't running. Miss Lana's down that path. I know it."

"Starr's already searched the empty houses. Get on."

"*Deputy Marla*'s already searched," I said.

He braced against the wind. "Daddy might be home, Mo. I got to go."

"Just a few minutes," I begged, stepping in front of the bike. "Remember how Miss Blalock's old water tower squeaks when the wind blows?" I said. "That's the sound I heard when Slate called." The wind raked his hair. "I got a foolproof plan. Take us five minutes is all. Five minutes to save Miss Lana's life."

He bit his lip. "I don't know. I hear the Blalock place's haunted, that everything's just like she left it. And Lavender says Miss Blalock's TV comes on at odd times, and she changes the channels herself."

I snorted. "Don't be a baby. Five minutes. You'll be a hero."

He sighed. "Five minutes, Mo, but that's all."

Ten minutes later we ditched the bike and hid behind a hydrangea. "Stay low," I whispered, glancing at the wooden water tower in the side yard. "Slate's been here sure as my name's Mo LoBeau," I added, nodding toward the tire tracks in the drive.

"Anybody could have left those tracks," he said. "What's your foolproof plan?"

"I'm getting to that," I said, trying hard to think of one. "First I do my surveillance. Then I'll explain my strategy, which is genius quality, believe me."

His shoulders slumped. "You don't have a plan, do you? I knew it," he said, his eyes filling with tears. "I knew not to come to a ghost farm with you during a hurricane."

"Shhh. I'm casing the place," I said, my gaze taking in the neat white house and lingering on the padlocked front door. "It's locked tight, just like people say."

"What was that?" Dale whispered. "Did you hear a TV?"

"No, I didn't hear a TV," I said. Still, an uneasy feeling settled cool hands against my neck. I swallowed hard and turned my attention to the side yard and the old water tower, with its bandied legs and potbelly. Its windmill had lost an arm, but it whirled to battle each gust of the approaching storm.

Faintly I heard it: *screeEEeek. ScreeEEEEK.*

"It was the water tower I heard, no doubt about it," I said. "Only there's no way you could hear it from inside Miss Blalock's house. Slate wasn't inside when he called."

"Thank you, Jesus," Dale whispered.

"He must have been closer to the tower." I glanced at the pump house. Its thick curtain of kudzu was torn. Someone had opened that door. "She's in that pump house," I said, my heart pounding. "Come on. We're on Search and Rescue. If you see Slate, give me a signal."

"I do a nice owl," he suggested.

"Fine," I told him. "If you see Slate, hoot like an owl. Now fan out."

Dale shook his head. "There's only two of us," he said. "You got to have three to fan, and that's at the very least."

"Okay," I said. "Forget fanning. We'll surround the pump house. You go around back, and I'll take the door."

"No," he said firmly. "It's too snaky in back. *I'll* go to the door. Snakes are mean enough in good weather; there's no telling how they think with a hurricane coming."

I took a deep breath. The Colonel says sometimes all a leader can do is see which way everybody's going, and try to get in front. This looked like one of those times. "Okay," I said. "We'll both take the door. Follow me." I crouched low and sprinted across the yard to the pump house, Dale on my heels.

"Miss Lana?" I whispered. "Are you in there?"

Scree-EEeeeek.

I grabbed the door's rusty latch. "Miss Lana?" A shaft of light pierced the shed's gloomy heart. Inside, I could just make out a case of old Mason jars, a rusted rake, and a wooden bucket rotted half through. "She ain't here," I said, my heart tumbling.

"No," Dale said, kicking at an old Nehi bottle. "I'm sorry, Mo. Let's go home." Behind us, a tree limb thunked against the side of the house. "What the . . ." He glanced back at the house and screamed, the sound slicing me like razors as he dove to my feet.

"What?" I shouted, falling to the ground beside him. "Did you see Slate? I thought you were going to hoot like an owl."

"It's Miss Blalock's ghost!" he cried, his face ashen.

"Where?"

"In the house," he said, his eyes glassy with fear. "She flitted past the window."

Thunk.

I squinted past the dancing broom straw. "That ain't no ghost," I told him. "Somebody's in there."

I sprinted across the yard, to the back porch.

Miss Blalock's heavy back door scraped across the kitchen's faded linoleum. The rumors were right. The kitchen stood just as Miss Blalock left it the morning she died: table set for one, a paper-dry daffodil in a Mason jar, a cast-iron frying pan on the stove.

"Miss Lana?" I whispered. The wind groaned and the roof rattled. "Let's try the living room," I murmured, looking away from the table. It looked too lonely, too abandoned, too close to being alive.

Dale grabbed my arm. "What's that smell?" he asked, sniffing the air.

I scanned the kitchen. Pizza boxes littered the counter.

"Pizza Hut delivers out here?" he gasped. He tiptoed to the boxes, opened the top one, and sniffed again. "Empty, but fresh."

"At least Miss Lana ain't hungry." I crept to the living room. The room sat prim and proper. A torn curtain fluttered by a cracked windowpane. "There's your ghost," I said. Then, as my eyes adjusted, I saw something else: Blood. Blood on the floor, blood on a shattered lamp, blood on the faded wallpaper.

"Miss Lana!" I screamed. "Where are you?"

We tore through the creaking house, yanking open doors, calling her name. "She ain't here," Dale panted, his face pale as his forgotten ghost.

"Follow the blood," I said, heading back to the living room's wallpaper and placing my hand against her handprint. "There," I said, pointing. We followed a faint smear of blood across the room, down a hall to a door. As I pushed the door open, the wind grabbed it, jerking me onto the porch.

Scuff marks scarred the dirt drive and disappeared in a crisscross of tire tracks. "She was fighting," Dale said, his voice shaking. "Fighting's good."

The pecan trees flailed at a darkening sky, and an old fertilizer bag cartwheeled across the yard. The storm's first raindrops spattered into the dust, the size of dimes.

"He's moved her. We got to get some help," I said.

"Come on. Mama's closest," he said, running toward his bike. "She'll know what to do."

Chapter 25
A Hurricane Party

"Mama!" Dale panted minutes later as we blasted through her door. "Help us!"

Miss Rose stood, phone to ear, in the living room. "Where on *earth* have you two been?" she cried, lowering the phone. "Where's Deputy Marla?"

"Miss Lana's hurt," I gasped.

"Lana? Where is she?"

"Blood," I said, my voice sounding far away. "At Miss Blalock's place."

"Who's on the phone? Is it Lavender?" Dale asked, reaching out. "Let me talk."

Lavender? I hugged the packet beneath my shirt and sobbed.

Miss Rose lifted the phone. "Lavender? They're back and . . . Hello? Hello?" She dropped it. "The line's gone dead." She pushed me gently onto the settee. "Tell me what's happened." Dale sat beside me, and she pulled a chair close. "Take a deep breath and start at the beginning."

I went through the story step by step. She listened, her green eyes searching our faces as the words tumbled out. "Where's Slate now?"

"I don't know," I said. "The Colonel said he'd lead him away from Miss Lana, and save her. The next thing I knew, Slate was in our house. That's all I know."

She sat back and stared out the window. The wind charged across the tobacco field behind a ragged band of rain and slammed the house, rocking it. In the distance I heard a crash—a tree hitting the ground. The lights flickered. A lawn chair tumbled across the yard, to a barbed wire fence. "If the Colonel said he'd rescue Lana, he's probably done exactly that," she said.

"But you didn't see the blood. On the floor, on the wall . . . We have to save her."

She put her hand on mine. "We don't know whose blood that was."

"I do know. I saw Miss Lana's handprint."

"If that *was* her handprint, we know she had blood on her hand. And that's all we know. We don't know whose it was or how it got there. If we're going to assume, let's assume in a positive direction. My money's on the Colonel," she said. She headed down the hallway, and returned a moment later with her shotgun. "But in case Slate wants to come calling, let's ready a welcome."

"What about Joe Starr?" Dale asked.

Her eyes went hard as emeralds. "Marla had me fooled," she said. "Joe Starr could have fooled me too. We'll assume they're working together until we know different, and hope he doesn't drop by."

"He won't. He's staying at Miss Retzyl's," I said. "He radioed in while I was flattening Deputy Marla's tires."

"You flattened her tires?"

She flipped into Mother Mode just like that, like a werewolf growing hair beneath a full moon. "Maybe," I said, sliding the Colonel's packet onto the coffee table. "Let me try to remember." I studied her a moment. "Just out of curiosity, how would you feel about flattened tires, if it was true?"

She narrowed her eyes. "Let's see. Marla sat at my table and plotted against us, helped kidnap my friends, and held a gun on you and Dale. If you flattened her tires, Mo, I believe I could take it in stride."

"She's on the rims, all the way around," I said, and she smiled, unleashing dimples. "So," I said. "What's our plan?"

"Our plan is to stay safe, and wait out the storm." She held up her hand like a traffic cop, stopping my words. "It's too late to go out there," she said. "It's too dangerous. We'll stay here until the storm passes, and then we'll find the Colonel. Would you put the candles around, please ma'am?" she said, handing me a box of matches as the lights flickered again. "Dale, I need a hand in the kitchen."

I hated it, but I knew she was right. I set the candles out just in time. The lights died as Miss Rose and Dale spread armloads of treats across the coffee table: Oreos, cheese puffs, chips, pretzels. Dale grinned. "We normally eat boring during a hurricane, but Mama's making you feel at home. She's a natural born hostess."

"Thank you, Miss Rose."

Miss Lana's hurricane parties are famous county-wide, as well as in Charleston. On hurricane days, when most women fill their grocery carts with bread and milk, Miss Lana loads ours with candy, cakes, and tapered candles. "If I die in the storm, I'll drift away in the arms of a sugar coma and candlelight," she always says.

Miss Rose pulled the card table out of the closet. "My pleasure, Mo. Dale, get the cards," she said. "I need a party."

For the next few hours Hurricane Amy battered the house and screamed through window screens. Razor-colored rain slashed sideways, shredding leaves, toppling trees.

Anybody that says he ain't scared in a hurricane is a liar or a fool. That's what the Colonel says. A hurricane spins up like you're nothing, and takes your world apart like it's nothing too. There's no time in it, no sense of the sun moving, no waxing or waning light. All you can do is breathe, and ignore the world flying to pieces beyond your door.

To keep calm, we played cards, ate junk, and laughed too loud.

After a parade of losing hands I found myself staring at four fat aces. Dale bit his lip, a sure sign he's bluffing. "All or nothing," he said, pushing his pitiful three chips into the pot.

"Fine," I said, nudging a double handful of chips to the center of the table.

Miss Rose stared from behind her mountain of chips. "I think you're both bluffing," she said. "All or nothing. What you got?"

Dale flipped his cards over. "A pair of fours," he said, looking pleased.

I snorted. "Four aces." As I reached for the pot, the door slammed open and the storm screamed into the room, snuffing out candles, knocking over lamps. Queen Elizabeth jumped up barking as Miss Rose leaped to her feet. "Dale! The door!"

Dale rushed the door, the wind pinning his shirt against his lean chest. A man stepped into the gloom, his face hidden by his hood. "Dale!" I cried. "It's Slate!"

Miss Rose lunged forward, yanking Dale behind her. "Get out!" she shouted, throwing her weight against the man's chest.

He staggered back, rocked forward, and grabbed her shoulders. "Shut up," he growled, and shoved her across the room.

As he stepped inside, his hood fell from his face.

"Daddy," Dale said, backing away. "What are you doing here?"

Chapter 26
Sorry

"What do you *think* I'm doing here, you little nothing?" Mr. Macon slurred, pulling the front door to. "You think I'm standing outside in this weather when I got a loving family to come home to?" He swayed like the pines outside, water dripping from his jacket.

"Dale," I said, making my voice soft. "Back up." Out of the corner of my eye I saw Miss Rose rise unsteadily to her feet.

Dale took a ragged breath and stepped back. Miss Rose pulled him behind her. "Macon," she said, "you're drunk. And you're not supposed to be here."

He looked at her the way a cat looks at a bird, his eyes glinting. "So?" he said. "Why don't you call that detective boyfriend of yours and complain? You think I don't know about him?" He leered at her. "Go ahead and call."

So that was it. "Detective Starr ain't Miss Rose's boyfriend, Mr. Macon. He's got the hots for Miss Retzyl. Of course," I added, "you don't need to take my word for it. He'll be back in a few minutes and you can ask him yourself."

"Shut up, Mo," he growled, keeping his eyes on Miss Rose. "You talk too much. If you were my kid I'd knock some sense into you, wouldn't I, Dale? Go ahead, Rose, call for help." When she didn't move, he sneered, "What's the matter? Phone out?"

She glanced at us. "Dale, Mo, light the candles. It's dark in here."

I reached for the matches. I'd seen Mr. Macon drunk plenty of times, but I'd never seen him like this. Not this mean, not this bold. Outside, a tree crashed to the ground, but the storm outside no longer mattered. "Macon," Miss Rose said, "if you insist on staying, we can at least sit down and act like—"

"Hey, boy, your mama tell you she took papers out on me?" he demanded, his face twisted. "Threw me out of my own house? She tell you that?"

Dale's hand shook as he lit a candle. "She told me you don't live here anymore."

"Well," he said. "Today's your lucky day. I just moved back in. You," he said to Miss Rose. "Get me something to eat." She hesitated. I knew she wouldn't leave us alone with him. "Did you hear me?"

The Colonel always feeds Mr. Macon when he comes to the café drunk. He says it sobers him up. "I'll get you something, Mr. Macon," I said. "How about a PB and J on Wonder Bread?"

"Am I talking to you?" he shouted, slamming his fist against Miss Rose's bookcase and setting her red vase rocking. "Did I *ask* you to get me something? Sit down and shut up. Don't, you'll find yourself tied up like that loud-mouth stepmother of yours."

My anger jumped like a flame to a wick. "What do you know about Miss Lana?"

"Macon," Miss Rose said, "if you've hurt Lana, I swear I'll—"

His hand snaked out. He grabbed the front of her blouse and yanked her forward, onto her toes. "You'll what?" he growled. "Get me thrown out of my own house?"

"Daddy!" Dale cried. "Let her go!"

Time shifted into slow motion. Mr. Macon's hand swooped down in a clean, vicious arc, slamming Miss Rose's face, snapping her head back. She staggered sideways, her knees buckling as she crashed to the floor.

"Dale!" I shouted. "Karate! Fighting stance!"

I leaped in front of Miss Rose, hands up. Mr. Macon laughed and swiped at me like a big cat. I danced back, ready to kick. "Dale!"

Mr. Macon smirked. "Dale won't help you. He's a coward."

That did it. I kicked with all my might—leaning, twisting my body and throwing my weight into it, sending a perfect round kick to the side of his knee. I felt his knee give, and saw his face twist in pain. He lurched sideways as Miss Rose struggled to her feet. I darted forward to elbow his chin, but she grabbed my arm. "Stop," she gasped. "He'll kill you. Macon, please. She's a child. Just . . . just sit down. I'm sorry, I'll get you something to eat."

His laugh came jagged as broken glass, and he stepped closer, fist raised.

The first shot rang out, and the vase on Miss Rose's bookcase exploded.

I turned. Dale stood by the settee, face pale, Miss Rose's shotgun pointed square at his father's heart. His eyes met Mr. Macon's. "Get out of this house or I swear I will kill you," he said.

Mr. Macon's laugh wobbled thin and uncertain through the stunned silence. "You won't shoot me." He stepped forward, and Dale backed up, biting his lip.

He was right. Dale was bluffing. He could never pull that trigger.

"He will too shoot you," I said. "And I'll swear it was self-defense."

"Hush, Mo," Miss Rose said, her voice scared. "Dale . . ."

Mr. Macon edged nearer. Dale eased back, stopping in the hallway door.

One more step and Mr. Macon would have the gun. Then what? I looked for a weapon. Nothing. I glanced at Dale's terrified face. "Pull the trigger," I said.

Mr. Macon snorted. "You ain't got it in you, boy."

"Maybe not," the Colonel said, stepping out of the dark hallway and into the door. "But you'd better believe I have it in me."

He reached across Dale's body and took the gun. "Good work, son," he said. "I'll take it from here." The Colonel pointed the shotgun at Mr. Macon. "Get on your knees and put your hands behind your head, you yellow-bellied traitor," the Colonel said. "Soldier?"

"Yes, sir?" I said, my voice full of tears.

"Find me something to tie this coward up with." He glanced around the room. "Where's Lana?"

"Isn't she with you?"

Fear flashed across his face like lightning. "Not yet," he said. "But she will be."

He glared at Mr. Macon. "I said, get on your knees. Soldier? Are you okay?"

I blinked back tears. "Yes, sir. You missed seeing me in battle," I added, squaring my shoulders. "Hand-to-hand combat with an assailant twice my size."

A smile whispered across his unshaven face. "I look forward to your report," he said. "Right now, we have a prisoner to deal with."

Mr. Macon barked out a laugh. "Prisoner? What are you talking about? Put that gun down." He licked his rough lips. "Rose, I'm sorry if I hurt you," he said, glancing at her. "You just make me so mad I can't help it."

"Dale, could you get your mother some ice?" the Colonel asked. "And secure the back door, please, sir. I'm afraid I jimmied the lock on my way in." His gun hadn't wavered. "Macon, on your knees."

Mr. Macon bumped to the floor, hands high. "Cripes," he muttered. "Your kid kicks like a mule." He gave Miss Rose a sickly smile. "I *said* I'm *sorry*."

"I agree," the Colonel said, taking the extension cord I'd yanked from the wall. "Sorry is precisely the right word for you. Sit back and tie your feet together. Soldier, see if you can find another cord."

As the Colonel bulldogged Mr. Macon's hands, Dale came back cupping a dishtowel of ice. "Macon," the Colonel said, "where's Lana?"

"How should I know?"

"Then where's Slate? Where's your partner?"

Miss Rose gasped. "His partner?"

"We ain't partners," Mr. Macon said. "Slate hired me to drive some pizzas to the Blalock place. That's all." He twisted like a snake on a stick. "I didn't know you and Lana were in trouble, Colonel. I swear I didn't."

"He's lying," I said, and the Colonel nodded.

Mr. Macon dropped the helpless expression, replacing it with his usual hard mask. "Fine," he snarled. "Turn me in. Delivering pizzas ain't a crime."

The Colonel sat in Miss Rose's straight-back chair and leaned close to him. "If anything happens to Lana, that's first-degree murder—for Slate, and for you."

"Macon," Miss Rose said. "For God's sake, if you know anything . . ."

"Try Jesse Tatum's place," he said, his voice sullen. "Slate said something about going back there. He probably took Lana with him."

"Of course," I said, watching Dale ice Miss Rose's eye. He moved easy and sure, like he'd iced it a thousand times. "A criminal always returns to the scene of the crime. I should have thought of that."

"Shut up, Mo," Mr. Macon snapped. "You got too much mouth. No wonder your mother threw you away." Dale froze, and I saw the Colonel's hands tighten on his gun.

Finally, someone had said it out loud. And out loud, the words felt surprisingly thin.

I looked Mr. Macon in the eye. "Maybe she did throw me away and maybe she didn't," I said. "But if she did, she only did it once. You throw your people away every day that rolls around, and it sure ain't because something's wrong with *them*."

I looked at the Colonel. "What's our plan, sir?"

He sat still and quiet as a rabbit, his long, fine-boned hands draped delicately across the shotgun. "We're going to ask to borrow Rose's Pinto," he finally said. "If she says yes, I'll wait for the storm to break. Then I'm going to find Lana."

Not by yourself, you're not, I thought.

But I nodded, and bided my time.

Chapter 27
Storm Break

The Colonel placed a pistol by the front door, next to Mr. Macon's chainsaw.

"My pistol won't help you," Mr. Macon sneered. "Ain't got no bullets."

"Slate doesn't know that," the Colonel replied, checking the gas in the saw.

Dale settled onto the sofa with a new bag of chips. "Deputy Marla conned us top to bottom," he said, eyeing his father. "Looks like she was working with Slate all along. Maybe we should change our name to Dimwit Detectives," he added, dropping a chip into Liz's mouth.

"She conned *me*," I said. "You figured her out. But why would Deputy Marla team up with a loser like Slate?"

"Only two possibilities," he said. "Money or love."

"Or in her case, probably both," the Colonel said, setting his pack by the door. "Soldier, were you able to find that packet in my closet?"

I pointed toward the coffee table. "I'm sorry, sir, but a

few clippings got away," I said. "It's hard to flatten tires and do paperwork at the same time."

"Truer words were never spoken, my dear," he said. He picked up the packet and disappeared into the kitchen.

I found him at the kitchen table a short time later. His candle flickered low, and he rested his forehead in his hands. He looked up, candlelight playing across the lines of his face. "Soldier," he said, straightening the clippings. I slipped into the chair beside him and waited. "I will be honest with you, my dear. When Lana told me about these papers, I hoped she was just being dramatic. But after looking at them, I realize I was somehow involved in Slate's robbery," he said, his voice thick with grief. "I can't imagine I'd have these notes if I weren't. Apparently, Slate had at least one accomplice. I hope I'm not that man, but we have to prepare ourselves. I could be."

I nodded. "You could run, sir," I told him.

His smile flashed even and white in the candlelight. "Running isn't in my nature any more than it's in yours. I'll accept responsibility for my past, whatever it is," he said, sliding the clippings into the packet. "We can't change the past, Soldier. We can only be grateful for the life of a new day, and move on."

"Yes sir," I said, leaning against him. "I'm proud of you, Colonel."

He smiled. "And I'm proud of you. You've kept your head and your heart throughout all of this. You've shown uncommon courage. We'll just need a little more courage to see this thing through."

As the storm wore on, Dale and Liz napped, Mr. Macon sulked, and Miss Rose prayed. The Colonel paced like a leopard. I picked up Volume 6, and a pen.

Dear Upstream Mother, I wrote. I crossed out the words.

> Dear Miss Lana,
> Hold on. We'll find you.
> Mo.

As the hurricane roared, the Colonel patrolled. Once he stopped by a window. He winced and leaned forward, his forehead gently bumping the glass. "Colonel?" I said, rushing to him. "Are you okay?"

He put his wiry arm around me. "I am. But this feels so familiar. The storm, the danger." Rain lashed the window. He looked across the room to Miss Rose, who'd settled on the settee with her eyes closed.

"She's praying," I whispered. He waited until she opened her eyes.

"Rose," he said, "I think the storm's breaking."

"Of course," she said, taking the Pinto's keys from her pocket.

"I'll take the back road to Jesse's rather than going

through town. I have less chance of downed trees in a forest than out in the open, where the trees stand exposed. I'll have to cross just one small cleared field, where the winds will be strongest. I'll come in by the Crash Pine, and drive the lane along the river."

He looked at Mr. Macon. "If Macon gives you any trouble, feel free to shoot him," he added, a smile in his eyes.

"Thank you, Colonel," she said. "That's very generous of you."

"I'm going with you, sir," I said.

"Thank you, Soldier, but no. You stay with Rose. That's an order."

I shook my head. "I lost my first mother in a hurricane. I ain't losing Miss Lana in this one. I'm going, Colonel."

Dale sat up on the settee. "There's no point arguing when she gets like this," he said. He sighed and scanned the cords binding Mr. Macon's hands and feet. "You're safe, Mama," he said, his voice soft. "And Mo and me are partners. I'm going too."

I won't say it was my finest hour, but it was stacking up pretty good.

I stood at attention, more or less, until the Colonel nodded. "Rose?" he said, his eyes questioning.

She hesitated. "Colonel, you have to promise . . ."

"With my life," he said.

"You're taking those kids with you? You're all crazy," Mr. Macon snarled as Dale trotted to his room for rain slickers. "That boy's a coward. He ain't going to be nothing but in the way."

The Colonel shook his head. "A coward? Dale's already twice the man you'll ever be," he said, slipping the pistol in his pack.

"Here, Mo," Dale said, tossing me a rain jacket.

The Colonel grabbed his pack and chainsaw, opened the door, and pushed his way onto the porch. As we watched from the window he staggered down the steps, the hurricane shoving him like a schoolyard bully. He pried open the Pinto's front door, swung the chainsaw in, and then folded himself into the car like a contortionist.

Miss Rose fussed with our rain jackets until the Pinto's headlights flared. "I'll hold the door," she said. "You hold on to each other and go to the passenger's side. The Colonel will help you." She tried to kiss Dale, but he ducked.

"Ah, Mama," he said, shrugging away.

"Don't you 'ah, Mama' me," she said.

She opened the door and held on as we scampered

into a wall of wind. It clutched at us, slid us across the porch like skaters. "Hold on!" she shouted. Dale grabbed my arm and we shoved our way down the steps, the wind pushing, tripping, grabbing.

"Well done," the Colonel said as the wind slammed the door behind us. Dale dove into the backseat and we took off at a snail's pace. The Colonel hunched over the wheel as he crept down the drive and onto the road. Hurricane Amy pounded our little car with both fists.

"It's like riding in a drum," I shouted, wiping the fog off the windshield.

"Help me watch for fallen trees!" he bellowed. Dale and I leaned forward. We were lucky to see ten feet ahead.

Twice we stopped to chainsaw trees out of our path.

"Are you okay, sir?" I asked as we drove around the second tree. He nodded, but he clenched his jaw and his fingers went white, he gripped the wheel so hard.

When we reached the small, open field near the Crash Pine, he stopped. "Double-check seat belts," he said, and edged out of the woods.

The wind grabbed our little car's nose and turned us. "Hang on!" he shouted as the wind pushed us sideways down the road, skidding, skidding, skidding. Our fender grazed the Crash Pine, and the Colonel gasped. Slowly we slid toward the bridge.

"Unfasten seat belts!" he yelled. "Prepare for emergency exit!"

I fumbled with my belt as he floored the gas. I couldn't hear our engine through the storm's howl, but I felt our wheels spin and finally catch in the wet gravel. We fishtailed past the bridge, the beams of our headlights dancing jagged through the trees as we bounced onto the lane leading to Mr. Jesse's.

The trees blocked the wind again, and I could hear Dale singing himself calm in the backseat. We inched on, to Mr. Jesse's drive. "We'll leave the car here," the Colonel said. He held his door as we struggled out after him. "No flashlights," he said. "Stay behind me. No noise. Be careful."

We bent low, crawling over fallen trees and slipping through wet grass to Mr. Jesse's porch. The Colonel rolled onto the porch silent as fog, and we followed. "There's Slate," I whispered, peeping over the windowsill. "Where's Miss Lana?"

"You two stay here," the Colonel told us. "I'll find her."

He disappeared into the rain.

Slate had balanced his flashlight on Mr. Jesse's La-Z-Boy, propping it in place with two pillows. His pistol lay by the flashlight, blunt-nosed and mean. Dale and I watched, barely breathing, as Slate peeled back Mr. Jesse's rug and picked up a pry bar.

His bald head glistened, and sweat ran crooked down the side of his face. He worried the pry bar under a floorboard and stepped on the high end of the bar. The board broke loose with a dusty scream.

"What's he after?" Dale asked.

"A half-million bucks," I whispered.

As I watched Slate work, my mind raced. What did I know about this house? Old, wood, sitting two feet off the ground on brick pillars. Or was it? "Is Mr. Jesse's house underpinned?" I whispered.

"Yeah," Dale said as Slate pried the third board free. "Solid brick. Why?"

Slate pried board after board free. When he had a gap large enough, he grabbed his flashlight and leaned into the space, peering into the darkness beneath the house.

"Attack," I whispered.

"But the Colonel said . . ."

"Field command. Attack!" We snuck through the door and across the room. Slate knelt before us, grunting like a pig as he shone the light beneath the floorboards. I pointed to Mr. Jesse's massive oak coffee table. Dale crept toward it.

"Go!" I shouted, placing a perfect flying front kick on Slate's backside. Slate bellowed as he dove headfirst beneath the house. "The table!" We dragged it over the hole in the floor, jumped on, and held on for dear life. The table, with its stubby legs, left just enough space for us to see the glow of Slate's light.

"Now what?" Dale gasped as the table bucked.

"We wait for the Colonel," I said. "You hear that, Slate? We got reinforcements coming."

Slate kicked, roared, and kicked again. "Let me out of here," he demanded, panting. I could hear him struggle to his back under the house. His flashlight beam darted around the table edges as he explored his new prison. His voice was cold and sly. "How about I give you kids a hundred bucks apiece to go away? Make it two hundred. You can buy anything you want. Hey, Mo, you could hire a real detective to find out who your mother is. How about it?"

Dale leaned toward me. "How does he know . . ."

"Deputy Marla," I reminded him.

"Don't care about your true folks? No skin off my back. Dale, what you gonna do with your money? I'll throw in a couple of tickets to Daytona. You'd like that, wouldn't you?"

"Forget it, Slate," he said. "What do you think, I'm stupid?"

"I think you're your father's son," he said, his light darting frantically around his prison. "Let me out of here!" Slate roared, pushing up on the table. The table rose into the air and tilted, toppling us to the floor. "You think you're taking me down?" he shouted, his hand closing around my ankle and dragging me toward him.

"Let her go, Slate!" the Colonel shouted, jerking me out of the way. He shoved Mr. Macon's empty pistol into Slate's face. "Tell me where Lana is. Now."

"How should I know?" he snarled. "I don't know where she is, and I don't care."

The overhead lights flickered on. "Wow," Dale said, blinking like an owl. "Even dead guys get their lights turned back on before we do."

I peered at the bloody bandage on Slate's hand, and the cut on his head. "Looks like you had an accident," I said.

"That lunatic mother of yours hit me with a lamp," he sputtered. "She nearly killed me."

I grinned. "I guess that explains all the blood at the Blalock place. Too bad you didn't bleed to death."

Dale nodded. "You might want to ask the prison doctor for some stitches for that head, Mr. Slate. That's one good thing about hard time. Free medical."

"Slate, put your hands behind your head," the Colonel commanded. "Mo?"

"Got it, Colonel," I said, yanking an extension cord

out of the wall. He tied Slate's hands and handed me the empty pistol. "Keep this pointed at him."

"Do you think it's safe, sir?" I asked. "I've been going through an awkward stage. I hope my finger doesn't slip," I said as the Colonel dragged Slate into the room.

"Dale?" the Colonel said. "Tie his feet, son."

"Yes sir. I have Boy Scout skills." Dale kills me. He went to Boy Scouts twice, before Mr. Macon refused to buy him a uniform and he had to drop out. Dale has Boy Scout skills like I got a Harley.

"Now," the Colonel said, taking the gun. "I'll ask again. Where's Lana?"

"She got away from me, and ran," Slate said, ducking away from the pistol. "I don't know where she is."

"I do," a voice at the door said.

"Starr!" I gasped. Starr stood in the doorway, his pistol drawn.

Friend or enemy?

The Colonel turned and pointed his empty pistol at Starr.

"She's right here," Starr said, stepping aside.

Miss Lana ran toward me, her arms open.

"Thank God," the Colonel murmured as her arms wrapped around me. "Thank God."

Chapter 28
Didn't See It Coming

We waited out the rest of the storm at Mr. Jesse's.

Miss Lana and I settled in on Mr. Jesse's hideous plaid sofa. I couldn't sit close enough, couldn't touch her hand enough, couldn't hear the sound of her voice enough. She told us how Slate had kidnapped her, how she and the Colonel had worked together to loosen the Colonel's bonds so he could escape. "When you didn't come back for me, I knew something was wrong," she told the Colonel. "And when Slate tried to move me, I knew my situation was dire. I attacked."

"You almost killed me," Slate whined.

"Maybe next time," Dale muttered. He smiled at Miss Lana. "Mo and I mostly captured Slate for you, Miss Lana," he said.

"Such lovely children," she said, rumpling his hair. "You'll get some type of badge for this, I imagine."

"Probably," he said, blushing.

She turned to the Colonel. "Once I escaped, I made

my way to Priscilla's. I assumed Starr would be there. Lavender had just called. . . ."

"Lavender?" My heart scrabbled around my rib cage like a wild kitten.

"Yes, sugar," she said. "He heard you tell Rose I was in trouble, before the phone line went dead. He was finally able to get through to Priscilla, and Starr. I showed up at their door, windblown and bedraggled. Starr and I drove to Rose's as soon as we could—only to learn you'd gone to Jesse's on the back road."

While we talked, Joe Starr cuffed Slate and peered beneath the house. "Well, well. What have we here?" He tugged a metal box up into the room.

"The loot from Slate's bank robbery," I said. "And the source of Mr. Jesse's Saturday night church donations."

"Why do you say that?" the Colonel demanded.

"Because the serial numbers from Mr. Jesse's donations match the cash from the bank robbery," I said, enjoying the shock on Starr's face. "That's the information Desperado Detectives has, anyway. I feel like it will check out."

"It does check out," Starr said. "But how did you know?"

"Sorry," I said. "We always protect our sources."

The Colonel frowned. "But why is there money under Jesse's house?"

"Because," I said, settling against Miss Lana's arm. "Mr. Jesse brought it here after Slate and Dolph Andrews stole it from the bank in Winston-Salem. Mr. Jesse was in on the heist too. Right, Slate?"

Starr watched Slate carefully. "Actually," Starr said, "I'm not sure Jesse *was* in on the heist. But his cousin was."

"His dead one?" Dale asked.

"That's right. Jesse Tatum's cousin was a guard at the bank. He got shot in the holdup and died a week later, Jesse Tatum at his side. Slate stood trial for his murder, but a slick-talking attorney got him off." Starr dusted his hands off and glanced at the Colonel. "Sound familiar?"

The Colonel didn't blink. "Why would it?" he asked.

I jumped in before Starr could reply. "So Mr. Jesse's cousin was in on your holdup," I said, studying Slate. "He told Mr. Jesse where to find the loot."

"Then, when Mr. Jesse wouldn't share, you killed him. That was mean," Dale said, heading for the kitchen.

"And stupid," I added.

Starr's gaze moved from the Colonel, to Slate. "Or maybe you killed Jesse just so he couldn't turn you in," Starr said. "What about it, Slate?"

Slate scowled. "You're all crazy," he said. "I didn't kill anybody."

"Come on, Slate," I said. "You might as well tell us before your girlfriend does."

Slate glared at me, his pudgy face blank. "What girlfriend?"

"Deputy Marla," I said. "The one that's gonna turn state's evidence on you to keep her own cold-blooded self off Death Row."

Slate winced. "Never heard of her."

"Balderdash," Miss Lana said. "I saw you with her at Lucy Blalock's."

"And I heard her explaining our Three Day Rule before you made me call home," the Colonel said. He glanced at me. "I'm sorry I called you Moses, Soldier. I was trying to warn you."

"Missed it, sir," I told him. "But Dale and me didn't miss hearing Slate and Marla talking together on our porch, just before the storm." I glared at Slate. "You're lying. You and Deputy Marla are in this thing together."

Starr scratched his head. "You and Marla Everette," he said, sitting on Mr. Jesse's piano bench. He wore the same look Miss Lana wears when she's working a jigsaw puzzle. "I have to admit, she had me fooled."

"Didn't you wonder why Slate was always one step ahead of you?" I asked. "Who set up roadblocks that didn't work? Who couldn't trace Slate's call? Who searched the Blalock place? Deputy Marla. She's been Slate's inside man all along."

Dale filed in from the kitchen with a bag of cheese puffs. He tipped the bag toward Miss Lana, who shook her head. Only Dale would eat a dead man's snacks.

"Priscilla warned me about Marla," Starr muttered. "She didn't trust her. Especially when it came to you kids." He stood Slate up and walked him to Mr. Jesse's old piano. "You and Marla Everette," he said again, anger twisting his voice tight as a piano wire. "I must be getting old. I never saw that one coming."

Poor Joe Starr.

"You *are* getting old," I said. "But don't feel bad. I'm only eleven and I didn't see it coming either. Did you, Dale?"

Dale shook his head, orange crumbs glistening on his face. "But I did know she was a con, Detective. And I only known her a few weeks."

Starr cuffed Slate to the upright. "Colonel, I'd like a word in the kitchen, please," he said, unfolding a news clipping from his pocket. Miss Lana went tense beside me.

The Colonel looked at us, squared his shoulders, and followed Starr, who closed the kitchen door firmly behind them. "What's going on, Miss Lana?" I asked.

"Everything will be okay, Mo," she said. She took my

hand, but her silence stretched like old elastic about to give. I'd never seen her so pale.

The kitchen door flew open.

"This is an outrage," the Colonel shouted, storming into the living room.

"Sir," Starr said, "this clipping confirms everything I've told you."

"No matter what the Colonel's done, he's innocent," I said, rising.

The Colonel grabbed the clipping out of Starr's hand. "This is rubbish," he said. "Me . . ." He glared at the news article, and then dropped it like it was stained with blood.

I stared at the paper.

A photograph of a younger, dark-haired Colonel filled the page. He wore an expensive suit, a ponytail, and a close-clipped beard.

The Colonel backed away like he'd seen the Devil himself.

"God help me," he sobbed, sinking onto Mr. Jesse's sofa and hiding his face in his hands. "I'm a lawyer."

Chapter 29
Dear Upstream Mother

The café reopened two busy weeks later.

In those two weeks Miss Lana, Dale, and I repaired the café's busted windows, swept the hurricane out of the dining room, and mended the roof. The old sign—No Lawyers—came down. A new sign—Welcome Friends—went up.

Miss Rose shocked us twice in those weeks. First by divorcing Mr. Macon. Then by starting her own business—a living history tour of a 1930s tobacco farm. "She has two bus tours a day booked for the rest of the summer," Dale told me. He grinned. "She didn't want to tell us until she knew it would work out. And until I repaired all that trash at the tobacco barn."

Other folks were busy too.

Slate and Deputy Marla were charged with kidnapping the Colonel and Miss Lana, and with murdering Mr. Jesse and Dolph Andrews. Mr. Macon turned state's witness.

Spitz the Cat disappeared in the hurricane. Again. And Thes hired Desperado Detectives. Again. "I'll find him this time, but that's it," Dale said, marking *Lost Pets Found for Free* off our sign.

Lavender came home a hero—but not the way I expected.

We learned about Lavender's race the day of the hurricane. The television stations were still out, but a voice sputtered through Mr. Jesse's radio. "And today at the Sycamore 200 . . ."

"That's Lavender's race!" Dale cried. "Come on, baby," he whispered, twisting the dial. The station crackled: ". . . dramatic finish . . . And with me now in the winner's circle, driver of the thirty-two car . . ."

"That's us!" Dale yelped. "We won! Lavender won!"

"Here's driver Hank Richmond," the announcer said.

"*Hank Richmond?* Who's that?" I gasped.

Hank turned out to be the driver Lavender sold his car to just before the race.

"A thirty-thousand-dollar bird in the hand is a tempting creature," Lavender explained when he got home. He put a thousand dollars in bank accounts for Dale and me, and handed the rest to Miss Rose. "I love building cars," he said. "I'll be ready to test a new one by Christmas."

What he didn't say was, he spent most of the race on the phone with law enforcement, trying to get in touch with Joe Starr, and to get help to Miss Lana.

And the Colonel? The Colonel missed it all, thanks to Joe Starr. Starr took him to Winston-Salem to unsnarl a host of legal details, and then to the hospital to get checked out head to toe.

"I'll never speak to Joe Starr as long as I live," I told Miss Lana the morning of our Grand Reopening. She handed Dale and me maroon berets, patted her wig into place, and smoothed her shimmering pink dress over her hips.

"Mo, everything's fine. The Colonel needs time to get the details of his life straight, and adjust to his memories," she said. "And *jamais* say *jamais,* sugar."

"What?" Dale asked, looking at his beret like it was roadkill.

"Never say never," she translated, opening the door. "Places, everyone."

We were packed by seven a.m. "Bonjour and welcome to La Café, Monsieur Mayor," I said, adjusting my beret. Dale had already stuffed his behind the jukebox.

"Bonjour, Mo," he said. He glanced around the room: Eiffel Tower salt and pepper shakers, catty-cornered tablecloths, lilting accordion music. "It's nice to be back in Paris," he said. He smoothed his ice-pink tie over his belly, glided across the tiles to his counter seat, and winked at the Azalea Women.

"Good morning, Anna Celeste," he said. Attila and her mother sat by a window sucking down soft-boiled eggs like a couple of well-dressed weasels. "I hope you're having a good summer."

"I am, thank you, Mr. Mayor," she said, tossing her sun-streaked hair. "We just got back from Myrtle Beach. It's so nice to get away."

I walked by, holding a glass of ice water. Suddenly, I felt shy. "Hey, Anna. I'm trying those blue bottles," I told her. "Thanks for them, and for . . . everything." I smiled at her pinch-faced mother. "Breakfast is on the house today, Mrs. Simpson," I said. "Go ahead and eat like you mean it. Both of you."

Attila glanced at the glass of ice water. "I suppose that's from Dale," she said. "Could you please tell him . . . I'm sorry, but I'm not thirsty."

"No problem," I said.

Especially, I thought, since it's not for you.

She nodded and looked away. A choppy silence stretched between us.

Without strife, we had nothing.

"Too bad you can't go on vacation, Mo-ron," she

finally said. "You look so . . . I don't know. Deathly pale."

"Pale's temporary, Attila," I said, grinning. "Putrid is forever."

I spun to the next table. "Hey Salamander," I said. "I appreciate what you did for me. Thanks." She smiled and bobbed her head. "Breakfast is on the house," I told her. I slid the ice water across the table to her. "And Dale sent this over for you," I said, winking. Across the room, Dale put his hands in his pockets and smiled.

Sal knocked the glass over, sending a flood toward Skeeter's law book.

I'd just handed them a clump of paper towels when Lavender strolled in. "Morning, Lavender," I said as he sat down with Grandmother Miss Lacy Thornton.

"Morning, Sherlock," he said, flashing me a wicked grin.

Sherlock! A pet name!

"Hey, Dale," Tinks called. "How about some coffee over here?"

"Okay-vous," Dale muttered. "Keep your pants on."

I drifted to Lavender, order pad in hand. "We got two specials today. Miss Lana's breakfast soufflé, and biscuits au red-eye jus. What'll it be?"

"Biscuits au red-eye," he said, stretching his legs out into the aisle and smiling. Lavender knows how to wear a pair of jeans. "When's the Colonel coming home?"

I grinned. "Any minute now."

"He's thoroughly unbewildered, then?" Mayor Little asked, and I nodded.

"I'm so glad for you, Mo. I know you've missed him," Grandmother Miss Lacy Thornton said. "And I'll have Lana's soufflé, dear, if it's not too much trouble."

The door swung open.

Joe Starr looked around the room, his eyes the color of a thin winter sky. "Table for two, please, Mo," he said. I waved him and Miss Retzyl toward a table by the jukebox as Miss Lana strolled in from the kitchen.

"Welcome, friends," she sang, tapping a knife against a water glass until folks settled down. "Thank you for coming. There are a few rumors flying around I'd like to address before the Colonel gets home."

The café fluttered itself still.

"You have created some interesting stories about the Colonel and me." She smiled—though she wasn't smiling when she first heard them. "I don't have time to address each one, so I'll just tell you our true story, to set the record straight."

"Feel free to use my Pepsi crate, Miss Lana," I said.

"Thank you, sugar," she said, and stepped up on my tiny stage. "The Colonel and I met in Charleston twelve years ago," she said. "It was love at first sight. We planned to elope, and honeymoon in Paris."

"Oooh-la-la," Mayor Little said, propping his elbows on the counter.

"At the time, the Colonel was representing Slate, who was accused of killing a security guard during a holdup. That guard, we now know, was Mr. Jesse's cousin. Thanks to the Colonel, Slate was found not guilty of first-degree murder, and convicted only of manslaughter and robbery. As he left the courtroom, he told the Colonel to find his loot and save it, or he'd kill every person connected with the case. The Colonel didn't take him seriously. Slate was going to jail! What could he do?

"The next morning, the Colonel found his secretary dead."

An Azalea Woman dropped a glass. Dale sped by with a broom and dust pan.

"The Colonel never forgave himself," Miss Lana said. "He believed his arrogance had cost that woman her life."

"No wonder he hates lawyers," Tinks muttered.

"The Colonel called me that afternoon. 'Pack your bags,' he said. 'We'll start a new life in Paris.' He warned everyone he could think of about Slate, and set out to meet me—even though a hurricane had just slammed ashore. Along the way, I believe he thought of Jesse Tatum and detoured to warn him too."

"The Crash Pine," Thes murmured, and she nodded.

"When I found him a week later, he held a beautiful baby—and not the first memory of me." She blinked back tears as she stood there, alone, curls framing her face. For an instant, she looked like the photo of herself as a young girl, prior to blossoming. "I did the only thing I could," she said. "I stayed, and hoped he would fall in love with me again."

Sal dabbed her eyes as Thes raised his hand. "Who killed the Colonel's secretary?" he asked. "Slate was in the slammer."

"Deputy Marla," I guessed. From the corner of my eye, I saw Dale peer out the window and frown.

"That's my theory too," Starr said. "Slate came here looking for Jesse Tatum. When Jesse said he didn't have the loot, Slate killed him. Then, when he recognized the Colonel, he hoped *he* had his money. And he kidnapped Miss Lana, to pressure him into giving it up. Only, the Colonel didn't remember Slate or the heist."

Dale went up on his toes and leaned against the window frame, staring outside.

Miss Lana's eyes misted. "And that's our story. I deceived you, my friends," she said. "But I acted out of love, and hope you'll forgive me."

The café hung breathless, like a pendulum at the top of its swing.

"Well, my goodness," Mayor Little said. "It's not like any of you have outstanding warrants. Is it?"

"They do not," Starr said.

As the café erupted into cheers, Dale turned to me, waved his arms over his head, and pointed outside. I threaded my way through the crowd. "What is it?" I asked.

"Follow me." He barreled through the kitchen, to the side door. "It's Thes's stupid cat," he said, stuffing cooked bacon into his pocket. "He's headed to the creek." We tore through Miss Lana's flower garden, to the creek bank. The flood mark from two weeks before darkened tree trunks a foot above my head. "There he is," Dale said as an orange blur sped through the reeds. Dale took off like a shot.

I started after him, but a flash in the creek caught my eye. A bottle bobbed along at a slant, its cap glistening in the sun. "Dale!" I called as the reeds closed behind him. I stared at the bottle.

Finally, my heart said. *Finally.*

It's trash, my mind argued. *Trash knocked loose by the storm.*

I splashed into the creek's black water and scooped up the bottle. Behind me, Spitz the Cat yowled. "Got him," Dale crowed.

My heart went still and quiet as I twisted the cap from the bottle and peered inside. A piece of paper curled there, just like in my dreams. A message.

It's what I'd always wanted.

Or was it?

I pictured the Colonel pulling me from the flood, smoothing a bedroll beneath the stars, sitting at Miss Rose's table with his forehead resting in his hands. I pictured Miss Lana struggling in with her arms full of hurricane candy, walking me to kindergarten, writing Mr. Jesse's eulogy. I pictured them laughing with me and scolding me, and teaching me to hold my own at the café.

Then I tried to picture somebody different.

"Mo?" Dale called. He stood on the bank, cradling Spitz in his arms. "Oh," he said, his gaze finding the bottle.

I shook the message out and unrolled it, my heart pounding as the dark water lapped against my knees. My hand shook. The words blurred as I read them.

"What does it say?" Dale asked.

I took a deep breath. "'Dear Upstream Mother,'" I read, and my voice floated away.

He sloshed into the creek to stand by my side. "I'm sorry, Mo."

I glanced up as the Underbird wheeled into the parking lot and rocked to a stop in the sycamore's shade. The Colonel unfolded himself from the car. He stared at the café a moment and stretched, the sun kissing his white shirt and short-cropped hair.

The café door banged open. Miss Lana ran toward him, her arms wide. He scooped her up and whirled her around as friends and neighbors spilled across the parking lot, laughing and crying, and then clapping the Colonel's back.

As I watched them together, my earth found its axis and my stars found their sky.

I crumpled the note. "Thanks, Dale," I said. I looked at him. "Thanks for saying you're sorry. But you know what? I'm not."

I splashed to the creek bank and zipped through the garden, Dale at my heels. "Colonel!" I shouted. "Welcome home."

He and Miss Lana started toward me. "Thank you, Soldier," he called, opening his arms. "It's good to be home."

Acknowledgments

Many people helped create this book, and I am grateful to each of them.

Thanks to Rodney L. Beasley for his love, and patient reading and rereading.

Also to author Patsy Baker O'Leary, for her encouragement and advice, and to the members of her creative writing class.

Thank you to my family and writing friends who offered feedback, love and support, especially: Claire and Mamie; Nancy and Brenda; Allison, Karen, and Eileen.

Last but not least, thanks to my agent, Melissa Jeglinski of The Knight Agency, and to all the talented people at Penguin/Dial, especially Associate Publisher and Editorial Director, Kathy Dawson, whose skillful editing made this a much better book.

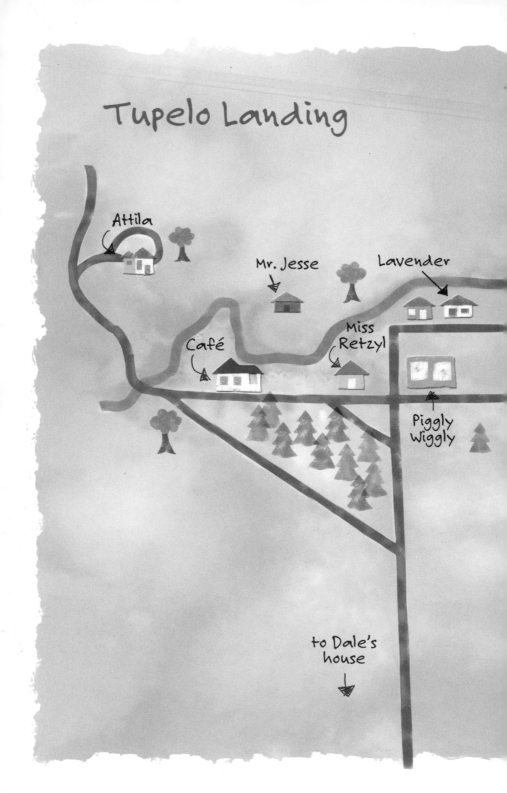